THE MESA

THE MESA

CHARLES ALDEN SELTZER

WILDSIDE PRESS

CHAPTER I

Jim Nolan, who had ridden down from the Calabasas country to Nogales the night before, was sitting on a rough bench in front of the Lone Star saloon, so named because Lee Hawkins, the owner, had once been in Texas.

Nolan was enjoying a holiday. At least, he had intended enjoying a brief vacation from work. But now that he was away from the home ranch he felt like a boy playing truant from school. He kept thinking of the Rancho Seco and the many things that were to be done there; and like all conscientious men he felt that he should be back there doing them instead of loafing around Nogales seeking diversion.

Nolan was serious minded, and few of the things that a man could do in a town like Nogales appealed to him. He had sat in at stud the night before and had won some money, which he had squandered before dawn. And the prospect of another day and night in town bored him. He turned a saturnine eye down Nogales's street. Immediately his gaze wandered out into the desert. He stretched his tall figure with a sigh of unutterable weariness of spirit, for Youth was still vibrant and eager in Jim Nolan's heart; and his twenty-seven years—twenty of them spent in the saddle—had not made an old man of him despite the fact that in various sections of the Southwest he was known as a man who was "plenty growed up."

Nolan's first action upon arriving in Nogales the night before was to visit a barber, and as a consequence his crisp black curls curved closer to his head than usual, and the shape of his head was more clearly defined. But the combing his hair had received after the cut had not lasted through the night, had not, indeed, survived the card game during which, many times, Nolan's fingers had been through it. It was now in a state of disorder. But so, for that matter, was its owner.

His saturnine eye glinted with disapprobation; one corner of his mouth drew down.

"Town's plumb disappointin'," he remarked.

"Shore is, stranger," conceded a voice from the doorway of the saloon.

"There's always too many folks breakin' in on a man's thoughts," added Nolan.

"After this I'm doin' my talkin' to myself," announced the voice from the doorway.

"It's safer," declared Nolan. "When a man's havin' thoughts an' speakin' them right out in meetin', he don't feel a hell of a lot like bein' interrupted."

"I'm talkin' to myself," said the stranger.

"Well, you're makin' considerable noise doin' it. An' I don't mind tellin' you that right now me an' noise ain't agreein'!"

"I've knowed a man to get right civil after gettin' outside of one of Lec Hawkins's bracers. It's right new," suggested the stranger.

"Why, you're beginnin' to talk intelligent!" said Nolan.

He turned his head and glanced at the other man. A whimsical smile appeared upon his lips. His eyes, which were softer and deeper with waywardness than a woman's, twinkled at the man in the doorway.

"Why, it's Bill Clelland!" he exclaimed with gentle mockery. "He's just got in from Sonoita. An' not bein' drunk last night he's figurin' on actin' superior. He's doin' his talkin' to himself. He's gassin' about Lec Hawkins's bracers when he don't need any, him havin' had no drinks of any kind for so long he's forgot the taste of them. Bill's got a habit of appearin' in doorways that way an' arguin' with folks."

"You damned old horse thief!" grinned Clelland. "You ain't forgot how to sling language!"

They entered the barroom now, and drank together. They said little of a personal nature, though old friendship was eloquently expressed in their glances at each other. They had not met in a year, but no one, watching them, would have suspected.

Clelland had been through his reckless days. He was now foreman of the Bar L outfit over near Sonoita, which was west of Tombstone, and was beginning to take life more or less seriously.

Jim Nolan had, since the beginning of their friendship several years before, been a governor upon Clelland's ebullience of spirit. Nolan, cool, confident, thoughtful, and imperturbable, had aroused in Clelland a desire for emulation, and unconsciously he had become remarkably like his friend.

For a number of years, however, both had been somewhat irresponsible and wild, and there were men who still gave them "plenty of room," having no faith in them in their new rôles, and remembering their previous shortness of temper and their swiftness and accuracy with the guns that both still carried in the low-swung holsters at their hips. But most of all they remembered the hard blueness of Nolan's eyes when his anger was aroused, and the strange flecks that appeared in Clelland's when his mood settled definitely upon violence.

Yet now Nolan had a settled air of solid value. Experience had tempered him until he had become dependable. No longer did one have to fear that Nolan would deliberately provoke a quarrel. His temper, while still as hot as formerly, was governed by a saturnine tolerance. He had become a solid citizen of the county. He owned a great deal of stock in the Rancho Seco; he was a grim, relentless figure to the lawless; he had qualities of character that caused men to trust him and seek his advice.

Nogales in the daylight was not attractive, nor were there places where men might relieve the dullness that settled heavily down over the town like a depressing atmosphere. And so at last, after several drinks together, and a game of cards which had no interest for either, Nolan and Clelland found themselves sitting on the bench outside the saloon, where Nolan had been sitting when Clelland had appeared in the doorway.

"Town's plumb disappointin'," said Nolan, again.

"Not like it used to be," suggested Clelland. "Once, we'd have tuned in on Nogales an' made her hum. Seems someone's mislaid the hummer. What's wrong? Is it us or the town?"

"It's us," said Nolan. "Things are here, waitin' for somebody to start them. Over there is Brinkley, the marshal. Walk over to him an' take his badge away an' you start somethin'. There's a box of dried prunes settin' on the stand in front of Licks's store. Go over an' kick them into the street an' shoot the glass out of the store windows an' you'll start somethin'."

"I reckon it's us," agreed Clelland. "I ain't got no desire to do them things no more. Not that I'm scared of Brinkley or Licks, but just because somehow it don't seem as engagin' as it used to be."

"Age is creepin' upon us, I reckon," said Nolan.

"I'm figurin' to grow whiskers," mourned Clelland. "I'll pass my spare time combin' them."

"We ought to be growin' children," suggested Nolan. "I'm gettin' so I'm longin' for an armful of them."

"Somethin's happened to you since I seen you before," said Clelland. "You ain't the same. You've got a yearnin' look in your eyes."

Nolan did not answer. Both men sat silent, gazing deeply into the phantasmagoric haze of space and flaming desert that stretched southward into the hills of Mexico.

Nolan's gaze grew reminiscent, troubled. He was trying to visualize something that he had forgotten, attempting to summon to memory an enchanting vision which had eluded him.

Clelland's voice aroused him.

"There's that hombre, Waldron, you had the trouble with two years ago!" warned Clelland. "The way he looks it still sticks in his craw!"

"Where's he been all this time?" questioned Nolan.

"Down Durango way."

"The oilers must have chased him out for stealin' their dogs," said Nolan.

Nolan fell to studying the southern horizon, while Clelland, less subtle than his friend, made no pretense of unconcern over Waldron's approach, but frankly and with unfriendly eyes watched him.

Somewhat to Clelland's amazement, Waldron grinned as he came near. He had approached from Nolan's left, which was east; and he came to a halt in front of them, so that if Nolan desired to continue to gaze at the southern landscape he would be compelled to gaze through Waldron. As this feat was physically impossible, Nolan looked up, and his gaze met the stranger's.

"Hello, Nolan!" greeted Waldron.

There was a breathless pause, for Clelland, who anticipated trouble. It was Waldron who avoided it. For Nolan's voice was slow and cold and provokingly gentle.

"You're back, eh?" he said. He got to his feet.

Waldron, a tall, slender man with deep, piercing black eyes, a rather full mouth, and a chin which receded slightly, reddened, paled, looked uncomfortable.

"That's past, Nolan," he said. "I've regretted it. Let's shake."

"So far as I'm concerned, it's plenty past," answered Nolan. "If your regret is sincere, you are showin' a flash of man. But I won't shake hands with you until you've proved it."

For an instant the two men stood gazing into each other's eyes. And then Waldron's wavered, glinted with some otherwise concealed passion, then drooped.

"Suit yourself, Nolan," he said.

He moved past Nolan, entered the saloon.

After Waldron entered the saloon Nolan, still standing, resumed gazing southward. Clelland followed Nolan's gaze and for a long time could see nothing but the dun-coloured land that swept away until it melted into some distant hills. But at last he detected a moving dot that seemed to be coming toward the town along a threadlike line that wound a sinuous course through the dun country; and after a while Clelland spoke:

"Oiler, I reckon."

Nolan nodded and resumed his place on the bench.

For an hour there was no word spoken. The moving dot grew larger in the vision and finally revealed itself as a horseman. And now, though each man's mind was alive with conjecture as to the probable identity of the rider, both continued silently to watch.

When the rider came down through a little gully close to town, Clelland spoke:

"Yep, an oiler."

"Vaquero," added Nolan.

When the rider struck the edge of town and rode straight toward the saloon he raised his right hand with the palm forward, making the Indian sign of peace. And when he dismounted at the hitching rack in front of the saloon he grinned widely at Nolan and Clelland.

"*Buenos dias*, señors," was his greeting.

The Mexican hitched his horse to the rack in front of the saloon and went into the building through the front door.

"Paloma brand," said Clelland, pointing to the Mexican's horse.

Nolan stared at the brand. His eyes gleamed. He strode to the doorway of the saloon and gazed into the room. There was an eager light in his eyes.

"H'm," remarked Clelland, "sight of that there dove on the oiler's horse seems to have stung you some!"

Nolan smiled at his friend, and the light in his eyes was so full of elation that Clelland almost gasped with amazement.

"Thought he was bored 'most to death," he ruminated. "An' all to once he looks like he'd swallowed a flock of songbirds! But a dove ain't a songbird, not by a long shot. Therefore I reckon Jim is thinkin' about a girl!"

Clelland's surmise was correct. Sight of the Paloma brand on the Mexican's horse had sent Nolan's thoughts skittering back to a scene that he had witnessed more than a year before. In memory he was again standing in a red sandstone colonnaded courtyard. There were pepper trees all around him, a garden, rows of date palms. Sweeping away from the sandstone floor of the courtyard, gradually dipping downward into the grasslands, was the most beautiful section of country he had ever seen. And there had been something in the atmosphere about him that suggested the knightly days of old, fabled in song and story.

The red sandstone walls of the house, its low, sloping roofs and wide, overhanging cornices, covered with faded red Spanish tile; the broad doorway with its sill level with the flagstone floor of the courtyard; a patio seen through the door, and beyond the columns of an arcade—all had to him a regal aspect. The shuttered windows suggested exclusiveness; the rare old bits of furniture he saw, the rich embroidered tablepiece, the heavy silver, the glistening goblets, the silver tankards, the candlesticks, the massive table of lapacho wood, all suggested opulence with a hint of power.

The gross man who sat at the massive table listening to him might have been a figure of those ancient days upon which Nolan's thoughts were dwelling, though he dazedly reminded himself that he was confronting Don Pedro Bazan, from whom he intended to buy cattle, and that Don Pedro had already agreed upon the price and the date of delivery.

But if Jim Nolan had felt the enchantment of the scene he was witnessing he was literally stricken dumb when he chanced to gaze beyond Don Pedro to see a girl standing at a little distance, watching him.

She was near one of the red sandstone columns, and the mellow sunshine coming down through a roofless section of the courtyard seemed to enfold her. She was slender, lissom. Nolan stared his amazement, his admiration. Her glistening black hair was drawn tightly about her head in bulging waves and coils, and the firm, slightly tinted skin of her oval face held a deep rich bloom and satiny smoothness that made Nolan instantly think of a ripe peach in a bower of leaves with the sun just touching it. Her neck had the rounded fullness of an adolescence not long past, and where it vanished into the folds of the rich brown lace mantilla she wore, it blended into ravishing curves.

Yet now that Nolan was again visualizing the scene, after having deliberately put it out of his mind for many months because pride of race had assured him that Mexican girls were not for him, he remembered that at the time he had seen her he had been aware of little but her eyes.

They had literally spoken to him; they had been as amazed and as full of admiration as his own. They had seemed to say to him, "At last we have met."

And now, all at once, Nolan knew why "town" bored him; he knew why he had been losing interest in his work, in the country, in his friends. The Paloma brand on the Mexican's horse had told him something that he had not suspected, that he loved Señorita Juana Bazan!

The Mexican was doing something inside the saloon. He was standing at the rear wall tacking up a paper, using the haft of a knife as a hammer.

Forgetting for the instant that Clelland was watching him intently, Nolan entered the saloon, strode to where the Mexican was tacking up the paper, leaned over his shoulder, and read:

To My Friends and Enemies. Greetings.

Too long has a spirit of animosity governed our actions toward our fellows; too long have we striven one against another in our efforts to garner the material things of life. We wound the flesh and we torture the souls of our fellow men from motives of hatred, of envy, and of greed. It is my wish that for one week each year we lay aside our grievances toward one another, our envies, our hatreds, and that we dwell for that brief time in amity and forebearance. Therefore:

Be it declared that beginning at six o'clock on the morning of the Tenth of August and continuing therefrom until the same hour on the Seventeenth, no person, man, woman, or child, shall be guilty of any hostile act toward another person. Since I have no jurisdiction over the entire world—though I wish for this purpose that I might—I designate a radius of one hundred miles in every direction from the Mesa del Angeles as sanctuary for the above time for all who have sinned or committed crimes against myself or others; for those who are hated and whose lives are sought, or whose persons are demanded for the infliction of punishment.

A person entering the zone of sanctuary during the aforementioned time shall be immune to molestation of any kind. He shall be free to go and come at his whim. Everybody is welcome, and there shall be no questions of a personal nature asked or answered.

"La Fiesta del Sanctuaire" shall be in progress on the Mesa del Angeles from the hour of beginning mentioned in this pronunciamento until the blessing is pronounced by Father Pelayez on the morning of the Seventeenth.

Given this day of Our Lord, August 8th; 18——

By Don Pedro Bazan.

When Nolan had finished reading he perceived that he did not lack company. Lec Hawkins was standing beside him, as were two residents of Nogales, and Clelland. And Waldron, having finished reading, was standing a little to one side, smiling.

"La Fiesta del Sanctuaire, eh?" said Hawkins. "Well, now, that old greaser does things up brown when he starts, eh? An' he ain't a bit modest, either. He takes in a right smart section of the United States when he goes to talkin' about the limits where he declares sanctuary. It ain't more'n sixty miles to the Mesa of the Angels. I've been there. An' cuss me if it don't seem there is angels up there if there is such a thing!"

Waldron was looking at the Mexican.

"That proclamation means that any man is safe within a distance of a hundred miles until the feast is over?" he asked.

"*Si*, señor."

"No one can shoot him or capture him, no matter what he has done?"

"That is what the pronunciamento means, señor."

"How will Don Pedro make sure of that? How will he punish anybody who breaks the rules of the pronunciamento?" asked Waldron.

Eager ears listened for the Mexican's reply. It came with a shrug of the shoulders and a broad, subtle smile.

"Señor the Magnificent has many men, señor. No man knows how many. Some are in Nogales. As far as Calabasas there are those that worship him and do his bidding. Beyond Hermosillo there are hundreds. There are many in the Chihuahuas. As far east as Juarez he is served. As far south as Jimenez. Whoever breaks the rules of the fiesta will not long survive the wrath of Pedro the Magnificent!"

Waldron smiled. "I have heard of Don Pedro's power," he said. He looked straight at Nolan. "Maybe that's why so many white men are knifed by Mexicans," he suggested. "They may have done something to arouse Don Pedro's temper?"

"The pronunciamento does not take effect until six o'clock to-morrow morning, Waldron," said Nolan. "If you are thinking thoughts, you won't be safe until then."

Waldron moved to the bar and drank. The Mexican drank also, flashed his white teeth from the doorway, mounted his horse, and rode eastward.

For a time Nolan stood at the bar and listened to the talk about the pronunciamento. He did not join the discussion. Later, he again sought the bench in front of the place, where he sat and stared into Mexico.

After a while Clelland joined him, though no word was spoken between them as they sat there. In the afternoon Nolan got up, stretched, grinned at Clelland.

"Bill," he said, "there's nothin' in town any more. I'm hittin' the breeze back to the Rancho Seco."

"You ain't goin' to Don Pedro's feast?"

"Nope. I ain't feelin' like I used to feel. You goin'?"

"Nope. I'm goin' home to grow them whiskers I was takin' about."

Nolan smiled. "Bill, I'm glad you rode in. See you some more. So long."

He walked to the hitching rail and mounted his horse.

Clelland watched him as he rode down the street. In front of a store Nolan dismounted. When he emerged from the store he placed something in his slicker. Then he rode eastward over a level, down a slope, into a gully, and so out of sight.

Half an hour later Clelland leaped on his horse and rode down the street. He stopped at the store in front of which Nolan had dismounted. Inside, he fixed the proprietor with a truculent eye.

"My friend Nolan was in here a minute ago," he said. "What did you sell him?"

"A can of airtights," truthfully answered the storekeeper.

"H'm," mused Clelland, "the Santa Cruz ain't all dried up yet?"

"There's always water in the 'Dobe Wells," answered the proprietor.

"An' Calabasas ain't far, I reckon," mused Clelland,

"No more than twenty miles."

"H'm," said Clelland. "Then airtights must give a man notions. I ain't had an idee for so long that I plumb need one. Give me a can of them airtights."

Clelland got his can of plums, went out, and climbed on his horse. He rode the trail Nolan had taken. Eastward he went, over a level. Down a slope, into a gully, and so out of sight from any who might have been watching him from Nogales.

CHAPTER II

Deep in a gorge that gashed the desert between the Cabeza Pireta and the Aja Mountains went two horses with riders. The horses moved slowly, as though spent, while the riders, gaunt and haggard, and so thickly covered with dust that their eyelashes were heavily rimmed with it, kept urging them on and frequently looked back as though fearful of pursuit.

And yet behind the two horses and their riders was no visible movement. Beyond the point where the gorge sank into the desolate land stretched a flat, unfeatured desert. Eastward rose the black summits of the Ajas, westward were the uncompromising peaks of the Cabeza Piretas. Southward, not more than a dozen miles, was Mexico in which, where they would enter if their pursuers did not reach them before that time, were lowland forests in which they might hide for a time without danger of discovery.

Half an hour later, when they had got out of the gorge and were riding around the shoulder of a hill, they got a glimpse of a green-brown land that stretched below them, southward.

"I reckon we'll make it, Galt," said one of the riders.

Galt merely nodded. His eyes were red as coals of fire with inflammation, his lips were thick and cracked. He was limp and saddle weary, and yet he snarled as he glanced backward into the yellow haze out of which he and his companion had ridden.

"Damn their hides, we'll shake 'em yet!" declared the man who had first spoken. "If the Picacho Kid hadn't let off his gun when he did, we'd have got away clean!"

The Picacho Kid was dead. He had been killed at Gila Bend, where the trio had held up a train. They had got away with ten thousand dollars in currency, which they had already divided, and which at that instant was safe in the pouches on their saddles.

A dozen times within the past two days they had discussed the robbery, had gone over every feature of it. And still their thoughts reverted to it as a subject which was of supreme importance. But always their final thoughts were of their chances of escape. For after the fight at Gila Bend they had discovered that two horsemen were on their trail.

However, they were natives of the country and were familiar with it, and they surmised that their pursuers were railroad detectives who would have trouble in tracking them. Their conviction of the ignorance of the two pursuers grew when they discovered quite a distance back that they were apparently alone in the desert.

"If we'd have pulled it off at Maricopa, where they'd have had a chance to get a posse together, we'd have been swingin' by this time," said the speaker. "As it is, if we can get into the lowlands we can hole up for a few days an' then slip down to Hermosillo or Guaymas. Then we can take a boat up to 'Frisco."

"Simms, you're talkin' sense," answered Galt. "There ain't no place in this greaser country where a man can spend cash like she ought to be spent."

"Right now I'm more interested in water," declared Simms. "I'm baked. My tongue is clackin' ag'in' the roof of my mouth."

"If we keep on goin' straight south we'll hit the north fork of the Altar pretty soon," predicted Galt. "That'll bring us onto old Don Pedro Bazan's land."

Two hours later the riders were deep in a lowland wilderness. Behind them, rising like a dun wall, was the slope they had descended. Secure in their green fastness they turned in their saddles and scanned the high, irregular horizon. Galt cursed when he observed a pin-point dot moving on the skyline.

"There's the critters!" he said. "Let's fan it! If we keep in the brush, they can't see us!"

Their horses scurried deeper into the wilderness. They reached a forest of cypress and eucalyptus which filled a flat. They went out of the flat into a prickly pear patch, miles wide, through which they sent their horses recklessly. They emerged with their clothing ripped and torn and the skin of their faces and hands scratched and bleeding. Again they turned in their saddles and surveyed the back trail. Where there had been one dot on the skyline there were now two.

Vitriolic profanity issued from their lips. They were saddle weary, and still they must press on.

"Them guys stick like burrs," said Galt. "They must be tough!"

At dusk, in the solemn shadows of a forest, they reached a small stream of water. Regardless of the riders who were pursuing them, they dismounted, removed their clothes, rolled in the water, and drank. For half an hour they luxuriated in the pool; then, refreshed, they again mounted and sent their horses southward. Just as darkness began to fall, they reached a small town, which Galt learned from a native was called Peza.

They entered a cantina and drank thirstily of the fiery liquors they found there. After a dozen drinks Simms found Galt standing with legs wide apart reading a notice that had been posted on a wall of the cantina. Simms approached Galt and looked over his shoulder. The notice was written in Spanish, and Simms could not understand it. But when Galt interpreted it, Simms laughed aloud.

Galt had stumbled upon a copy of Don Pedro Bazan's pronunciamento!

"Why, hell!" he declared. "We're free as kings! Them hombres that's been on our trail won't dast touch us! That there pronunciamento has been in effect since six o'clock this mornin'!" He emitted a whoop of delight and grabbed Simms around the waist. Together they danced about the room and at last brought up against the bar.

"Haw, haw, haw!" laughed Galt. "Let them hombres come! Just as soon as I collect a couple hundred more drinks I'm headin' for the Mesa del Angeles!"

CHAPTER III

Thirty-five miles southwestward from Cananea, the terminus of the C. Y. R. & P., Daniel Dean, engineer in charge of the construction work which would ultimately link the new railroad with the Sonora Line, stood in the doorway of the corrugated iron shack which answered as his temporary headquarters and gravely contemplated the result of his efforts. He also did some careful calculating. He finally decided that at the rate the work was going forward he would still have to remain for something more than a year in Mexico.

The prospect was not inviting. He had been accustomed to something vastly different. Right now he was longing for green fields, placid rivers whose waters ran over moss-covered rocks; cities where a man could renew acquaintance with a bathtub and drink things from thin glasses that tinkled with little chunks of ice.

"Ice!" he ejaculated. "Lord! I wonder if it still freezes anywhere?"

On the vast level across which he gazed a white-hot sun was baking the surface of what seemed to Dean to be a dead planet. There seemed to be no atmosphere such as a planet should have swirling around it. The sky was cloudless; not in months had a spot the size of a man's hand floated between the sun and the earth. There was dust which seemed to have been floating in the air for centuries—a dun-coloured dust which incessantly hovered, night and day. It glittered in the sunlight like a great yellow curtain shot through with particles of gold, and at night it formed a dusky pall through which the stars shone hazily.

Dean gazed through the shimmering heat waves at the Mexican labourers who were stolidly working on the right of way a mile or so southwestward. They seemed not to mind the sun or the heat or the dust. And Dean had observed that they drank very little water.

As for the last, he did not blame them, for he himself drank as little as possible. But while the Mexicans appeared to be flourishing, Dean was convinced that he was rapidly drying up. He had lost weight amazingly, and though he was lean and brown and rugged, and knew he could work all day in the sun with no ill effect, he was continually tortured by thoughts of various cooling drinks.

"If a man's never had them he won't miss them, of course," he decided as he stood in the doorway. "But if he has had them he'll never quit longing for them."

Dean was thirty and unmarried. He had no serious love affairs to haunt his leisure moments; no girl's picture was among his effects. He had carefully avoided committing himself, because, until he got something "big" at home he would not be able to support a wife. Yet there were several faces that occasionally flashed into Dean's memory, and he was beginning to look eagerly forward to the completion of the present job.

Dean made an attractive picture as he stood in the doorway. His chin was that of a man who feels the urge of ambition and who has the tenacity of purpose necessary to achieve it; his mouth was rather large but firm; his nose was distinguished with a rather high bridge, and his eyes, gray and clear, were set under brows that arched but very little. Dean was a man who was accustomed to being obeyed. He knew how to use the heavy revolver that reposed in the black holster that hung at his right hip.

Standing in the doorway of the corrugated iron shack, he observed two riders leave the group of Mexican workers on the right of way and start toward him.

A short time before, a lone rider had appeared from out of the dust haze. The rider had halted near where the Mexicans had been working, and within a few minutes the workers had all grouped around him. They appeared to be listening to him.

Now the first rider and another were coming toward the shack.

Dean knew the second rider was Bill Carey, his assistant, for he could recognize Carey as far as he could see him.

Also, Dean felt that the first rider must either be a man of importance or was the bearer of news of importance. For the Mexicans had not resumed their work but were still grouped and gesticulating.

Dean's lips tightened. Such interruptions would delay the completion of the work still more. Dean decided that he would have something to say to the rider who was coming toward him with Carey.

Yet, as the two riders continued to approach, Dean was conscious of a growing curiosity. For the rider was a gaily arrayed vaquero, and he rode a horse that was magnificently proportioned.

When the two riders drew close it was Carey who spoke. The vaquero sat quietly in the saddle smiling at Dean as though certain of his reception.

Carey was short and heavily built. His hair was the colour of a cock's comb, and unruly. His face was freckled and his eyes challenging.

"This hombre is a rider for a man named Don Pedro Bazan," he told Dean. "Ever hear of him?"

"Yes," answered Dean. "He's rich and powerful. He owns the Rancho Paloma on the Altar."

"H'm," said Carey. "I thought at first that this guy was talking tall and wide. But if you know his boss I guess it's all right. He's got the gang milling. Says he's got a note from Don Pedro. It's in Spanish, or Mexican. He read it to the gang, and they're all wanting to quit for a week. So I brought him to see you."

He waved a hand at the vaquero and the latter urged his horse closer to Dean. He dismounted, bowed, and presented Dean with a paper.

As Dean read, the expression of his face changed. A new interest gleamed in his eyes, and he smiled faintly.

"The feast is to be held this week, beginning this morning," he said. "And while the feast is in progress everyone is granted immunity. Tell me, señor," he continued, looking at the Mexican, "what is the nature of this feast?"

"No comprehend, señor," smiled the vaquero.

"What happens?" asked Dean, in the Mexican at his command.

"Ai, señor, everysing," smiled the vaquero.

"Everything, eh," said Dean. "It has a diverting sound. And the Mesa Del Angeles *is* between the two forks of the Altar?"

"*Si*, señor."

"Well," mused Dean. "I have never yet known a Mexican who could resist a feast. If I don't agree to let the gang off, they'll sneak. Tell them to vamos, Carey." His eyes twinkled. "We'll shut up shop and trail along. Maybe Don Pedro will have some ice!"

CHAPTER IV

From Nogales southwestward, the land had a downward trend. When dusk came Nolan was descending a big slope. Below him were systems of gorges, basins, low hills, mesas. A dead dry land. Beyond the desolate country, though, was a vista of green, stretching far along the horizon. That was the lower country, stretching away to the Gulf of California.

Nolan was descending the slope of a vast tableland. As he continued to drop, the atmosphere gradually changed. By the time he had reached the floor of the first of a series of basins the air had grown heavier. Also, darkness had come.

Yet Nolan rode on. More than a year ago he had made this same trip, and he had an eye for landmarks and a tenacious memory. He followed the course of the Altar, most of the time riding over the well-packed sand of the river bed.

At midnight, finding a small pool of stagnant water, he permitted the horse to drink sparingly. He pried open the can of airtights and moistened his own lips with the bittersweet plum juice. Then he rode on.

He regretted leaving Clelland. He liked Clelland. They had been together a great deal, and between them was a friendship that had survived more than one hazardous undertaking. And yet, after reading Don Pedro's pronunciamento and seeing again in memory the face of Juana Bazan, he had suddenly lost interest in everything else. Nogales had bored him, thoughts of going back to Calabasas had sent a shiver of repulsion over him; he had even found Clelland uninteresting.

He rode all night, and the dawn found him descending a wooded arroyo which led into a little basin covered with a wild growth of nondescript trees and brush. The North Fork of the Altar ran through the basin. He followed it to an open space, where he found another pool of water. There again he watered his horse. Sitting on a huge rock near the water he drank the rest of the contents of the can of plums. He threw the can from him and watched it roll down a short slope into the river bed. For a time he sat, watching it. Then as a sharp sound reached his ears, he twisted around, slid down the rock, and landed between two huge boulders at the bottom of the slope near where the empty tin can had stopped rolling.

When he finally came to a halt one of his heavy Colt revolvers was in his hand; and with his body concealed between the boulders he listened for a repetition of the sound he had heard.

His horse had not moved, for the animal had made no sound. And yet, though Nolan was curious, he did not raise his head above the rock. One never knew what might happen in this section of the country. This was Mexico, and the outlaw, Zorilla, might have men in the vicinity. Or any other Mexican, filled with the Mexican national antipathy for Americans, might have developed notions.

Nolan was taking no chances. He kept himself concealed and strained his ears to catch all sound.

For a time he heard nothing. And then, when he had almost decided that the sharp sound he had heard had been made by some roaming animal breaking a twig, he heard it again.

The second sound resembled the first. It was sharp, crackling, near. This time Nolan established the direction from which it came. He peered cautiously around the boulder at his right and saw a man stealthily moving down the opposite slope of the river toward him.

The river bed at this point was not more than a dozen feet wide, and its banks were heavily studded with brush.

The man was lurching down the slope, holding to the trees and brush to keep from falling. His knees were sagging, his head was rolling; he seemed to have barely enough strength to walk. And apparently he did not see Nolan's horse, for not once as he descended the slope did he gaze at the animal. His eyes, wild and inflamed, seemed to see nothing but the little pool of water, and he made queer little throat noises as he continued to half walk, half slide down the slope.

Nolan's pity was instant, but still he did not move. This might be a ruse to bring him out of his concealment.

He waited, watching. The man reached the bottom of the slope, threw himself flat upon his stomach, and buried his face almost to his ears in the water.

Still Nolan did not move. He was aware that in his extremity of thirst the man might drink himself to death, and yet Nolan must crouch there and permit him to do so. For another sound had reached Nolan, and after a short interval another man came into view at the crest of the opposite slope.

The second man was big, florid. He wore black trousers, high-heeled black boots, a gray flannel shirt, a gray, wide-brimmed Stetson hat. Around his waist was a cartridge belt which bore at the right hip a holster. In the holster was a revolver of small calibre. The weapon had an ivory handle, for the man now drew it and levelled it at the drinking man. The big man's eyes were glowing with an evil light. He meant to kill.

Then Nolan broke the silence.

"Sure, stranger," he said, "shoot him in the back! There's no chance of you gettin' hurt that way!"

Nolan did not expose himself, and the man with the revolver stood erect and rigid, trying to discover from which direction the voice had come.

He had changed his mind about shooting the man who was drinking, for he had involuntarily raised both hands until the fingers were about level with his shoulders, and he looked harassed and uncertain. Meanwhile, the man at the bottom of the river bed continued to drink, as though completely oblivious to all things save the quenching of his thirst.

"Go down there an' stop him!" ordered Nolan, speaking to the would-be killer. "He won't stop until he kills himself!"

The other man slid down the slope. He seized the drinker by the collar and dragged him back. The drinker instantly stretched out on the sand of the river bed and drew a deep sigh of contentment.

"He's had plenty," said Nolan. "Now, stranger, put up your gun an' tell me why you go around tryin' to shoot men in the back. Talk fast!"

Nolan stood erect at the side of the boulder which had concealed him. He was irritated, and his gaze was level and steady.

"You're interfering with the law!" declared the stranger. "My name is Ben Lathrop, and I'm a revenue officer from El Paso. This man"—he pointed to the drinker—"is a moonshiner. The Department has been after him for months. I have orders to bring him in. I've chased him from El Paso."

"H'm," said Nolan, "the one thing I admire about you revenue fellows is the way you hang on. But what makes you think you've got a right to play tag with your man when he's in Mexico? You got extradition papers?"

"Don't need them," answered Lathrop. "We catch our man first and get the extradition papers afterward."

"H'm," said Nolan. "Laws don't cut much of a figure with you as long as you get your man, eh?"

"I always get him!" declared Lathrop.

"I've noticed you tryin' to get him. When you pulled that toy pistol you was figurin' on givin' him extradition papers to heaven, I reckon. Mebbe for the good of his soul, eh?"

Lathrop reddened. But there was malice in his gaze.

"Look here!" he said. "What business is this of yours? You are an American, ain't you? You live close to the border or you wouldn't be here right now. Well, I'm telling you this: if you keep on interfering with me, I'll lay for you when you get back to the States, and I'll haul you up for interfering with an officer!"

"Sometimes I get pretty close to losin' my temper when I meet a man like you," said Nolan. "I sure do. Here's a poor devil that's dragged himself to this water. He's already half dead. Accordin' to you, he's a criminal. Well, say he is. No matter what he's done in that moonshine deal he don't deserve killin'. You ever been shot? You ever feel the burn of a bullet when it tears into you? You didn't? Then you've got no right to do any shootin'." Nolan was fingering his gun; he now lifted its muzzle until it gaped at Lathrop. Into Nolan's eyes had come a glint of intolerance.

"I've got a notion to let you have the feel of a bullet," he said. "The feelin' will amaze you. If one even hits your arm, it feels like someone had busted you with a sledge hammer. If it goes into your chest it feels like someone was workin' on you with a red-hot drill while somebody else is whackin' you on the head with a mallet. If you're shot in the back it feels like someone was stickin' you with a fence post an' shovin' you forward on your face. Yes, shootin' is an amazin' thing; an' it's just such miserable shorthorns like you that's always wantin' to do it. I reckon I'll just bore you once to give you the feel of it!"

Lathrop's face whitened. He smiled stiffly.

"You're talking high and mighty," he said. "But if you think I run into this deal without anyone to back up my play you are fooled. There's two of us. My partner, Abe Pennel, is back in the brush right now. He's got you covered with his rifle. If you try any monkey business you'll do some feeling yourself. Abe!" he called. "Tell this hombre where to head in at!"

"He'll do his heading in if he lifts that gun any higher!" came a voice from the brush at the crest of the slope behind Lathrop. "I've got a dead bead on him."

There came a ripple of cold laughter from another point in the brush. Lathrop started. Lathrop's confederate, in the brush behind, cursed.

Nolan did not move, yet his eyes gleamed and a guilty smile curved his lips.

He knew that voice, even though it had merely emitted a ripple of laughter. He even caught the note of derision in the laughter, the taunt.

The owner of the voice was Bill Clelland!

"It's curious how smart a man can talk when he thinks he's got the drop on you, ain't it, Jim?" said Clelland. His voice was so close that the sound of it now made Nolan almost jump.

"This guy in the brush, now," Clelland went on. "While you an' this Lathrop man has been talkin', this guy's been up here grinnin' to himself. He's been thinkin' that when the time comes he'd bust in an' salivate you. But right now he's standin' there with his knees knockin' together. He's dropped his rifle. You can go ahead with your talk, Jim; it was right interestin'. You was sayin' somethin' about shootin' Lathrop. You go right ahead, just as though nothin' had happened!"

Lathrop's face was gray with fear. The ivory-handled gun dropped from his fingers; he stood facing Nolan, his eyes bulging, his mouth open.

Nolan grinned.

"Bill," he said, "how did you know where I was headin'?"

"I was born with a cawl in one hand an' a can of airtights in the other," answered Clelland. "Besides, I've seen her."

"An' I thought I was sneakin' away right clever," mourned Nolan.

"A man in love is never clever, Jim," said Clelland. "He's blind an' foolish an' gentle. An' when he goes to gazin' into distances he's got to have someone around him to see that he don't go off an' get himself killed. That's why I'm hangin' around, Jim. Go ahead an' do your shootin'."

But Nolan did not shoot. While Clelland had been talking, the beating of hoofs at a little distance had attracted Nolan's attention; and now the sound grew louder and closer, and the four men at the river held their positions and waited, listening.

Presently a band of horsemen came into view from among the trees and rode directly toward the water. There were thirty or forty men in the band, and they were mostly Mexicans who rode mules or ewe-necked horses. But ahead of them rode two men who were evidently Americans. One of them was red-headed and freckled; the other was tall and austere, with a look of being accustomed to giving orders.

The tall man halted his horse as he reached the crest of the slope behind Nolan. His swift glance took in Nolan, Lathrop, and the fallen moonshiner. He looked straight at Nolan and held up a hand to halt the Mexicans, who were swarming forward.

"Sorry to break in on trouble this way, gentlemen," he said. "But you should have warned us. If you feel like explaining, go ahead. If you don't, we'll keep right on riding."

Nolan grinned at him.

"You're that engineer I've been hearin' about, I reckon," he said. "Your name's Dan Dean. Well, I've been tryin' to convince this hombre an' his friend, who is back there in the brush, that it ain't decent to try to shoot a man in the back, especially when he's flat on his stomach gettin' himself a drink."

Nolan explained further, and when he concluded Dean smiled.

"Unfortunately this is Mexico," he said. "Lathrop and his friend Pennel have no authority to make a prisoner of the moonshiner. Of course, they couldn't take him with you and your friend preventing them, and since our coming their chances have grown exceedingly slender, indeed. For our friend Don Pedro Bazan has issued a pronunciamento which immunizes from molestation a great many people, the moonshiner among them. I shouldn't like to be near if Mr. Lathrop tried to take the moonshiner while the Mexicans are here. These feasts are sacred to them. I should advise you to grin and bear it, Mr. Lathrop."

"What is the pronunciamento you are talking about?" asked Lathrop.

Dean told him, and Lathrop made a wry face.

"We quit," he decided. "We'll hang around until the week is up, and then we'll grab our man."

"Mebbe," said Clelland. "Anyhow, if this hombre can fork a horse we'll take him to the Mesa del Angeles. An' when I tell him how you tried to shoot him in the back mebbe he'll be tickled to death to know you're hangin' around."

CHAPTER V

"So you have been caught, Señor Valdez?" said Don Pedro in a dulcet, almost a caressing, voice. The rounded labials of his language flowed liquidly from his tongue, and he lingered over them as though enjoying their timbre, like a drinker and a connoisseur of wine inhaling its bouquet.

"You came once too often to my potrero seeking your choice of my horses, and my vaqueros took you! Last year you appropriated three of my best and left only the *grullas Diablo*. Did you not know that I would be expecting you? Did you think that I would let it happen again? Do you not know that since you made off with my horses last year there has not been a night when my *ranchites* or my vaqueros have not been watching for you? *Bastante!* Señor Valdez, I shall have you flogged. Afterward, you shall be shot!"

The culprit, a tall, slender Mexican, seemed unaffected by Don Pedro's threats. He stood near one of the roughly rounded red sandstone pillars of the colonnaded courtyard, his arms folded across his arched chest, his booted feet set wide apart and firm, his black eyes gleaming with an expression in which was more of amusement than of concern.

And yet the concern was tempered by respect; the amusement was not provoked by derision but by Señor Valdez's contempt of himself for having permitted himself to be taken into custody by Don Pedro's men. Valdez was aware that his position was precarious and that Don Pedro's threat to have him shot had not been idly uttered.

Don Pedro Bazan was powerful. One need only to gaze as Valdez was now gazing into the vastness of Don Pedro's domain to understand how unlimited was the authority he exercised. Don Pedro's possessions could not be comprehended by glances from any given point. A month's riding would hardly suffice to cover the limits of his land.

Perhaps for the first time Valdez was assailed with a proper conception of Don Pedro's position, for his gaze now wandered, seeking the pepper trees below him, their yield just beginning to colour in the blighting heat of the sun. He looked from the pepper trees to the bright green palms that grew everywhere; he studied the thickets and coppices towering over prickly pear hedges. Near by a garden caught his eye, and he was amazed at the orderliness of the rows of onions, garlic, cabbages, melons. Beyond the garden was a forest of cypress, eucalyptus, and lapacho wood. On a broad level adjacent grazed countless cattle, knee deep in sedge grass. (That was where Valdez had been caught.)

The lowlands were vivid with colour. Vermilion, scarlet, crimson, claret, purple, lavender, plum, green, orange, gold-brown, lemon-yellow were splashed over the face of the lowlands in such harmony of design that Valdez, who appreciated beauty, was conscious of a pang in his chest and of a queer constriction at his throat. Associated with his strange physical pains was a thought that perhaps not many more times would he look upon the beauties of the earth.

And yet, as Don Pedro continued to remain silent, merely watching him, Valdez glanced at the two branches of the Altar that came from their cañons eastward to mingle at the confluence; and his gaze travelled the upland reaches of Don Pedro's land until a ragged horizon of distant peaks loomed hazily in his vision.

To the peaks and beyond stretched Don Pedro's domain. Up, up, to the sky. Down through the lowlands to the Gulf of California. Northward five days' travel. Southward as many more. Scattered over the face of this kingdom—it was nothing less, Valdez assured himself—were the jacals of Don Pedro's ranchites, the dugouts of his vaqueros. One could not travel half a dozen miles in the daylight without encountering one of Don Pedro's minions. Why, at Pezon, which was a collection of jacals on the Altar a dozen miles distant, Don Pedro maintained a private cuartel where he arbitrarily confined wretches that offended him. And what was worse, Valdez was aware that somewhere behind the colonnaded red sandstone courtyard in which he was now standing was an iron-barred structure of the same material into which, he anticipated, he would be confined until such a time as it suited Don Pedro's whim to have him executed.

A glint of awe somehow got into Valdez's eyes. A feeling that weakened his knees so that he cast a glance around as though searching for something to sit upon. A conviction of Don Pedro's omnipotence had struck him suddenly, and for the first time since he had been captured he was beginning to doubt the power of his leader, Zorilla, to aid him.

"*Que desa Usted?*" asked Don Pedro, observing the changing colour of his captive's face.

"A place to sit, Magnífico," blurted Valdez, amazed to find that his voice was quivering as uncertainly as his knees. "I am faint; I have had no food since yesterday at noon!"

Between Don Pedro and Valdez was a huge table with legs like clumsy posts. Its top was covered with a heavily embroidered native cloth with a deep-tasselled fringe. Upon the table were openwork silver trays bearing native bread made of maize and manioc. Clustered about were fruits, tarts, sweetmeats—candied—a silver pitcher of milk, little bowls of honey, and platters of new cheese. Goblets, aguardiente, a bowl of glittering panales, another of lemons.

Evidently Don Pedro had been about to gorge himself when Valdez had been brought to him, for upon the table near him was a huge vessel of carne con cuero—roast beef with peppers and spices, and a ragout of stringy mutton, half garlic.

"*Ya se ve*," answered Don Pedro. "But you should have thought of that before you tried to steal my horses. Pedro the Magnificent does not eat with thieves, but none the less he does not deny food to those who hunger. Philippe!" he called to a servant who had been standing near a column in apparent indifference to the presence of Valdez.

The servant approached and stood, waiting.

"Philippe," said Don Pedro, "escort Señor Valdez to that bench at the corner column and give him some of that most excellent olla which was left over from yesterday. Also give him a cup of mescal. But see that the mescal is not too strong, Philippe, for Señor Valdez is faint, and I fear he will collapse under the stimulus of strong drink." Don Pedro smiled very faintly at his captive.

With a wave of his hand he dismissed both servant and Valdez, drew a chair up to the table, and began to eat.

From his distant bench Valdez furtively watched his host.

Don Pedro was a gross figure. He was a giant of a man, and in his youth must have been an heroic figure. For his shoulders were broad and still retained a military squareness; and his features were of that mould which from time immemorial have been termed patrician. Yet age and abnormal appetite had coarsened his face and laid a sheath of flesh at his jaws and at the back of his neck which sagged flaccidly. His nose had grown more prominent; it was becoming bulbous with moles and other protuberances, so that of its patrician shape nothing was left except the bridge. His mouth, especially the upper lip, had a blatant flare, while the lower receded but still held a rather attractive curve. His teeth, like those of all gourmands, were white and even and had the appearance of having been ground off so that they formed a straight line.

His eyebrows were shaggy and prominent, and the eyes under them were full and brilliant such as reflect a sensuous spirit seeking the complacent enjoyment of fulfillment. The lobes of his ears were fat and pendent, with a bluish cast.

As Don Pedro sat at the table his enormous stomach rested on his knees. And yet his stomach was not flaccid, like the flesh of his face; it seemed to form the lower bulge of a mass that swelled out under his armpits, firmly, completely encircled him, and then ran down his hips and legs to feet so small that they might have belonged to a woman. His arms were short, and with his fat stomach against the table edge Pedro had some difficulty in reaching the food that was spread before him. But he had hardly seated himself when a swarthy servant appeared and hovered over him.

Don Pedro's attire was rather startling for the rural region in which he lived.

He wore the uniform of a Spanish general of viceregal days with its blue coat with red facings and narrow gold lace, its white waistcoat, knee breeches, and silk stockings with gold buckles on the knee straps, and the low shoes which accompanied it. He wore a big cavalry sabre in a black leather scabbard, which dangled almost to the floor as he sat at the table.

He had come out of the house wearing a tricolour-cockaded rather flat hat. Whenever Don Pedro was forced to sit as judge and jury, as in the present instance, he appeared in the panoply of power and authority.

Valdez had heard tales of Don Pedro's achievements at the festal board, and yet, as he sat there covertly watching, it seemed that the tellers of the tales had not done justice to the man's appetite.

Under Valdez's eyes, as though through some weird feat of legerdemain, the platter of roast beef vanished. Portions of lamb, fish, ham, and boiled pigeon followed, and an aroma, pleasant to Valdez's nostrils, permeated the atmosphere of the courtyard. Don Pedro's garlic was pungent; it made Valdez's mouth moist.

Don Pedro paid no attention to Valdez as he applied himself to the viands before him. He ate noisily, eagerly, enjoying every mouthful, lingering longer over some dishes than others. Frequently he drank deeply of the thick white wine of Mendoza. There seemed to be no appeasing his appetite.

"*Diablo!*" breathed Valdez, "two such eaters would bring famine into the country! I think I know now why he is called Pedro the Magnificent! Bah! He is magnificent only at the table!"

While Don Pedro attacked the fruits, tarts, the candied sweetmeats, the honey, and drained a silver tankard of dark Benicarlo wine, Valdez found time to gaze around him. His glance went through a broad doorway whose sill was level with the sandstone of the courtyard into a patio. The sun shining through a window beyond the patio revealed another open door and a room. In the room Valdez could see a tall *bufete*, a chest of drawers, a writing desk, filing cabinet, and bookcase. Standing fairly in the sunlight that entered a window of the room was a *seron* of tobacco. Near by was a wine cask. In the patio was swung a gigantic hammock, knotless, broadmeshed, with a broad silk ribbon affixed to a ring in the wall of the house. With the ribbon the occupant of the hammock could pull the latter back and forth.

The *casa*, or house, was a great structure with sloping roofs of Spanish tile and many squat gables. Like the colonnades and the floor of the courtyard, the house was built of red sandstone. Vines climbed its walls. Flowers bloomed near its foundations and in spacious beds arranged among curving walks. Rows of palms formed a lane that ran down the slope westward into the garden. The air, except for the scent of the lingering garlic, was fragrant. The sun beat down brightly, but not with such intensity as elsewhere. A vaquero, gaily caparisoned, was riding leisurely down into the sedge grass of the level where the cattle grazed. Some ranchites were lounging around a jacal at a distance. Half a dozen lazy peons were making a pretense of working in the garden. A corsetless Mexican girl with a brilliantly embroidered girdle was turning some peppers that were strewn on the floor of the courtyard at a distance. Her black hair was agleam with oil; twice had Valdez caught the flash of her dark eyes.

A heavy somnolence was in the atmosphere. Two or three vultures sat on the azoteas—flat roofs—of the outbuildings near by. A vagrant breeze stirred the leaves of the palms close to the courtyard. Don Pedro had leaned back. He was filled to repletion, and a drowsiness was stealing over him. His head had sagged forward, and he was watching Valdez through heavy-lidded eyes. Pretending that he was not aware of Don Pedro's gaze, Valdez viewed the tinted gauze of the southwestern haze where the sun was working its magic above a distant stretch of desert.

"Señor Valdez," said Don Pedro suddenly, "why do you persist in trying to steal my horses?"

"They are good horses, Magnífico," answered Valdez, startled into telling the truth.

"So they are. And thieves must ride only the best. *Por Dios!* That is an insolence, Señor Valdez. You might say the same thing about my wines, my silver, my hacienda. All are good. But because they are good it does not follow that they should be appropriated to the use of Señor Zorilla!"

Valdez started; his gaze fell.

"That is the truth, is it not, Señor Valdez?" said Don Pedro in a voice which was almost insinuatingly derisive, but which had in it a note of gentleness.

Valdez was silent.

"Come, señor," insisted Don Pedro, "be frank. Zorilla is your chief, is he not?"

Valdez looked straight at Don Pedro.

"*Si*, Señor Magnífico," he answered.

Don Pedro stiffened. He had hoped Valdez would deny the charge. For in spite of himself his heart had been warming toward Valdez. That, he supposed, was because Valdez had not blustered or exhibited venom and had not been impertinent.

For a time Don Pedro did not permit himself to speak. His passions were aroused, and he knew that if he permitted himself to give voice to his thoughts his rage would grow and he might order Valdez to be shot immediately. And despite his rage against Zorilla, the outlaw chief, he did not feel viciously disposed toward his captive.

When he felt he could control his voice he spoke.

"Señor Valdez," he said, "you know that Zorilla is my despised and contemptible enemy?"

"*Si*, Señor Magnífico."

"And having tried to steal my horses for Zorilla you do not hope to escape being shot, Señor Valdez?" queried Don Pedro, leaning back and surveying his captive with brilliant, scowling eyes.

"I have no such hope, Señor the Magnificent," answered Valdez, an edge of bitter irony in his voice.

"Ah!" exclaimed Don Pedro; "then you have heard that when once I say a thing I do not reconsider?"

"That is common knowledge, Señor the Magnificent."

"So it is," said Don Pedro, his great chest swelling a little. "It is as such a man that I have become known. People talk about me in that manner, eh? They know of my determination, my unalterable will, my——" He paused, searching for further words.

"And they know you for your justice, señor," supplied Valdez, cunningly.

"So they do, Señor Valdez. No man can say I am not just. It is true that it is Zorilla I should have taken out and shot. But since Zorilla is not here, and since you were fool enough to permit yourself to be taken in his place, it is, of course, you who will have to be shot. You see the justice of that, Señor Valdez?"

Valdez's cunning expression faded.

"*Si*, señor," he was forced to say.

"Yet the affair will be conducted with great ceremony, Señor Valdez. As an agent of Zorilla, you will be accorded every courtesy that would be accorded Zorilla. There will be six men in the firing squad. But only three of the rifles will bear bullets. And the men will be instructed to fire at your heart, in order to make the affair as merciful as possible."

"*Gracias*, señor," said Valdez, thin irony in his voice.

"Do not thank me," said Don Pedro. "I try to end these affairs quickly." He lifted a goblet of wine, drained it, and leaned back again, his arms folded across his ponderous stomach as he gazed somewhat meditatively at Valdez.

CHAPTER VI

Strange emotions were assailing Valdez. The death threat had sounded in his ears, and he anticipated nothing less than facing a firing squad whenever Don Pedro willed. By all the traditions of the country and his experience in such affairs, he had no right to expect any other fate. Yet, somehow, he was not depressed by the prospect. Something had happened to him. Something subtle, insidious, was stealing over him. Whatever it was, it was so elusive that his senses could not grasp it, though it welled up inside of him, slowly, gradually, filling him with a tingling sensation of pleasure and gratification.

As he sat there watching Don Pedro he was puzzled and amazed, and yet he was half angry with himself because he was not able to understand his feelings. It was not until Don Pedro's eyes narrowed and twinkled that he knew.

He liked Don Pedro!

Ai! Even though Don Pedro had promised him a firing squad, he liked him!

A miracle? Well, so it was. In such a short time; only while he had been sitting here, the emotion had stolen upon him. The gross figure, the heavy head, were pleasurable in his sight.

Yet, no! It went deeper than that. It was all in Don Pedro's manner, in his eyes, in the curve of his lips, in that imponderable and elusive thing called personality.

Don Pedro exuded something besides the odour of garlic. A something that, like a faint and delicious perfume, permeated the atmosphere around the man and enveloped you, held you. You were at first repelled by the fat cheeks, the prehensile upper lip, the knotty nose. You thought, decided Valdez, that so gross a man must have gross thoughts; that basically he must be a beast.

And then, just as it had happened to Valdez, you discovered charm behind the grossness.

Valdez had discovered something more. He was certain that Don Pedro was reluctant to shoot him. He did not know how he had obtained that knowledge, but it had grown slowly upon him until now it was more than a half-formed conviction. Perhaps Don Pedro's voice had something to do with it; it was possible that the twinkle in Don Pedro's eyes might be responsible.

To be sure, men had been shot at Don Pedro's orders, and undoubtedly more would be shot; but for just this once, Valdez was certain, Don Pedro had decided to be merciful.

"Señor Valdez," said Don Pedro, "do you know my daughter, the Señorita Juana Bazan?"

"*Si*, señor."

"And what is your opinion of her, Señor Valdez?"

"She is beautiful beyond expression, Señor Magnífico!"

Don Pedro beamed, but his eyes were full of guile.

"Señor Valdez, I perceive you are a remarkable man. You do not confine yourself to comparisons, lest they bring confusion upon you. You do not say that her colour rivals that of the poppy, for you might discover that I detest poppies; you do not compare her to any other flower, because you do not know which flower I favour or dislike. Like the wise man you are, you say neither too much nor too little. Yes, señor, you are a wise man, but you were not wise when you tried to steal my horses!"

Valdez was silent.

"But the Señorita Juana adds lustre to her father's fame, Señor Valdez?"

"*Si*, señor."

"And you have found that fame extensive?"

"Men bend the knee when your name is mentioned, Magnífico."

Don Pedro drew a deep breath.

"You will show me how they do it, señor," he said.

Valdez rose and made a bow by doubling a leg under him.

"That low, Señor Valdez?"

"Even lower, Magnífico. I could not properly accomplish it, for I am weak from fasting and confinement."

"You shall be well fed presently," promised Don Pedro. "They bend low, do they? Well, that is proper, to be sure. For not one in the country, save perhaps his excellency Porfirio Diaz, is greater than I. You have remarked the extensiveness of my possessions, Señor Valdez? And you are aware with what cleverness and wisdom I rule my domains?"

"It is everywhere recognized, Señor Magnífico."

"Philippe, a goblet of Benicarlo for Señor Valdez!"

Don Pedro refilled his own glass. He drank, smiling afterward when he observed how Valdez licked his lips.

"And you, yourself, Señor Valdez, how do you account for my greatness?"

"It is almost impossible to say, Señor Magnífico."

Don Pedro frowned.

"That is to say," went on Valdez quickly, "that no one ingredient makes a food we like acceptable to the taste. It is a combination of ingredients that make a perfect whole. And who is there that can say which one spoils the food when it is omitted?"

"Ai." Don Pedro meditated. "Then I am a food that the people like, Señor Valdez? And I am to understand that no one particular trait of character accounts for my greatness."

"You have many, Señor the Magnificent."

"Name the foremost, señor!"

"It is your mercifulness, Señor Magnífico."

Don Pedro frowned, and Valdez perceived that he had made a mistake.

"And your greatness of heart."

"Ai!"

"But I perceive I embarrass you, Señor Magnífico."

"So you do, Valdez. Already I am blushing! The wine never flushes me this way, Valdez; so you must know that I am deeply moved through learning from you what the people think of me."

His face now assumed a woeful expression, and it was plain to Valdez that thoughts of gravest importance were in his mind.

"Now he will order the firing squad!" decided Valdez. "He has heard all he cares to hear and is wearied. He will have me shot immediately! *Madre de Dios!*"

Don Pedro continued his meditations, and Valdez slumped to the bench and continued to watch him, stealthily making the sign of the Cross.

"I much regret it," finally said Don Pedro.

"Yes?" Valdez's voice was very eager.

But Don Pedro did not volunteer to mention what he regretted.

Valdez waited for a time, and then, thinking that he had better keep Don Pedro's mind centred upon the immediate subject, he asked softly:

"You regret my capture, Magnífico? I assure you that I also——"

"Ai," softly said Don Pedro, as though he had not heard Valdez, "it is too late!"

"Yes, too late," echoed Valdez, still hoping.

"Too late to do anything. The execution must take place. The pronunciamento does not take effect until the day after to-morrow. And you are to be shot at dawn."

"The pronunciamento?" queried Valdez, all eagerness and curiosity. "What pronunciamento, Señor the Magnificent?"

"Mine," answered Don Pedro. "La Fiesta del Sanctuaire. You have not heard? *Pero, mas,* of course not. For I have told no one. My riders have gone forth to bear the news of the pronunciamento. I shall read it to you,

Señor Valdez, that you may know what a pity it is that you did not postpone your raid on my horses for at least one day."

Don Pedro drew a great sheet of folded paper from a pocket of the blue military coat he wore, opened it, and gazed over the top of it at Valdez, who watched him with open mouth and new hope.

"You are aware, Señor Valdez, that I am relentless in the prosecution of wars against my enemies. I am known as a just though ruthless antagonist. Men tremble when my wrath is turned against them. My passions are the passions of a demon, and when I am aroused there is none who can withstand the fury of my onslaught. Singly and alone I have done deeds that have brought awe to my enemies. I do not recount them to you in detail for I dislike boasting in any form. Yet note this: in all my battles no adversary has succeeded in giving me a wound. I bear no scars!

"Yet, though I love to fight, I weary of it. I am not bloodthirsty, and of late I have been wondering if I have not been too energetic in warring upon my enemies. In other words, Señor Valdez, I have had an impulse of mercy. And not desiring to be selfish, I have declared an all-embracing truce. But you shall hear! Listen."

He then proceeded to read from the paper.

For a time after the reading of the pronunciamento both captor and captive were silent. Don Pedro gazed at Valdez above the edge of the paper, while Valdez sat with bowed head staring at the red sandstone of the courtyard.

At last Valdez sighed.

"*Los muertos*," he groaned hollowly. Which, interpreted, means "the dead one."

"Yes," said Don Pedro, "you will undoubtedly be dead. It cannot be changed. My riders are at this moment bearing the news abroad. The date cannot be altered. And having already set the hour of your execution, I cannot set it forward or back. My word once given is final. Señor Valdez, you are unfortunate."

Valdez groaned again. Then he glanced rather wildly around, as though wondering if he could escape.

Don Pedro interpreted the glance and smiled grimly.

"It is useless, Señor Valdez," he warned. "You would be shot before you had taken ten steps. A squad of my vaqueros is concealed, watching you."

"Mercy, Magnífico!" begged Valdez.

Don Pedro shook his head.

"You should have thought of that before you tried to steal my horses, Señor Valdez. You shall be well fed to-night, but to-morrow at dawn you shall be shot. Yet I promise that on the first day of the feast I shall have Father Pelayez say a mass for your soul."

"*Los Diablos!*" breathed Valdez.

"*Que es eso?*" asked Don Pedro, who had not caught the low-uttered words.

"I was thanking you for your thoughtfulness, Señor Magnífico," answered Valdez. "Yet I would much prefer that my soul and body remain as they are."

"That is an insolence, Señor Valdez!" reproved Don Pedro.

He now motioned to Philippe, who had been standing near. At a signal, some vaqueros appeared and Valdez was led away, toward the barred windows he disliked.

Don Pedro sat at the table and watched his vaqueros and Valdez until they turned a corner. Then, in the sudden dead silence which descended upon him, he poured himself another goblet of wine, drank slowly and steadily until he could see the sun through the bottom of the glass, placed the glass upon the table, and fell to spreading the fingers of his hands on the table edge. He seemed interested in the movement of the muscles which guided the fingers wherever his mind willed them.

"Marvellous!" he declared. "Perfect! To-morrow Valdez will have no control over his fingers. It is a pity!"

Late that night, in the shadows of the azoteas, along the prickly pear hedges, under the broad palms where the giant leaves rustled in the cool night breeze, around the eroded bases of the crumbling sandstone colonnades, and stealing perilously close to the peppers strewn about the courtyard by the girl who had flashed a brilliant smile from her black eyes at Valdez, went a gigantic figure. There was a slight metallic clinking, and the barred door of Valdez's cell swung open.

Valdez stepped shrinkingly into the moonlight. He saw Don Pedro, still arrayed in his military clothing, standing just outside the door, the big keys in his hands, looking at him.

Valdez was about to speak when Don Pedro motioned him to silence. And when Don Pedro motioned for Valdez to follow him and began to walk away, toward the courtyard, the prisoner followed him, amazed, incredulous. For Valdez could see no guards about, and there had been one, who had been sitting for hours on the bench which was placed immediately in front of the barred door of the cell.

There was a heavy silence in the courtyard. The grinding of the dead sand under the feet of the two men was the only sound that Valdez heard.

Don Pedro led Valdez to the table where in the afternoon Don Pedro had dined.

The table, Valdez observed with a sort of dazed astonishment, was loaded with food and wine.

Don Pedro motioned Valdez to a chair. He sat down opposite his prisoner.

"Eat and drink!" he commanded.

Don Pedro sat for some minutes watching Valdez while the latter ate and drank.

"It is midnight, Señor Valdez," said Don Pedro. "In a few hours you will have no further use for food. It is because I dislike to see a man die on an empty stomach that I have brought you here."

"*Diablo!*" gasped Valdez, almost choking over a mouthful of food. "Why torture me? You bid me dine, and as I eat you remind me of what approaches. *Peste!* My appetite is with me no longer! I choke with emotion!"

"Ai," said Don Pedro silkily; "now you admit that when you became aware that I was bringing you here to eat you had hopes that I would release you?"

Valdez was silent.

"Behold the feast that an honest man is able to set before you, Valdez," said Don Pedro. "And mark how a man of wisdom shows you that there is no profit in crime. So long as freedom and life are beckoning to you, you have a remarkable appetite. But just as soon as I mention quite casually that you are to die at dawn, the thought of food repulses you. By being honest you could not, perhaps, have such food as this. But even plain food is better than death, Señor Valdez. And appetite! How many dead men enjoy the flavour of pulque and manioc, Señor Valdez?"

Valdez had ceased attempting to eat.

"Take me out and shoot me this minute," he begged. "*Madre de Dios!* I had rather be shot instantly than be tortured like this!"

Don Pedro laughed.

"Thoughts of death and eternity are not pleasing, eh, Señor Valdez? It is when we begin to realize that we shall wake to no more dawns that remorse and dread begin to annoy us! No more shall we thrill to the thought of a well-cooked dinner, eh, Valdez? No more eager looks at the wine flagons? No more of filling our eyes with pretty girls? No more of lying in the shade on some remote hillside enjoying the beauties of nature and wondering about ourselves—where we shall go when death overtakes us—why we were put here in the first place—what is the basis of the scheme of things? No more of anything! That is the thought that awes us, eh, Valdez?"

Valdez hid his face in his hands and groaned.

"That *is* a picture, eh? At any rate, it is the only one we are able to see. And after the dawn comes you will not even be able to see that. Do you know why, Señor Valdez? It is because you are able to comprehend only the material things. You drink, you eat, you sleep, you love, you hate, you envy, you steal. You attempt to satisfy appetite. I eat, Señor Valdez, and likewise I drink. And yet I thrill to thoughts of the mysteries beyond this life. I do not fear to die. I am wise and powerful, and yet I observe the work of the Infinite Being in the petals of a flower."

"Bah!" exclaimed Valdez, driven to desperation by his thoughts. "I begin to understand you. I begin to realize why you are called the Magnificent and the Glorious. It is because you are a magnificent fool, a glorious fool!"

"A while ago you were growing to like me, Señor Valdez. I observed it in your eyes!"

"I like you no longer!" declared Valdez. "I hate you! You are a gross monster! Call your minions and have me shot this minute! I shall die cursing you!"

Don Pedro laughed.

"And yet this gross monster gives you your life, Señor Valdez. This vile being whom you would die cursing gives you once more to the sunlight and freedom. Go you right this instant to your horse. He stands in the shadows of the palms at the far corner of the courtyard. He is saddled and bridled. A better horse than the *grulla* you rode when you entered my potrero. Go! Take your life and your freedom to your friends and tell them what a gross creature is Don Pedro Bazan. I taunted you——"

But Don Pedro got no further.

Valdez was on his knees before the gross figure, abasing himself, kissing the booted feet. He shivered when Don Pedro laid a hand softly upon his head, and when he spoke there was a great quaver in his voice.

"Ai, Señor the Glorious!" he exclaimed, "may I die proclaiming your greatness!"

CHAPTER VII

More brilliant than the eyes of the girl of the peppers who had looked at Valdez when he had sat on the bench in the red sandstone courtyard were the eyes of Señorita Juana Bazan as she rode southward through the afternoon haze.

And yet there was a softness in the brilliance of Señorita Juana's eyes which the eyes of the girl of the peppers lacked. A softness with fire in it, and depth in which a beholder was lost. Veiled by long black lashes, her eyes had a way of calmly appraising one, of laughing at one without a movement of the lips, or of sending a message of quiet derision, or of conveying interest. Don Pedro maintained that the Señorita had "talking" eyes, though, of course, Juana did not gaze as expressively at her father as she did at the good-looking young men who crossed her path.

And yet Juana was not frivolous. To be sure, there were times when a glance turned the heads of certain young men—and even of older men whom she considered worthy of admiration, but on the whole Juana was steady and sedate and circumspect, and the inhabitants of the country in which Don Pedro ruled knew well enough that Juana's conquests were mere incidents which were forgotten with the next breath.

She was riding homeward after having paid a visit to her *padrino*, Don Bernardo Francisco, who owned a large rancho near Hermosillo; and she was riding through a vast green basin which would bring her eventually to the south fork of the Altar when, halting her horse for an instant to breathe him after a climb out of a gorge, she observed a dot moving through the green of a far slope.

One of her father's vaqueros. She had reached the Bazan domain, she knew, and before nightfall she would be sitting opposite Don Pedro at the big clumsy table in the courtyard. Afterward there would be the stars and the moon and the soft melody of a guitar on the breeze that always swept up the valley and into the courtyard. And perhaps there would be that young Vittorio Cerros, from Peza, who occasionally found some excuse to visit Don Pedro on business.

Juana did not blush at thought of Cerros. For since, a year ago perhaps, she had seen a young gringo named Nolan, whose black hair curled tightly against his head and whose eyes were as blue as the velvet of a night sky, she had blushed only when her thoughts were of him.

Señor Nolan had not stayed long in the valley. He had been segundo of a gringo cattle outfit which had ridden down to Paloma ranch in search of yearling cattle; and Señor Nolan had stood only for a little while in the colonnaded courtyard talking with Don Pedro while Juana had watched him from a distance which was not so great, after all. For Señor Nolan had seen her, and it had been when he had doffed his broad-brimmed hat that she had observed the raven-black curls that snuggled his head so tightly that they seemed to have been stuck there. Only over his brow were the curls in disorder, and there, with a negligence which was most attractive, drooped a curl which almost swept Señor Nolan's eyebrow.

Señorita Juana observed that Señor Nolan made no effort to brush back the refractory curl; he appeared to be entirely unconscious of it, just as, at the instant he caught sight of her, he appeared to become unaware of the fact that he was supposed to be talking—and looking—at Don Pedro. The drooping curl, Señorita Juana thought, gave to Señor Nolan a singularly reckless and saturnine appearance. At any rate, there had been in Señor Nolan's eyes when he gazed at her an intentness that had sent the blood racing through her veins. And what was remarkable about the thing was that her heart beat faster every time she thought of Señor Nolan.

She was thinking of him now, and that was why she kept the horse under her standing so long. She had forgotten that she was riding homeward, had forgotten the moving dot she had seen on the far slope of the basin; she was standing again in the courtyard of the Paloma ranch-house, looking at Señor Nolan as he stood talking to her father.

Where had Señor Nolan gone? Whereabouts in the gringo country did he live? How many girls did he know? Would he ever return to Paloma Rancho?

These mental interrogations flashed one after another through her consciousness, and because she could find no answers to them her brows drew together in a frown and she impatiently tapped the high pommel of the saddle with her gloved fingers.

Her gaze rested on her small booted foot, the right one, which she had withdrawn from the tapadero, and travelled slowly up the embroidered skirt, laced at the hips, to the tight-fitting green waistcoat she wore, with its wide, befrilled sleeves.

Gringo women dressed differently. They preferred the quieter colours. They were fair haired, with milk-white skins. There was no fire in them— visible fire, that is—and yet, somehow, they managed to ensnare men. And they loved devotedly and with fidelity. That was proof that they had fire in them.

Señor Nolan was handsome. Not long could he resist the gringo women. One day she would hear that one of them had won him, and then——

"*Adios querido*," whispered Juana regretfully. "May she be worthy."

She had delayed long, and when she sent the horse on again she observed that the sun was low. She would have to ride hard to reach Paloma Rancho before dark, for she was still about twenty miles distant, and after she crossed the basin in which she was riding she would strike the upland country with its difficult gorges and its impenetrable sections of wilderness.

She rode down into the bottom of the basin and followed a small stream that flowed down the slope near where she had observed the moving dot which she had decided was one of her father's vaqueros. At the head of a shallow gorge which she reached a few minutes later she saw several horsemen cutting down the sides of the gorge ahead of her.

She was startled, for she perceived that the horsemen were not vaqueros. They wore jackets of cheap calico, wide trousers supported by sashes of various colours, and red Barcelona liberty caps of knitted silk. In a scabbard on the skirt of each saddle was a rifle, and in a holster at each hip every horseman wore a heavy revolver.

Once before, from a distance, she had seen men so arrayed. And now she pulled her horse up quickly, rapidly calculating, though chilled by a fear that seized her.

"Zorilla's men!"

With the exclamation, she wheeled her horse, sent it scampering over the back trail a few paces, intending to get out of the gorge and make a try over a level northward, which she knew would bring her to a narrow trail between two mountains.

But now she saw other horsemen at the lower end of the gorge! They had concealed themselves until she had passed and had then fallen in behind her!

Again she brought the horse to a halt. She was surrounded! She saw the red liberty caps on the crests of the two slopes of the gorge!

Desperately she headed the animal under her up the north slope. But the slope was precipitous, and the horse had not climbed a dozen feet when he slid back, toppled, and almost threw her out of the saddle.

Still, she tried it again and again at various points, with equally futile results. And all the time the red caps were coming closer. The final try at the slope winded the horse, and so she sat defiantly in the saddle as the horsemen closed in on her, grinning their amusement over her repeated failures to escape.

She was silent, though her eyes were flashing contempt at them, and she was attempting to unbuckle the flap of the holster in which she carried her revolver. The weapon had a trick of working up out of the holster while she rode, and so she kept the flap fastened. Now the fastening stuck and resisted her efforts long enough to permit her hand to be seized by one of the horsemen who spurred against her.

By the time the horseman had wrenched the weapon from her, the others were crowded around her. They were swarthy, evil-looking, dirty, and unshaven, and they seemed delighted over their feat in capturing her.

Juana's eyes flashed, but she said nothing until a rather handsome rider spurred forward and brought his horse to a halt directly in front of her.

The horseman was picturesque. He was cleanly shaved, so that the skin of his face had a blue-black sheen; he wore a heavy black moustache under which his white teeth gleamed as he smiled at her.

He was arrayed in a black velvet jacket with bell-like cuffs heavy with embroidery and lace; his velvet trousers were laced with white cord which was almost like that at her own hips; and the trousers were studded down the seams with lumps of turquoise stones set in silver. He wore long-rowelled silver spurs, soft-top boots with extraordinarily high heels, and his bell-crowned hat was a-glitter with bits of metal. There was a green sash about his middle, out of which stuck the butts of two heavy revolvers. His eyes were heavy-lidded, but Juana observed a dancing gleam in them which seemed to indicate a Satanic humour.

This, she suspected, was the outlaw Zorilla.

Zorilla removed his bell-crowned hat and pressed it against his chest as he bowed.

"*Buenos tardes*, señorita!" he greeted.

"*Que desa Usted?*" she asked coldly.

"But little, *caro mi*," he answered, silkily smiling. "Just a little talk, maybe. Who can tell?"

"You will talk quickly, if you please!" declared Juana. "And you will order your men away!"

"Vamos!" snapped Zorilla.

The riders scurried out of sight. But Juana observed that they merely dispersed to the points from which they had appeared, and so she knew that she would be given no opportunity to escape until Zorilla willed it.

She was now very little disturbed over her predicament, for she doubted that Zorilla meant to harm her. He must know that if he molested her in any way Don Pedro's vaqueros would search him out and exact vengeance. His action in halting her would arouse Don Pedro's anger should she finally decide to inform him of what had happened, and if he so much as touched her Don Pedro's wrath would be terrible.

After the riders vanished, Zorilla urged his horse close until the animal and Juana's touched. Juana did not try to draw away, but sat very rigid, looking straight at the outlaw.

"You observe how quickly I am obeyed, Señorita Juana?" he asked, smiling.

"By jackals," she replied, her lips curving. "How flattering must be such power!"

"Yet it *is* power, señorita. In my humble way I am as powerful as any. I bend the knee to no man. My men obey me. When I say 'come,' they come; and when I order them to 'go,' they go. I live on milk and honey. The fattest goats are in my mountain fastnesses. I have my choice of the best horses in the country——"

"Through stealing them!" she said scornfully.

"——And my herds grow larger every day," he went on. "Men pay me tribute——"

"When you do not take it by force!" she charged.

"What matters the method, señorita?" he asked, smiling. "We have only to do with results. I am powerful. I am feared."

"Not by me, Señor Zorilla!"

"Forbid!" he said softly. "It is for the beautiful Señorita Juana Bazan that I every day increase my power and my possessions. Señorita, until now I have said nothing. But for years I have watched you. I have seen you grow from a child into the wonderful creature you now are. And every steer that has been added to my herds, every peso that I have added to my store, every improvement I have made to my mountain home has been with the thought of you. I have told myself that some day, when you stand on the threshold of my hacienda, you will understand how great has been my effort to please you!"

She gave him a slow smile of derision.

"I perceive that Señor Zorilla has dreamed impossible dreams," she said.

Zorilla's face paled.

"You mean that you have never thought of becoming my wife, señorita?" he said, as though amazed.

"Ai!" she exclaimed softly. "Señor Zorilla becomes intelligent!"

"You reject me!" he cried. "*Peste!* Am I not as handsome as any? Handsomer than that young Vittorio Cerros who makes up absurd excuses of business in order to visit Paloma Rancho? Or that other springgald at Hermosillo, who draws you on the pretext of visiting your *padrino*?"

Juana was not angry. She was greatly amused at Zorilla's earnestness because she did not seriously consider either Vittorio Cerros or the young man at Hermosillo to whom Zorilla had referred. The only face that Juana could see at this instant was Señor Nolan's, with its intent eyes and the negligent curl upon his brow.

She sighed and blushed.

"Ah!" exclaimed Zorilla, observing the blush with the quick eye of jealousy; "there is another!"

Juana smiled. It was the sad smile of martyrdom; for she felt that she would never see Señor Nolan again; and it did not matter that Zorilla should be jealous. And yet, because Zorilla had discovered her secret, she longed to torment him.

"Ai," she said, "Señor Zorilla has sharp eyes. And yet he cannot see as far as my memory."

"*Diablos!*" snarled Zorilla. "It is someone who lives at a distance!"

"In a land whose people are fair, Señor Zorilla," she said softly.

"A gringo!"

"With blue eyes," she went on, looking straight at the outlaw. "And hair which is blacker than yours, *amigo*, and curly. It caresses his head like—like—ai! it is impossible to describe it!"

"*Peste!*" growled Zorilla. "Tell me his name that I may go and kill him!"

Juana laughed long and lowly, and Zorilla writhed at the mockery in her voice.

"You kill him, Zorilla? You? *Puf!* I doubt if he would look at you a second time. But if he did, I assure you *muchacho*, that he would notice you merely to tweak your nose! He is a man, Zorilla!"

The outlaw choked over unintelligible words.

"My nose is not tweaked every day, Señorita Juana!" declared Zorilla when he could make himself understood. "And your gringo dog would not dare attempt it! Nor your father! That gross beast who gorges himself until he resembles a fat pig!"

"Don Pedro eats sufficient because he possesses sufficient," said Juana, her voice further irritating the outlaw. "He is not forced to subsist upon goat's meat and pulque. Nor does he have to seek a raven among the rocks when he dines. And also, he is served by honest men. But I have already abased myself in holding speech with you, señor; and now I ask you to withdraw yourself to your mountain fastness and permit me to go. Instantly, Señor Zorilla, lest when I reach Paloma Rancho I tell my father of what has occurred and he have his vaqueros whip you!"

Zorilla's dark face became purple with rage. Yet he forced himself to calmness, realizing that the girl was deliberately provoking him.

"You grow impatient, Señorita Juana?" he mocked. "Yet you are not to see the Rancho Paloma this night, perhaps not for many nights. It is my intention to hold you to insure the safe return of Señor Valdez, a most estimable man who at present is occupying the cuartel at Paloma Rancho."

"One of your men?"

Zorilla bowed.

"Then I vow he has committed some depredation."

"Señor Valdez desired to look over your father's horses, señorita. Of late the poor mounts he has been forced to ride have vexed him, and he sought better. But unfortunately your father's vaqueros took him. Word was brought me that he was to be shot this morning. I am awaiting confirmation, and if Señor Valdez has been shot the Rancho Paloma will never again be beautified by your presence!"

The outlaw's eyes grew avid.

"Perhaps I shall keep you anyway," he went on. "It is Zorilla's way to keep what he values. In time you might become convinced that I would make a good substitute for the blue-eyed gringo you love. And now, señorita, if you will be so good as to dismount we shall try to make you comfortable."

"Then you really mean to hold me?" asked Juana.

"As one holds a flower," he answered.

"Then, señor——" began Juana.

Her body had stiffened. She meant to make a last desperate effort to escape. But at the instant her muscles were on the verge of action she heard a shout from a distance; observed that the liberty caps were coming into view again and that a chorus of voices rose around her.

"Ai!" exclaimed Zorilla.

He stared northward, where upon a distant level a rider came.

Some of Zorilla's men were in motion, leaping their horses out of the gorge to a little level beyond, where they could get a better view of the rider.

Zorilla did not move except to grasp the bridle of the horse Juana rode. He stood there, facing the coming rider, listening to the cries of his men, who proclaimed the rider to be Señor Valdez.

Juana smiled.

"You will permit me to go now, Señor Zorilla?" she asked.

He turned to her, and his eyes were soft with a glow she had not seen in them before.

"Zorilla keeps what he values," he laughed.

He mocked her attempts to break his grip on the bridle rein. And then she desisted and sat very still in the saddle, for the rider was now close and the other men were welcoming him with vociferous shouts of joy.

Valdez came on rapidly. He grinned at those who rode close to him to welcome him, but he kept straight on until he reached a point near Zorilla and Juana. There he halted his horse and smiled at the girl and the outlaw.

"*Buenos tardes*," he greeted. "I bring you news."

He then related what had happened to him, adding the news of Don Pedro's pronunciamento.

The other men laughed, shouted, and felicitated with one another. But Zorilla stood frowning.

"Señor Valdez," he said, "you tell us that the pronunciamento becomes effective at six o'clock to-morrow morning. There is nothing in the pronunciamento which changes our status toward one another. It does not take away a man's possessions? What he holds now he holds after the pronunciamento takes effect?"

"There is nothing said about that, so I presume that to all men belong the things they held before the time named in the pronunciamento," said Valdez.

Zorilla smiled whimsically and turned to Juana.

"Then, Señorita Juana," he said, "together we shall attend the Fiesta del Sanctuaire!"

CHAPTER VIII

For days before his interview with Señor Valdez, and for some time preceding the pronunciamento, Don Pedro's underlings had been preparing for the feast. Two days before his riders had gone forth bearing the written word, other riders had made their way up the green slopes to the Mesa del Angeles. Pack trains of mules heavily burdened had followed the riders. Ox teams drawing picturesque two-wheeled carts had followed devious trails from various sections of the Bazan domain. The carts were burdened with supplies for the feast, the various items having been officially requisitioned by Don Pedro in time to insure their delivery.

Cattle, goats, sheep in droves were plodding the upland, coming from all points of the compass. Crates of duck, wild pigeon, and chicken in wagons were moving toward the mesa of sanctuary. From the wine-makers on the western slopes came heavy casks bound by mouldy wooden hoops and bearing a dank appearance; from tobacco growers on the far hillsides came *serons* of the fragrant weed. Other wagons bore bags of frijoles, calabash, peppers, onions, garlic, cabbages, and other products of the garden. Crates of melons, ripening, came from the hot lowlands; salted fish went inward from the coast. Bales, trunks, plank boxes, were packed in carts that went careening over the upland, accompanied by sweating drivers who wore grins of anticipation on their swarthy faces.

Fruits, honey, cheese; sweetmeats prepared for the occasion found places in catch-alls. Tables, benches, chairs, hammocks, bedding, tents, moved toward the mesa. On the evening of the day preceding the beginning of the feast there was movement upon every trail in the country within a radius of one hundred miles.

Ox teams, heavy treaded, with sometimes four or six oxen to a vehicle, dragged their loads on distant hillsides, upon the levels, in the gorges. They that were first in arriving at the mesa saw, in the growing dusk of the evening before, the floating dust that marked the progress of those who were seeking sanctuary. Oxen were yoked by a beam fastened with rawhide thongs across the front of their long horns, which were adorned with gay ribbons, pink, yellow, blue. Two-wheeled carts and four-wheeled wagons, springless and jolting, deep with soft mattresses and cushions, over which were erected gaily striped awnings for ladies, came to a halt at the western slope of the mesa where the trail ended and where all must ascend afoot.

Men on horseback dismounted at the foot of the slope and picketed their mounts in the forest which ran westward from the mesa. Strangers, friends, enemies. They mingled, talked together, laughed, and gazed with glances of anticipation at the high brow of the mesa looming above them. They knew Don Pedro would not come until the morning, when the camp would be organized and all things ready for him.

Most of the guests, knowing Don Pedro better, perhaps, than he knew himself, were aware that he loved a dramatic appearance. He would come when the stage was all set, when all eyes might be directed toward him.

No one class predominated in the mass that gathered at the foot of the mesa, or climbed the slope to its top, or pitched tents in the forest to await the coming of the patron.

Families of *hacendados* mingled with *tenderos*, with *comerciantes* and *paysitos*. Peons came on foot, barefooted, barelegged, with no visible clothing except long, rain-faded, threadbare ponchos and narrow-brimmed, saucer-crowned hats hideously bedecked with ribbons. Musicians, peons, and dressed like peons, led various bands, blowing on tuneless and discordant pipes, flageolets, and oboes. Running pages with red handkerchiefs knotted around their greasy heads were leading horses with lariats upon which rode gaily bedecked ladies.

Fat tonsured friars, smugly smiling, came from various points. One could observe Franciscans in brown; Dominicans in white; Recoletanos in gray, with small, bare sandalled feet. There were horses of every breed and quality, banded and tasselled with housing to match their saddles, which were gaudy and high-peaked, some of them velvet or plush covered in green, red, yellow, or blue.

A band arrived, mounted on mules, carrying their instruments. They were playing the "Jubilate." Other musicians came, with fiddles, 'cellos, clarinets, hautboys. Then came a *guitarreros* band. Arrived some peons from the low country, wearing *potro* boots. Women arrived astride donkeys, with extra donkeys bearing panniers. Occasionally came a horse bearing twin panniers, loaded with produce.

Upon the level top of the mesa arose trestle tables under festoons of lanterns. Hammocks were swung between trees; tents were erected, blankets were spread. As the dusk settled lights began to appear upon the mesa and in the forest at its base. Music from hundreds of instruments filled the desert air; the hum of voices, singing, laughing, talking, created a babel of sound. When the moon rose over the brow of the mesa a heavy dust from the hoofs of arriving horses had floated skyward, and the mesa was obscured by a yellow haze through which the festoons of lanterns gleamed hazily.

Some of the talk and laughter did not cease during the night, and when the dawn came the western slope of the mesa was a living thing, teeming with climbers.

By five o'clock everyone, with the exception of a dozen of Don Pedro's vaqueros, who awaited their master's arrival, had mounted to the mesa. And at exactly a quarter to six a caravan appeared out of the western haze and came toward the bottom of the slope.

The caravan was led by Don Pedro.

Don Pedro was resplendent and bestrode a magnificent horse. The animal wore a spangled concho, a thin-braided leather bridle with silver studs, and a gold frontlet band; an embroidered saddle skirt hung from the saddle, whose high pommel was inlaid with silver, and the tapaderos were clever specimens of the pyrographer's art.

The garments that adorned Don Pedro's huge person drew low gasps of admiration from those who beheld him as he rode up and dismounted.

Don Pedro wore a light drab coat with dove-coloured facings and large, cloudy, mother-of-pearl buttons, a gold embroidered, dove-coloured waistcoat, pearl-gray satin knee breeches, and pale silk stockings. A brilliant scarlet capote—riding cloak, all-enveloping, and worn for ornament only—was hanging down his back between his shoulder blades.

The cloak gave to Don Pedro a somewhat rakish air, and the waiting vaqueros grinned and winked at one another as they saluted him.

But Don Pedro did not observe the winks. His manner was impressively calm and judicial as he gazed at one Testera, who was chief of the vaqueros.

"Is everything prepared?" he asked.

"Everything, Magnífico," answered Testera, who was a handsome, slender fellow. "Your quarters are ready. Your cooks await only your presence before serving breakfast."

"How many people have taken advantage of my invitation?"

"*Diablos!*" smiled Testera. "The whole country is here!"

"Good!" declared Don Pedro. "And the Señorita Juana?"

"She has not yet arrived, your excellency."

"*Peste!*" Don Pedro frowned. He looked at a great silver timepiece. "It is six," he said. "Is Padre Pelayez here?"

Testera nodded.

"There has been no trouble?" questioned Don Pedro.

"*Pero mas*, there is always trouble," frowned Testera. "Observe, Your Excellency!" He spoke sharply to his men, and presently there was brought to the spot two men who were lying face down upon the backs of donkeys. The men were bound with rawhide thongs to the backs of the animals. The bodies of the men were limp, and Don Pedro started.

"*Muertos!*" he exclaimed.

Testera smiled. "Not dead, Magnífico," he said. "Merely too much mescal. They were brought here from Pezon, where they attempted to drink everything in the cantinas. Of course, they ended flat on their backs, not knowing anything. In that condition they were set upon by two other men—Americanos—who claimed them as prisoners, accused of having robbed a train in Arizona. Their names are Galt and Simms." Testera pointed to two other men, who sat upright on other donkeys, likewise bound, but sitting their animals and looking spitefully at Testera.

"And those men?" said Don Pedro.

"Are the captors of the first two," answered Testera. "Knowing about the pronunciamento, the people of Pezon would not permit the captors to take the men away, but insisted that they all be brought here for judgment."

"It is right," said Don Pedro. He looked at the two men bound in upright positions. His gaze was severe.

"It is six o'clock," he said. "It is the hour of the beginning of the Fiesta del Sanctuaire. During the next week the persons of the men you have captured are inviolate. Afterward you may take them—if you can. Meanwhile, you are invited to attend the feast. Testera, release all of them!"

All were released and led away.

Testera barked a sharp order to his men, and presently Nolan, Clelland, Dean, Lathrop, Pennel, Carey, and some Mexicans were standing before Don Pedro.

"More trouble?" asked Don Pedro.

Testera related the story of the attempted shooting of the moonshiner by Lathrop and Pennel. He studied the faces of all of those who were connected with the adventure, at last looking long at Nolan.

"I have seen you before, señor?" he asked. "Are you not that Señor Nolan who last year came to Rancho Paloma to buy cattle?"

"I am, Magnífico," answered Nolan.

"Myself and my men came upon them at the river," said Testera. "We heard what had happened, and we thought Your Excellency should judge."

"Good!" said Don Pedro. "You say the capture was made before six o'clock?"

"At dawn, Magnífico."

"The prisoner belongs to Señors Lathrop and Pennel," decided Don Pedro. "However, he cannot be taken away or molested until the end of the feast. He is free while he remains within the limits that have been named as sanctuary. Señors Lathrop and Pennel will try to remove him at their peril! Dismiss them!"

Dean, Carey, Lathrop, Pennel, the moonshiner—whose name was Manville—and the Mexicans who had accompanied Dean, moved up the slope of the mesa. Nolan and Clelland sat down in some grass at the base of a tree. Clelland looked at Nolan and wondered why the latter did not follow the others. He himself had no intention of going anywhere unless Nolan preceded him. For Clelland suspected that trouble would soon raise its head among those who were gathered here, and he intended to be as near as possible to Nolan when the clash came.

Don Pedro and his vaqueros were grouped at a little distance. A few of the guests that had come for the feast were scattered among the trees, delaying their ascent to the mesa. Their reasons were their own, and Clelland was not bothering about them. He watched Nolan without appearing to do so. And when, after a while, he observed Nolan gazing at the head of a gorge about two or three hundred yards distant, where a band of horsemen was emerging, he saw a flood of colour stain Nolan's face. Searching for the cause of his friend's sudden embarrassment, Clelland saw a girl riding a horse near the head of the column.

"So that's why he's losin' interest in the old life, eh?" was Clelland's thought. "H'm. Well, I'm glad I'm here! That's old Bazan's daughter, and the wild, handsome guy that's ridin' so close to her is Zorilla! An' Don Pedro's cork has gone under! He's got a bite that he can't scratch! If the old boy knowed anything about apoplexy, he'd sure throw a fit of it right now!"

Don Pedro had recognized his ancient enemy and his daughter. Apparently he suspected what had happened, for his face was the colour of a ripened pepper and his eyes were darting venomous glances that were definitely centred upon Zorilla.

Zorilla was grinning. He led his band of horsemen to a point near where Don Pedro stood, ordered them sharply to halt, and sat in the saddle bowing to his enemy.

"We have come to attend the feast, Magnífico," he said.

Don Pedro's red-pepper complexion was fading. Perhaps he felt that a show of temper in this situation would not be dignified. Perhaps he felt that with a superior force behind him he could well bide his time. At any rate, he had grown calmer, though Clelland, who was watching him intently, observed flecks of passion in his eyes.

He did not answer Zorilla; his gaze went to his daughter, who met it steadily, with a suggestion of laughter in her eyes.

"The Señorita Juana Bazan will please tell me how it happens that she arrives at the fiesta in the company of mongrels," he said evenly. "Is it possible that in this country there are no longer any gentlemen with whom she might ride?"

"There are times when one has no choice, Señor Magnífico," answered the girl.

"Do you mean to say that Zorilla forced you to ride with him?" thundered Don Pedro.

Señorita Juana's laugh tinkled with amusement.

"Worse than that, Señor the Magnificent," she answered. "At frequent intervals I have had to listen to Señor Zorilla's declarations of love. He insists, señor, that he cannot live without me. He declares that he will marry me despite all objections. He threatens to carry me to his mountain fastness to feed me upon goat meat and pulque. And, ai, there was to be love for dessert. Señor Zorilla would not permit me to forget that!"

"*Peste!*" growled Don Pedro. "And has this dog dared to offend you otherwise?"

She shook her head with a quiet negative.

"Señor Zorilla knew better than that," she declared. "I must confess that he has acted the gentleman."

"*Puf!*" sneered Don Pedro.

"At any rate, he has not offended me," the girl went on. "He and his men captured me yesterday before sundown as I was riding through the *tierras calientes*. We spent last night in a wood on a plateau. I had a tent to myself, Señor the Magnificent. I slept on the softest robes, in vast security. I had the best of treatment and the choicest of foods."

"And yet you were not at liberty to ride here alone. You were Zorilla's prisoner!"

"There is no doubt of that," conceded the girl.

"*Diablos!*" ejaculated Don Pedro. His gaze sought out Testera.

"You will place this dog under arrest!" he ordered. "He shall be tied up and flogged! And after he has been punished until he realizes the greatness of the crime he has committed, he shall face a firing squad!"

Testera paled, though he sat erect and wheeled his horse so that it faced Zorilla and his men.

Zorilla smiled.

"I fear my men will object, Señor the Magnificent," he said. "You will observe that they are all armed. Perhaps there are some among them who would object very little if I were to be flogged and shot, but all will resent discovering that your pronunciamento means so little."

Don Pedro paled and stood silent. He had given his word. He had ruled that the moonshiner and the two train robbers were immune during the period of the space of time set aside by him, and if he had a thought of being consistent, and, what was more important, of retaining the respect of the people in his domain, he must permit his enemy to enjoy the immunity he had granted to all others.

He stood, looking at Testera and frowning. His face reddened again when he felt all were watching him; it paled when he glanced at Zorilla.

So far Zorilla had the best of it. For one thing, he had kept his temper, had concealed the rage that must have beset him at having been termed a "dog" and a "mongrel." Zorilla was keen about the advantage he held, an advantage which was his through Don Pedro's generosity. Also, Zorilla was enjoying Don Pedro's discomfiture. Don Pedro knew that, and the knowledge inflamed him still further. And yet, mastering himself, he spoke calmly:

"So be it, Señor Zorilla. You have played a keen trick. And you have possession of Señorita Juana during the days of the feast. Yet you are not to molest her in any way, even though you control her actions. But, beware, Zorilla. When the feast is ended you shall pay heavily for your impertinence!"

"*Si*, Señor Magnífico," said Zorilla, his voice soft as silk.

At this instant Don Pedro became aware of Nolan standing beside him. He looked sharply at Nolan, who looked straight back at him and smiled a tight-lipped smile.

"Señor the Magnificent," said Nolan, "a man does not have to accept sanctuary, does he?"

"It is not compulsory, Señor Nolan," answered Don Pedro, astonished that anyone should think of refusing to accept.

"I'm not accepting it," said Nolan. "Not right now. There are some things to be done." He looked at Zorilla, and Clelland saw that over his face was settling the recklessness that had marked him in the old days.

"I'm not accepting it," repeated Nolan, "and I'm wondering if the dog, Zorilla, chooses to hide behind it!"

Clelland got stealthily to his feet and dropped his right hand to the holster of the heavy revolver at his hip.

Clelland was conscious of an odd thrill. Before him stood the old Nolan, the man he knew; the quiet, confident, imperturbable fighter who took no thought of odds or of consequences, and the emotion that filled Clelland found expression in his voice:

"We're goin', Jim!"

CHAPTER IX

With Nolan's utterance came a new atmosphere. It was as if a vital and electric force had suddenly been unleashed upon a quiescent, passive, and half-humorous group of people, finding them unprepared, incredulous, and leaving them amazed and stunned.

There were many men gathered at the base of the slope leading to the mesa, and even though Don Pedro's magnificent figure stood out among them, there had seemed to be no leader, no one with sufficient strength of personality to assume authority. Don Pedro had brought the group together, and he was given a certain respect, which was almost a half-humorous tolerance. But Don Pedro's authority was without dignity, and in the hearts of those whom he had brought together was no awe for his power.

Behind Nolan was the sinister threat of the heavy revolver with its black stock lying naked just below his right hip. And still more sinister was the frosty, steellike glint in his blue eyes, the straightness of his lips, and the freezing calm of his manner. The instant he spoke he dominated the group. He became a dread figure from which, at the slightest suggestion of resistance, death might leap in any direction.

And Nolan was not perturbed by the risk he was taking in baiting the outlaw. At any instant one of the latter's men might draw a gun and attempt to kill him. No such probability concerned Nolan. The cold confidence of his manner proclaimed him in his own estimation supreme. And at such moments a man is very likely to be accepted at his own valuation.

Nolan looked straight at Zorilla. The heavy silence that had fallen endured, grew oppressive. Clelland watched with an inclusive stare which took in, mainly, all of Zorilla's men. Don Pedro's complexion became again the fiery hue of red pepper. Testera grew paler. Don Pedro's vaqueros stiffened and wheeled their horses so that they faced Zorilla's men.

Señorita Juana alone seemed immune to the general tenseness which, at a stroke, had overtaken all the men. She sat quietly on her horse during the silence, darting glances into the faces of the three—her father, Nolan, and the outlaw chief. Nor was there in her eyes even a hint that she sensed the tragedy which Nolan's words had made imminent. Her colour had not changed; the amused smile which had been on her lips when she had drawn her horse down to confront her father had not vanished. It appeared to grow more expansive as her gaze sought Nolan. And her long lashes seemed to veil mischief.

"*Ay de mi!*" she exclaimed softly, "is it not the gringo señor who came last year to the Rancho Paloma to buy cattle?"

With his left hand Nolan removed his wide-brimmed Stetson and swept it toward his knees. The hat had been tight about his head, and when it came off there was revealed the impression of the hatband where it had pressed the raven-black short curls. The curls were abundant but in disorder. And as when Juana had seen Nolan before, there was one curl which drooped over his forehead with singularly defiant negligence.

The mischief in Juana's eyes grew deeper, even though she drew a long breath.

"One does not forget such a visit, señorita," answered Nolan. He flushed a little, whereat the girl's eyes grew distinctly brighter.

But Nolan had started something which he meant to finish, and he replaced the hat upon his head. His voice was several degrees colder when he again spoke.

"And now, if the Señorita Juana will excuse me, I shall——"

"Proceed to pursue trouble," interrupted the girl. "You are intent to kill Zorilla. *De veras*, how bloodthirsty you are! And why should you seek to kill Señor Zorilla?"

"Zorilla plucks roses that do not belong to him," said Nolan, a glint coming into the frostiness of his eyes.

"Ai," she said, "and do you blame him for wanting a thing he can never possess? I assure you, Señor Nolan, it is quite a universal fault. And I shouldn't want Señor Zorilla killed because he admires me!

"Also, I am certain that Señor Zorilla will not refuse to accept sanctuary, even to fight with you. For in that case he would forfeit his right to entertain me for a week. In addition, he would very likely be killed. For I have heard that you are a terrible fighter, Señor Nolan. Besides, Señor Zorilla amuses me; he is so original and vehement."

"If Señor Nolan will compose himself until after the feast I will give him all the fighting he wants!" declared Zorilla. "I accept sanctuary because it is my right and because I choose to do so. And if Señor Nolan does not vamos before dawn on the last day of the feast I shall flog him as I would flog any other little boy!"

"Zorilla is brave when he talks of the things he is goin' to do. Yet, with a gun at his hip, he does nothing," answered Nolan.

"Zorilla does nothing in my presence to offend me," said Juana. "Does Señor Nolan respect me as much, or will he fight and distress me?"

Nolan bowed and his eyes flashed. A smile curved his lips.

"The señorita commands," he said. His smile was now for Zorilla. "On the last day you shall make good your boast," he promised.

"If you do not run before that," said Zorilla, his smile smooth and bland. "Or if I find an opportunity to strike sooner," he thought.

Juana flashed a bright smile at Nolan, while Zorilla, observing the smile, frowned ferociously and promised himself to make opportunity.

At this instant Don Pedro, who had been standing by helplessly, feeling the futility of interference and twisting his features into grimaces which he felt were expressing a judicial attitude, noisily cleared his throat and spoke pompously:

"*Bastante!* Señors, I command you to be silent! I shall adjust this matter! And you may be assured that both will receive justice. I am not called Pedro the Wise for nothing!"

A ripple of admiration in which there was a hint of amusement ran through the group, and Don Pedro swelled with pride.

"You are both within the zone of sanctuary," he declared sonorously. "Therefore, although I should have Zorilla dragged away and shot for the crime he has committed, and though I should reprimand Señor Nolan for attempting to fight in my presence on a sacred day, I do neither! Our differences shall be forgotten until the last day of the feast. Then I shall strike!"

"Señor Zorilla, I warn you! Señor Nolan, remember I am master here! Ascend to the mesa—all of you! And let me hear no more of this quarrel until the last day! Vamos!"

Don Pedro turned his back and moved toward the ascent with what dignity his huge body would permit. He looked neither to the right nor the left, and strutted like a peacock displaying its glorious iridescent feathers.

But though Juana and Zorilla and Nolan and Clelland and all the rest of them followed closely after Don Pedro, not one of them looked straight ahead.

Clelland stayed back of Nolan to guard him from harm; Juana gave Nolan a witching smile which brought a crimson tint to the young man's face. And Zorilla watched, frowning.

CHAPTER X

Nolan had heard much of the Mesa of the Angels, and when he reached the edge of the great, high level land he paused and drew a deep breath of amazement.

The mesa top stretched, green and beautiful, to a distance of several miles. Through the aisles of the trees—cypress, eucalyptus, lapacho, and palms, some of them with a filmy lace veil of Spanish moss—he could see, glittering in the sun, the waters of a small stream that flowed from a gorge between two mountains at a point where the mesa jutted from their shoulders. In another and smaller gorge, not so distant, he could see the stream again, gleaming in the sunlight that filtered down through the trees. And to his left, as he stood facing eastward, he observed the stream a third time, where it went foaming down a miniature fall to the country below.

To his left, also, he observed a large clearing. The clearing spanned the watercourse, and there was a place where the stream had been dammed so that a pool had been formed in a hollow. Near the pool a number of large tables had been built, and at the tables worked a great number of men and women who were preparing food for the first meal of the feast. Farther back in the clearing were ovens and stoves out of which floated appetizing aromas. Bales, crates, boxes, serons, casks, panniers, bundles, were piled in tiers around the edge of the clearing. There was an abundance of supplies.

On every hand were tents, tent houses, rough board shacks, canopies, hammocks. Whole families were clustered around bedding upon which they had slept during the night. Among all the guests was an eagerness to get their effects into shape for the week's sojourn. Whether by prearrangement or by instinct, the various paraphernalia of shelter was stretched out in rows resembling streets, with some attempt to establish parallel lines.

As Nolan and Clelland walked eastward along one of the streets they observed men and women in various stages of deshabille. Women in loose negligee, barefooted, uncombed; men bare to the waist, washing their faces, shaving, combing and oiling their hair. Some were arraying themselves in gaudily coloured garments; others, already dressed, were pirouetting before women also gaily attired and ready for the festivities. Couples—lovers by their actions—were deep in shaded aisles, far from the streets, walking arm in arm.

Nolan and Clelland heard no word of discord, but to their ears came much laughter and banter.

For a moment after reaching the mesa Nolan had stood watching Zorilla and Juana and the outlaw's men. He was wondering if Zorilla meant to exercise his right to hold Juana prisoner during the festivities. It seemed that Juana also was wondering, for as Nolan watched from a distance he observed Juana straighten as she looked at the outlaw. Zorilla's face was toward Nolan, and Nolan observed a smile upon his lips.

Then the outlaw jerked a thumb toward the southern side of the mesa, indicating in pantomime that Juana was to accompany him.

The movement was a command, though no doubt his smile was meant to be cajoling. Nolan could not hear their voices, though he observed Zorilla's lips moving.

For an instant it seemed Juana meant to refuse, for she drew herself more erect and tightened the mantilla where it folded about her neck. Her manner was imperious. In the next instant, however, just when Nolan was thinking that he would now have an opportunity to shoot Zorilla, Juana tilted her chin in the air and sent a rippling laugh over the mesa. A laugh of irritating mockery. Then, kissing a hand to her father, who was standing at a little distance silently regarding her, she followed Zorilla through the trees, southward.

After reaching the crest of the mesa she hadn't looked once at Nolan, and Nolan, who was expecting at least a glance, was disappointed.

Followed by Clelland, Nolan walked eastward half a mile. Then, halting among some trees, he half smiled at his companion.

"We'll camp here, I reckon."

Both men had brought the slickers from their saddles. Nolan dropped his to the grass and seated himself near it. Clelland did likewise. The two men gazed at each other, and into Clelland's eyes came a subtle glint.

"In the old days you'd have salivated him," he remarked.

"Meanin' Zorilla," said Nolan. "Yes, I reckon I would have. He's a mighty annoyin' man."

"Nice girl," said Clelland. "Knowed her long?"

"I saw her when I bought cattle from Don Pedro. Last year."

"H'm." Clelland rolled a cigarette. "She knowed you right away. Must have took a good look at you when you was there."

Nolan did not answer.

"You must have got a good look at her, too," said Clelland. He smiled reminiscently. "That explains it," he added.

"Explains what?"

"Them plums at Nogales. That talk about raisin' a family. Your gettin' tired of the old life." Clelland sighed. "Well," he added, "I don't know as

I blame you. She's a mighty sweet-lookin' girl." He seemed to meditate. "You reckon she's just foolin' with that there outlaw?"

"She's helpin' Don Pedro to carry this thing off in style," declared Nolan. "She knows that if she backs out of the Zorilla deal the whole country will be laughin' at her dad."

"She's game," conceded Clelland. "Most girls would have been yellin' for help an' bawlin' their eyes out."

Nolan got up.

"I reckon we'll have a look around," he said.

"I've been hankerin' to look at the layout," agreed Clelland.

They moved eastward, then southward, and Clelland's eyes gleamed with knowledge. And when a little later the two were standing at a little distance looking at a row of tents around which were some of Zorilla's men, Clelland smiled.

Where the tents had come from Clelland did not know. Nor did Nolan. The outlaws had not brought them, for they were nomadic and travelled with little impedimenta. They might have been brought in one of the many wagons which for days had been moving toward the mesa.

Most of the tents were small. They were compactly grouped, as if the outlaws desired to be close together. But there was one big tent which, though near the others, was distinctly apart.

This tent had a coloured canopy in front of it, and under the canopy was swung a hammock in which were gaudy, fluffy pillows and soft blankets. Lying in the hammock, her hands clasped behind her head as she gazed into the hot, flaming country southward from the mesa, was Señorita Juana.

Nolan and Clelland had left their slickers in the wood which they had selected for their camp, and both observing Juana at the same instant they stopped at a little distance and stood, unencumbered, slightly embarrassed.

"Far as I'm goin'," said Clelland. "I'm bushed, sort of, ridin' all night."

He dropped into some grass at the base of a tree and reclined against the trunk. Nolan grinned at him in appreciation and strode toward the hammock.

He was within half a dozen feet of Juana when she heard his step and turned her head. She blushed and sat erect, folding her mantilla, tucking in stray wisps of hair at her temples and at the nape of her neck. She was trying to pretend unconcern, but there was a breathlessness in her manner that no pretense could conceal, and Nolan's blood leaped in his veins in strange ecstasy.

Their eyes met, and they were silent, and in that wordless conversation she knew why he had sought her out, just as Nolan knew.

"Señor Nolan is brave," she said. "Or perhaps he does not know that Zorilla's men are near, watching him; and that Zorilla himself may return at any minute."

"Nolan has come to ask if you were in earnest when you declared you meant to stay with Zorilla during the feast," he said.

"And if not?" queried the girl, her gaze holding his.

"I shall take you back to your father, instantly!"

Juana's lashes drooped. She turned her head and gazed at Clelland, who still reclined at the base of the tree at a little distance. Clelland had his heavy six-shooter in hand and was carefully rubbing it with the bandana he had removed from around his neck. The girl's eyes gleamed. Her gaze went to Nolan's slim waist and the heavily studded cartridge belt. She observed at his hip the heavy revolver with its black stock, naked and projecting. And then her gaze roved upward to Nolan's eyes. Something she saw in them caused her to pale and draw a long breath.

Then she smiled again.

"Would Señor Nolan have me bring confusion upon my father?" she asked.

"Yes, if the señorita objects to Zorilla's attentions."

"Ai, that is another matter," she smiled, giving him a glance full of mischief. "Señor Nolan, I am amazed at my emotions. I had heard that Zorilla was a beast, a brute, an ugly man with uncouth habits. I find he is almost a gentleman. And he is handsome. What do you think?"

"He is handsome," conceded Nolan, with no change in his expression. "And yet, if you do not care to be his prisoner for the week, you shall go back to your father."

She laughed and drooped her lashes. She was amazed at the boldness of Nolan's gaze, at the simple directness of his manner, and at his evident eagerness to plunge headlong into trouble on her account. And she loved Nolan. His face had been in her thoughts for more than a year; she had yearned for him, had sighed for him, and there had been desolation in her heart because he had not come again to see her.

And yet he was an American; he was handsome—handsomer than Zorilla and infinitely more desirable than the outlaw—and she was not quite certain that his intentions were serious. She had heard that young Americans were inconstant in their relations with girls of her race, and she was quite certain she would not permit Nolan to divine how much she liked him until he proved that he was not trifling with her.

She looked again at Nolan, and her eyes were dancing. Yet, even though Nolan did not see it, there was tragedy behind the glint of mischief. The tragedy of doubt. The tragedy of regret that she must hurt him.

"But Zorilla amuses me, Señor Nolan. He is so—so original. He makes love like Popocatepetl! He rumbles and roars and threatens. And there is fire in him!"

There was fire in Nolan, too, she knew. The fire of jealousy. For she saw his eyes flame. And then she observed the flame die as he smiled with straight lips.

He bowed.

"The Señorita Juana will excuse me for meddling in her affairs," he said stiffly. "*Adios.*"

"And yet," said Juana as if she had not heard Nolan, "Zorilla annoys me. It is presumptuous of him to think that the daughter of Don Pedro Bazan could consider him. He is a great clown, for all his ridiculous pretensions!"

"Yet he amuses you, Señorita Juana!"

"So he does. Popocatepetl amuses me. Isn't it amusing to have something near which threatens but seldom acts? A danger that does not come, señor? A fire that never breaks into flame? A rumbling that thrills you to your very toes but which cannot harm you because you are at a safe distance?"

Nolan smiled. He had been so interested in watching the changing expression of Juana's face and in observing the eagerness in her eyes—an eagerness, he was certain, to assure him that her only motive in mentioning Zorilla was that of mischief—that he had forgotten Zorilla and the presence near him of the outlaw's men.

And now, just at the conclusion of Juana's speech, and at the instant she was about to speak again, he heard Clelland's voice from behind him.

"Easy there, Zorilla!" It came, cold and sharp. "Don't pull it if you want to keep on headin' your gang of pirates!"

Nolan stepped slowly backward and turned so that he could observe the drama that had been enacted without his knowledge.

Zorilla stood in front of his tent. It was evident that he had been listening. His eyes were blazing with rage, his lips were loose and pouting, and his right hand was hovering close to the butt of the pistol he carried at his right hip.

Clelland had ceased rubbing his weapon with the bandana. The heavy stock of the pistol was lying in his right hand, which was supported by the left, which in turn was resting upon his drawn-up knees. Clelland's back was against the tree, and he was still half-reclining. And the pistol was not pointed, though it was apparent that a quick flip of the wrist would bring its muzzle toward Zorilla. Clelland knew how to make that flip, and because of Clelland's very unconcern in holding the weapon, Zorilla was aware that he knew how to make it. Therefore, Zorilla did not draw his gun but stood in front of the tent, uncertain. He had seen Nolan under the canopy; he had not observed Clelland reclining under the tree.

Nolan smiled with straight lips which had grown a trifle pale.

"Zorilla listens," he said coldly.

"Zorilla also speaks!" declared the outlaw. His face was a poisonous red. "And Zorilla is tempted to speak to his men, to tell them to shoot you like the dog you are!"

"Zorilla speaks but he don't say anything," interrupted Clelland shortly. "An' Zorilla ain't sayin' nothin' to his men because he knows that if he does his days of talkin' are ended!"

A silence came. Zorilla slowly regained his normal colour; Juana breathed more deeply, Nolan smiled crookedly at the outlaw; Zorilla's men were motionless.

Zorilla held his life in his hands. He knew it, and he decided to keep it. For upon his lips a smile was born—a smooth, silky smile, which told Nolan and Clelland that the incident was ended, though there would come a time when it would be carried further.

"It pleases Señorita Juana to play with you, it seems, Señor Nolan, just as it pleases her to play with me. She loves me! Her glances have told me. Señor Nolan does not know women. But before the week is ended Señor Nolan shall stand near and watch her face the Padre with me at her side!"

"You will go to your father now?" asked Nolan, ignoring Zorilla.

She blushed. "You know why I cannot, Señor Nolan," she answered.

Nolan bowed to her.

"*Adios*," he said, and turned on his heel.

CHAPTER XI

Eastward, toward the middle of the mesa, Nolan and Clelland came upon Dean and his friend Carey. Don Pedro had seen Dean at the base of the mesa before they had ascended, and after Don Pedro had established himself in the permanent house which years before had been built for him on the mesa, he had sent for the engineer and had supplied him with a tent and bedding for himself and Carey.

Dean's eyes lighted when he saw Nolan.

"The old codger has a way about him," he told Nolan. "He really is respected by these people. They swear by him. It seems to me that they all know he is a boaster and a braggart, but he does things on such a grand scale that they are impressed. Did you ever see such a stack of supplies! There is enough food piled around to feed an army for a month!"

"And," said Carey, "they've even got ice."

Dean moistened his lips reminiscently.

"Ah!" he exclaimed.

"Where is Don Pedro's house?" asked Nolan.

The house was visible from where Nolan stood. It was a square affair, rather large, with a portico across the front, which was gaily decorated. The house sat in a grove of palms on a slight eminence from which Don Pedro could view a great part of the mesa.

"Don Pedro is concerned about his daughter," said Dean. "He doesn't say much, but he keeps looking toward Zorilla's camp; and I wouldn't be surprised to discover that he has some of his vaqueros watching the outlaw. And, by the way, Nolan, that was a mighty fine thing you did down there at the foot of the mesa. I noticed that several of Zorilla's men had nervous trigger fingers. They might have shot you. That took nerve!" He smiled into Nolan's eyes. "I just want you to know that if any trouble develops I'll be ready for a call."

When Nolan and Clelland approached Don Pedro's house they saw Don Pedro seated in a chair of monstrous size on the portico. There was a big table in front of him, upon which were a silver platter of sweetmeats, some pastry, a silver decanter, and some tall goblets. A glass, half empty, was standing at Don Pedro's elbow. Don Pedro himself was sitting back in his chair meditatively frowning.

He did not see Nolan and Clelland until they were at the edge of the portico, and then he started and sat erect.

"*Buenos dias*, señors," he greeted.

He motioned grandly for them to take chairs and draw themselves to the table, and while they did so he filled glasses for them from the silver decanter.

"*Peste!*" he exclaimed after they had drained their glasses. "I am enraged! That dog Zorilla has tricked me! You observed that, Señor Nolan—and you, Señor Clelland? You observed how he took advantage of my generosity to steal my daughter, knowing well that I had already committed myself and could not harm him! *Pero mas*, señors, there was a time when I could hardly restrain myself. I was moved to shoot him as he sat there grinning his apish grin. I had my pistol out—did you notice? Señors, I was ready to risk death at the hands of his men! They might have killed me, but they could not intimidate me! Not I! Death will be nothing to me, señors. When it comes I shall meet it with a smile upon my lips. I was about to shoot Zorilla. I had steeled myself! And then I caught Testera winking at me, warning me. He has not yet hinted the reason for his warning, but I have no doubt that a dozen or so of Zorilla's men were ready to shoot me. *Ai*, that mongrel, Zorilla!"

Nolan's face at this minute lacked expression. But Clelland, though schooled to repression, was compelled to avert his gaze that Don Pedro might not see the mirth in his eyes. For his own recollection of the incident that Don Pedro referred to was that Don Pedro had been frightened to silence. In fact, it had not been until after Nolan had threatened Zorilla that Don Pedro had opened his mouth or moved a muscle.

"But, señors," Don Pedro continued, "you are my friends. I can see that. Señor Nolan, you were magnificent! You are as brave as I! You faced that dog without a sign of trepidation! I could not have done better myself! And you, Señor Clelland! I observed you! You were ready, too. I saw your fingers touching your pistol! You would have backed Señor Nolan up; you would have died right there! Señors, I am glad you came to the feast. And you will stay to the end, will you not? You will stay to help me save my daughter from Zorilla?"

"We stay," said Nolan.

Don Pedro smiled expansively. He refilled the glasses. Clelland drank, but Nolan merely sipped his. Again the glasses were filled, and again Don Pedro and Clelland drank. Meanwhile Don Pedro talked in his grandiose manner, assuring his guests that his power was so great in the country that men trembled when his name was spoken. He even got up and essayed to imitate the bow that Valdez had shown him while the latter had been a prisoner at the Rancho Paloma—the bow that Valdez contended the inhabitants of the country used to express their awe and veneration of the lord of the domain.

"They bow low, these people," he said. "Yet their bowing is not as low as it shall be when they learn of my real greatness! Come, let us drink!"

Disastrously, Clelland attempted to keep pace with Don Pedro. There was an hour of drinking and listening to their guest, and then Clelland limply slipped down in his chair and rested his sagging chin upon the table top. Amazed, Don Pedro called his servants and had Clelland taken into the house, where he was placed in a hammock and his face covered against the flies.

Nolan took his leave. The wine that Clelland had consumed would keep him in the hammock for many hours, and on the morrow he would be worthless.

Nolan made his way over the mesa alone. Around him moved Don Pedro's guests. Everywhere were colour and movement and noise. Walking northward Nolan came into a clearing where some fat, tonsured friars reclined on the grass, eating and drinking. A convent band under some trees near by was playing the "Jubilate." There was much laughter here, for a fat friar was telling stories. One of Zorilla's outlaws, his red liberty cap brilliant in contrast to the sombre colours worn by the friars, stood at the edge of the clearing, watching and listening.

"*Peste!*" Nolan heard him exclaim as he passed: "*Es verdad?*" (Is it true?) "In that case me and my companions do not do so bad. We are not worse, anyway!"

Near the northern edge of the mesa a band of peon musicians were blowing on pipes. Others were yelling and laughing and dancing. Everywhere discordant melody assailed Nolan's ears. Flageolets and oboes were groaning and shrilling.

Seating himself near a clump of brush from where he could see the cooks working at the long tables, Nolan leaned back on an elbow and watched the scene. And as he sat there meditating and listening, voices reached his ears. The voices came from behind the brush clump near where he was sitting, and he had no difficulty in overhearing. As a matter of fact, he could not help hearing, for the voices were sonorous, argumentative.

"You guys don't dare pull off any monkey business here!" said one voice. "You can hang around all you please, an' keep an eye on me. But you don't dast do no shootin'. 'Cause why? 'Cause everybody'd know who done the shootin', an' yore throats would be cut before you could get away. Now, set there, cuss you, an' watch me 'still this here whisky!"

Nolan smiled. He had no need to look around, for he was convinced that he was listening to Manville, the moonshiner. And from the defiance in Manville's voice he suspected that the latter was talking to Pennel and Lathrop, the revenue agents.

"Where I got the mash is my business," said Manville. "I got it. An' I got the kettles. You seen me buildin' the fire. Watch her steam!"

Nolan peered through the brush, for his curiosity was aroused. Squatting beside a little fire back of the brush was Manville. Over his fire was a small copper kettle with a conelike lid. The lid was inverted, and in the depression was a cake of ice, slowly melting. Near Manville, on the ground, was more ice.

Manville was grinning. His eyes were bleared from his impotations, for now and then he would reach down into the copper kettle and dip a tin cup into the liquor.

Lathrop and Pennel were sitting near him, sullenly watching him.

Manville licked his lips after each drink and grinned widely at the revenue agents.

"She's simple when you know how," he said. "Anyone can make whisky. This here kettle has got water in the bottom of it. There's a flat stone on the bottom, too, which is just high enough to clear the water. There's a little kettle settin' on that stone. The mash is in the water. The cone of this lid is right over the kettle settin' on the stone. When the mash boils it sends steam ag'in' the cone of the lid. The ice on the top of the lid condenses the steam, an' the steam falls down the cone into the little kettle—drop by drop. That keeps goin'."

"Keep drinkin' it," said Lathrop. "I hope it kills you!"

Nolan was not interested in this conversation. He got up and walked away.

The sun had grown high. Nolan was hungry, and he approached one of the long tables in the clearing near the stoves and the stores and helped himself to the food that was set out there. He ate only some bacon and bread and drank some vile coffee. Around him Mexicans were devouring *bacalao* (salt cod); red herrings; hashes of mysterious ingredients; ham, carne con cuero; armadillo flesh, which looked fresh and luscious, resembling opossum; roast javelina; maize and manioc; peppers; frijoles; kid meat stuffed with olives; calabash stew, and various other viands the names of which Nolan was not familiar. They were drinking boiled sour wine in prodigious quantities.

A band of men from the lowlands, wearing *potro* boots, was devouring food taken from the tables with their fingers. A *guitarreros* band near by were vigorously strumming their instruments. Under a tree were two fiddlers. Another group played 'cellos, clarinets, and hautboys.

Nolan spent the day watching Don Pedro's guests disport themselves. Several times he saw Dean and Carey, the two train robbers Galt and

Simms, and the two detectives who had trailed the robbers. The detectives were named Belden and Colton.

And Nolan also saw "Slim" Waldron, his old-time enemy. Waldron had become friendly with the Mexicans. Twice when Nolan observed him he was seated upon the grass under a tree with a Mexican girl; and another time he was drinking with a group of men. He did not see Nolan.

But Nolan was in no mood to talk to the men of his race. In the midst of all the gaiety he was lonesome and thoughtful. For Juana's manner disturbed him. He knew Juana's blushes could mean only one thing, and yet she had proclaimed to him that she intended staying with Zorilla because he amused her. How much of her attitude was filial loyalty and how much was pure mischief, he did not know. But he knew one thing. He loved her and he meant to have her.

Yet not once again during the day did he go near the outlaw camp. He spent a tiresome day, and when dusk began to fall he went to the grove where Clelland and he had left their slickers and seated himself on a flat rock under the trees.

For an hour or more he sat there watching the fading colours of the afterglow as they dimmed in the solemn twilight.

Lanterns began to glimmer on the mesa top. Near the centre, where Don Pedro's house stood, were the greater number of lanterns, though here and there all along the mesa they appeared singly and in clusters.

The laughter, the hilarity, and the noises continued until nearly midnight, and until nearly midnight Nolan sat and watched and listened. He had made mental note of the location of the outlaw camp, and now he observed that there were few lights near it.

He was glad when the sounds of hilarity began to diminish. Here and there still sounded the shrill notes of a solitary pipe; now and then the liquid music of a guitar reached him, and rippling laughter, as of some Mexican señorita teasing her lover.

Presently even these sounds ceased, and Nolan was enveloped in a profound silence which settled down over and around him like a vacuum.

The moon, which had been swimming low over the western horizon at dusk, had now vanished, leaving a mellow golden flood to fade and sink after it. Only for an hour or so had the moon been visible, but in that time it had worked its enchantment upon the country surrounding the mesa. It had caused the peaks of distant mountains to shimmer with a golden radiance, it had wrought soft purple shadows in the silent gorges, it had sent long lances to penetrate remote cañons, it had drenched the plains with an effulgent mellow flood. Its rays had tinted the foliage of the trees upon the nearer hills, turning the dark green leaves into silver; it had made of the land a mystic place of quiet, rich tones and soothing beauty.

Gradually receding, drawing its light and its radiance with it, the moon left a brooding darkness which was little relieved by the velvet blue of the sky glittering with the cold points of the stars.

It grew dark on the mesa top, with a blackness that hovered close and that the eye could not penetrate. Only the lanterns on the mesa could be seen, and they, one by one, went out. After the last lantern light faded the darkness seemed to hover closer.

And yet there still remained in Nolan's mind a picture of the land as he had seen it by moonlight. It was to such a place as this, he decided, that angels would come if they were to visit the earth. Nowhere else had he seen the moonlight so beautiful.

He sought his slicker and blankets, and found them where he and Clelland had left them, under a tree. He sat down upon his own slicker and fell to reviewing the events of the day.

He was disappointed. Remembering still the way Juana had looked at him more than a year before, he felt that he should have made some progress. He hadn't made any. Juana was interested in him, but the interest she had shown was not the sort of interest he sought, and he wondered if he hadn't presumed upon the glance she had given him when he had seen her the first time.

He was aware of how the mind plays its tricks, and of how memory persists in magnifying everything. No doubt her glance at him when he had seen her at the Rancho Paloma had betrayed interest in him, and perhaps he alone had invested the glance with a deeper meaning than she had meant to give it. But, if that were the case, how could he interpret the glances she had given him to-day—especially the first glance, which had lasted long, and which had seemed to tell him that she had been waiting for him?

Mischief? Coquetry? Well, perhaps. Most girls succeeded in making a man understand their interest. Yet he had never encountered a girl who had looked at him like that, nor had he ever seen a girl who had made him feel as he had felt each time he looked at Juana. She had made him lose interest in his daily tasks, in his old friends, in his old pleasures. She had changed him from a reckless youth to a thoughtful, serious-minded man with all the conservativeness of middle age.

He drew off his boots and stood them against the trunk of the tree, feeling around in the darkness. He unrolled the slicker, laid it on the ground, stretched out on it, unfolded his blankets, pulled them over him, wrapped his feet in the bottom, laid his Stetson under his head, and stretched out to gaze at the sky.

He was not yet done with his thoughts of Juana, and for an hour or more he watched the stars while his thoughts dwelt upon her face. Thinking of her was delightful.

He must have fallen asleep quickly, for he came suddenly out of oblivion with all his senses alert and acute, as they had been trained to do by the life he had led all his days.

He did not move except to slip his right hand down along his side until the fingers came in contact with the naked butt of the gun that hung there.

Around him was the soft and all-pervading silence that had encompassed him when he had drawn the blankets around him. The darkness, he felt, had grown denser, and there were more stars in the sky. There came to his ears no sounds except the night noises to which he had grown accustomed; and though he heard nothing strange he was aware that a strange sound must have awakened him.

As he did not know from which direction the sound had come he could not decide in which direction to listen for a recurrence of it, so he remained flat on his back with his head propped up a little with his left hand, listening, while his right hand drew out the heavy pistol.

Presently, from an easterly direction, which was on his left, came a sound which resembled that which might be made by the snapping of a twig on the ground.

The sound was not sharp, but dull and sodden, as if a foot had rested heavily upon the twig and had pressed it into the soft earth. And yet it was not like that, precisely; it was more as if something softer than a booted foot had pressed upon the twig—a hand, a knee, or a beast's paw. Still, he could not be sure, for a moccasined foot would yield the same sound, or a *potro* boot, which is made from colt hides, without soles. Yet *potro* boots were worn only by lowlanders, who were peons, and he could think of no reason why any lowlander should be prowling around in the darkness near his camp.

Nor could he understand why anybody should be prowling around at this hour, though now that he had ascertained the direction from which the sound had come he was prepared to meet the intruder and make things interesting for him if he meant to attack. Therefore he twisted himself slightly until he was lying partly upon his left side, with the pistol outside the blanket and lying rigid along his right hip, his finger on the trigger.

He had estimated that the sound had come from a distance of perhaps fifty or sixty feet, and he was now interested in discovering whether what was making the sound was coming toward him or going away. And when a little later he heard the sound again, though it was slighter this time, he was convinced that whatever it was, man or beast, it was approaching him. Also, it was approaching with the utmost stealth.

Nolan smiled mirthlessly in the dark. Man or beast, the big pistol would finish it.

Yet he did not believe it was an animal that was stealing upon him. He was gazing in the direction from which the sounds had come, and he knew that an animal stalking its prey never removes its gaze for an instant, and if the intruder was an animal he would by this time have caught the gleam of its eyes even in the faint star haze.

The prowler was a man.

Nolan listened more intently, seeking other sounds which would tell him whether there were more than one presence near him. He heard nothing from any other direction.

Nor did he hear the sounds of other twigs breaking. For a time he heard no stealthy sounds at all. And then, a little later, he was aware of a slight slithering noise, such as might be made by a snake writhing through dried leaves.

That sound ceased. All sound ceased. There came a silence so dead and calm that Nolan's ears ached with it. And then in that silence came a slow, long exhalation of the Thing's breath.

A man!

The prowler was breathing hard and fast now, as though under stress of excitement or of passion, and the sound appeared to come from a point not more than half a dozen feet distant, and to Nolan's left.

Still the darkness was so dense that Nolan could not penetrate it, though he had grimly shifted his weapon so that the muzzle was pointed directly toward the prowler.

He had thought of Clelland, that the prowler might be his friend. And he had dismissed that thought, for it was unlike Clelland, drunk or sober, to move by stealth anywhere, at any time. Also, his final look at Clelland, there at Don Pedro's house, had convinced him that many hours would pass before Clelland would be able to stand. Clelland would not show his face out of the house until daylight at the earliest. And if the prowler were Clelland he would have made his presence known.

Yet Nolan did not mean to fire at the prowler unless he was convinced that an attack was intended. His senses strained, his muscles tensed, he waited.

He could hear the man breathing, could hear the leaves and dried grass softly rustling with the prowler's progress toward him.

And now, thinking the time had come, he carefully slipped out of the blanket and sought to get to his feet. With the movement came a sudden threshing from the point where the prowler crouched, a stifled grunt, a muffled groan of agony! Distinctly Nolan heard the creaking of bones, the straining of sinews, the heaving of bodies locked close together. Murder was being done close to Nolan, and he was powerless because of the density of the darkness to interfere!

He heard a sound, such as might be made by someone sitting down heavily upon dried leaves and grass. Then followed a silence which was presently broken by the snapping of a twig at a distance. Another silence came. Crouching there, motionless, leaning forward a little the better to listen, Nolan heard nothing more, saw nothing. He felt that whoever had been moving toward him had gone.

And then out of the silence came sound. Such sound as might be made by drops of water falling singly and regularly upon a sheet of dry paper. A slight and persistent tapping which Nolan felt was singularly like water dripping slowly from the eaves of a roof. A damp tapping, a dull and sodden sound accompanied by a liquid splashing; an after-note suggesting the breaking up of the falling drops.

Nolan did not move. He crouched there, listening, waiting. There was nothing he could do. If a murder had been committed he could not hope to capture the murderer because he did not know which way he had gone. Plunging aimlessly through the darkness in the hope of grasping someone would be a ridiculous performance, would betray panic.

Nolan was far from being unnerved by what had happened. It was his opinion that there had been a quarrel possibly over some beautiful señorita, and that one disappointed lover had trailed the successful one and killed him.

For Nolan had decided about the tapping noise. It was blood dripping upon the leaves with which the ground under the tree was strewn.

He was curious, but not curious enough to be foolhardy and reveal himself to the murderer, who might be lurking near, waiting. He did not intend to become involved in the affair. He knew how Mexicans fought, and he was aware that the knife had been used.

Yet after a while his curiosity impelled him to move cautiously forward toward the point from which the tapping noise still came. As he drew closer he heard stifled breathing, a low groan. Then he felt that there might still be hope for the stricken man.

Deliberately he lighted a match, held it in his left hand, and peered downward.

At his feet, sitting, and leaning forward upon his braced and extended arms, was a man arrayed in a jacket of cheap calico, a wide scarlet sash, dun trousers, light boots, and a red liberty cap. In one of the braced hands was a long-bladed knife which gleamed brightly in the flickering light of Nolan's match. The knife had not been used, but Nolan had an uncomfortable conviction that it had been intended for him. For the man was one of Zorilla's men, and his action in stealing stealthily upon Nolan could mean only one thing.

But the man would never again seek to kill. His throat was cut clear across, and he died as Nolan leaned over him, pitching forward limply so that his head struck Nolan's boot.

CHAPTER XII

Nolan's match went out, and he stood for some seconds motionless, wondering.

It was now quite evident to him that the man in the red liberty cap had not been killed as a result of a quarrel but by someone who knew that he was stealing upon Nolan. Very naturally Nolan decided that whoever had struck the blow at the red liberty cap was his friend. But he had no clue to the identity of that friend.

It could not have been Clelland, nor would Clelland have cut the outlaw's throat. Clelland would have shot or struck with the butt of his pistol, or would have shouted to him, to warn him, before the prowler could have got close enough to use the knife.

So far as Nolan knew, he had no other friend on the mesa. He knew Dean, to be sure, but only slightly. Likewise he knew Carey and Don Pedro and Juana. But none of these, he was certain, would have used a knife. Waldron might do so, but the weapon would have been used upon Nolan rather than upon one who was seeking to do Nolan injury.

Nolan was puzzled. He would have given some credence to his original theory had he not seen that the prowler was one of Zorilla's men, but he knew that no disappointed lover would be prowling around in the vicinity of his camp seeking a rival.

Nolan drew his boot away. The man's head had struck it, and after pitching forward the man's shoulders had sagged against the boot top.

Nolan had no desire to finish his sleep so close to the man's body, so in the darkness he picked up his slicker and blankets, placed his hat on his head, and fumbled around until he found Clelland's slicker. Then he walked away a little distance, dropped Clelland's slicker, spread his own upon the ground, rearranged his blankets, and stretched out to consider the incident.

As before, he went to sleep slowly, and awakened quickly to feel the dawn in his eyes. He sat up and gazed about him.

Already people were stirring on the mesa. He heard voices, which were resonant in the morning air. From a distance he heard a fire crackling, and an appetizing aroma reached him.

He got up, rolled his blankets into a compact bundle, searched in his slicker until he found his shaving tools, and strode off through the trees toward the stream which ran through the clearing where the kitchen had been established.

At the farther edge of the clearing, after passing around the kitchen, he found a shallow where a small pool had been formed. Half a dozen Mexicans were at the pool, washing and dressing and animatedly talking. When they saw Nolan they became silent. It seemed to him that, as he strode toward the pool, they betrayed extraordinary interest in him, for they all stood watching him, chattering in their own language.

Nolan paid little attention to them because he knew that among themselves they are voluble, and since there were few Americans at the feast their curiosity would be keen.

Nolan walked to the pool, greeted them with a low: *"Buenos dias,"* and began to roll up the sleeves of his shirt preparatory to washing his face and hands. And then he discovered why the Mexicans had been attracted to him. His hands were stained with blood!

He felt he knew how that had happened. When during the night he had picked up Clelland's slicker he had felt a moisture upon it, but at that time he had decided the moisture was dew. Now he remembered that Clelland's slicker had been near the murdered man. The man's blood must have dripped upon it.

Nolan looked down at his right boot, against which the man had fallen. A big, dark stain soiled the leather.

Nolan said nothing. He kneeled at the side of the pool and washed his hands and face, observing how the action discoloured the water. The Mexicans jabbered excitedly, but he paid no attention to them. He finished washing his hands and face, dried himself upon a towel he had brought from his slicker, and strode away toward the grove in which he had passed the night.

Reaching the grove he restored the towel to the slicker, placed Clelland's beside his own, and set off through the trees toward Don Pedro's house.

Don Pedro was walking under the trees near the house when he saw Nolan. He grinned and motioned for Nolan to approach.

"Your friend is still asleep, Señor Nolan," he greeted. "And he drank only a little. *Diablos!* He hardly more than tasted the wine. And he sleeps the sleep of *los muertos*, and will not awaken, though I have shaken him twice! As for myself, Señor Nolan, I drank two decanters after you left, before I dined. And afterward I sat on the veranda until nearly midnight sipping Benicarlo and dallying with sweetmeats. And this morning I am wide awake, and am as full of spirit as a young man arraying himself to visit his lady! And you know that I do not drink to excess, Señor Nolan. Merely a sip now and then, just enough to keep me going. For I am a connoisseur, señor; it is the quality that I enjoy and not the quantity. But you have seen that!"

"Ah," thought Nolan, "who is the judge of quantity? Appetite, certainly." Aloud he said:

"Señor the Magnificent, I am the bearer of bad news." And he told Don Pedro what had happened during the night, calling his host's attention to the fact that he never carried a knife.

"Ai, Señor Nolan, you do not need to tell me that," declared Don Pedro. "It is plain that the dog Zorilla set that man upon you! I am delighted that he did not succeed in murdering you! *Peste!* I shall have Testera gather my vaqueros together and punish Zorilla!"

"Pedro the Magnificent cannot violate his pronunciamento," Nolan reminded him. "He has promised immunity to everyone."

"Not to a murderer!" declared Don Pedro, his fat face mottled with the purple of anger almost ungovernable. "I shall charge Zorilla with this crime! He shall be punished! I will not permit my guests to be in danger of their lives! I am the court and the judge here, Señor Nolan, and I tell you that I shall have Zorilla tried this very morning!"

"And your proof, Señor the Magnificent?" asked Nolan.

Don Pedro frowned.

"I had forgotten that you did not see the murderer," he said. "And yet the fact that one of Zorilla's men was prowling around your camp with a naked knife in hand proves that he sought your life!"

"Proves it to us," said Nolan, "but to no one else."

While they had been talking there were sounds of a commotion from the direction of the grove in which Nolan had camped; and now there came toward them from the direction of the grove a crowd of men, bearing a burden. Near the head of the group was Zorilla.

Don Pedro paled.

"Do not say anything about my charging Zorilla with the murder," he whispered. "Perhaps it would be better to hear what he has to say before taking any action. There is more virtue in wisdom than in violence!"

When the men had approached to within a little distance of Don Pedro and Nolan, they halted. At a word from Zorilla they placed the body of the slain man on the grass and stood silent.

Zorilla came forward. His eyes were stern and accusing, but Nolan observed that his lips were curved as though grim humour was tugging at them. He came forward stiffly, without looking at Nolan, keeping his gaze on Don Pedro. And when he stopped within half a dozen feet of the huge figure of his host he bowed extravagantly.

"*Buenos dias, caballeros*," he said unctuously. "I bring one of you news. It is you, Magnífico. One of my men, a fellow named Benico, had his throat cut last night. He is there." He pointed to where the body lay.

Don Pedro's cheeks swelled; the muscles of his neck expanded and quivered with his efforts to maintain his self-control in the presence of his sworn enemy.

"The devil, Zorilla!" he said in his own language; "how do you know that my friend Señor Nolan killed your man?"

"Ai!" returned Zorilla, "you will observe that I have not accused him. I merely said that I had news for one of you—for you, Magnífico. And instantly you charge me with accusing Señor Nolan. Is that not strange?"

He spoke more to the group of men standing near the body than to Don Pedro, and he smiled as though calling the attention of the men to the proof of Nolan's guilt and to his own forbearance.

"Yet it is not strange that Señor Nolan should be suspected," he added. "He slept in the grove last night, and this morning he was seen washing blood from his hands. And there is blood on Señor Clelland's slicker. And Señor Clelland has disappeared."

"Señor Clelland was my guest last night," answered Don Pedro.

At the mention of Clelland's name there came a sound from inside the house and Clelland appeared in the front doorway.

Clelland's hair was tousled; he was pale and still slightly drunk, and he held to the door jambs as he gazed at Zorilla and the others. Yet his eyes blazed fiercely.

"Whoever says Jim Nolan cut anybody's throat is a damned liar!" he declared, his right hand falling to the butt of his gun. "Nobody but a Greaser would cut anybody's throat! If anybody's throat was cut I'm bettin' Zorilla did it. Don Pedro, you just step aside a little an' I'll bust that damned outlaw wide open!"

"Señor Clelland will please leave this matter to me!" said Don Pedro sternly.

Clelland's face reddened and he was about to speak when he caught Nolan's eye. Instantly he grinned.

"I'll put off shootin' the skunk if you say so," he said. "But you're sure wastin' time. Somebody'll have to shoot him sooner or later. He's got a bad case of swell head!"

Zorilla paid no attention to Clelland except to show his teeth in a slight smirk as Clelland subsided. But he cast a look of concentrated hate and malignance at Nolan, who answered the glance with a chilling smile.

"Since Señor Clelland was a guest at Magnífico's house during the night we do not accuse him," said Zorilla. "But unless Señor Nolan can explain how the blood came to be on his hands and upon his boots and his friend's slicker, we must assume that he was very close to Benico when Benico was murdered. Has Señor Nolan an explanation?"

"None that I will give Zorilla," answered Nolan.

"Señor Nolan has already explained the matter to me," pompously stated Don Pedro. "That should be enough. Señor Nolan is innocent. He carries no knife; he does not, like your men, prowl around in the dark carrying a naked knife."

Don Pedro cleared his throat and straightened importantly. "That should be enough," he repeated.

"Enough for Señor the Magnificent," smoothly said Zorilla. "But my men are uneasy and vengeful. Perhaps you can observe the interest they are taking in what we have been saying." And Zorilla smiled until his teeth glistened as he waved a hand toward a thicket of brush at his right, at a little distance southward from Don Pedro's house.

Don Pedro turned. Nolan, less trustful of Zorilla, did not remove his gaze from the outlaw. For ever since Zorilla's appearance Nolan had suspected he was keeping something back. He had been too polite, too bland, and too unconcerned.

Nolan heard Don Pedro draw a quick, sharp breath; he heard Clelland curse softly; he observed the flash of exultation that leaped into Zorilla's eyes. Still he did not remove his gaze from the outlaw, though into his own eyes came again the frosty glint that warned all who knew him that his passions were aroused.

He was now standing near the edge of the portico at the front of the house. Don Pedro was standing at his left, slightly behind him; Clelland was standing just outside the doorway; Zorilla was directly in front of Don Pedro, and a little to Nolan's left. The men grouped around the body of the outlaw had not moved; they were perhaps fifty feet distant, straight out from the front of the house.

Nolan heard Don Pedro breathing heavily; he could hear Clelland muttering profanely, but his gaze was on Zorilla with a steady watchfulness that the outlaw could not mistake.

Standing thus, he heard Don Pedro speak.

"So this is the way you take advantage of my generosity and trust? You come with all your men! They are armed with rifles! They crouch behind bushes and take aim! They are ready at your word to kill your host and his guests! You dog! You buzzard!" He stood erect and raised his voice, calling loudly:

"Testera! Testera!"

Zorilla laughed.

"Testera will not come, Magnífico. Your vaqueros are leaderless. For during the night Testera descended to the forest to see how the horses left in his charge were faring. And while there a noose fell around his shoulders and he was dragged away."

"Your work?" asked Don Pedro.

Zorilla bowed.

"One has to look ahead," he said.

CHAPTER XIII

Nolan knew, as well as Don Pedro and Clelland, what was meant by Zorilla's show of force. He had accused Nolan of murdering Benico, and he was intent upon revenge. And though Nolan still did not look toward the bushes he was certain the outlaw's men were there and that they would fire upon him at their leader's word, or perhaps at his own first aggressive movement, possibly by prearrangement. Yet he gazed as steadily as before at the man who at a stroke could bring death upon him.

"Zorilla is careful," he said, speaking to the outlaw. "He surrounds himself with many men so that no harm may come to himself."

"Zorilla is cautious," answered the outlaw. He bent forward in a sardonic bow. With the movement Nolan turned his head and looked at Clelland. But he had no need to signal to the latter, for Clelland had stepped back into the room, out of sight from the men concealed in the bushes, though he was still visible to Zorilla. And when Zorilla completed his bow and again stood erect he was gazing into the muzzle of Clelland's pistol.

Clelland's brain, still slightly stimulated by his drinking, was on the verge of obeying a vicious impulse. His finger pressed lightly on the trigger of the weapon in his hand; for an instant Zorilla's life was in danger of being snuffed out. Yet as Clelland, his eyes red and inflamed but sinister with an implacable resolution, aimed at Zorilla's heart, he had a flash of comprehension of the consequences that would follow his killing of the outlaw leader. His men, concealed in the brush, would instantly shoot Nolan and Don Pedro.

Clelland hesitated. At the same instant he heard a light step behind him, and before he could turn, a hand gently gripped the arm holding the pistol and pushed it downward.

Clelland stifled the half-formed curse that leaped to his lips as he glanced sidelong and saw Señorita Juana standing beside him.

She smiled at him.

"Foolish!" she whispered. "Shooting now would bring on a massacre! Wait!"

She smiled at him again and instantly stepped out upon the floor of the portico.

Unconcernedly, as though she had no knowledge of what impended, and as if she were ignorant of the presence of the outlaw's men in the brush, with their rifles trained toward the portico, she crossed the floor, stepped down to the grass, and walked directly to Don Pedro.

With her back to the concealed riflemen and her slender body poised lightly as a partial shield for her father and Nolan, she bowed gracefully to them.

"*Que es eso, caballeros?*" she said, laughing. "*Caro mi!* You look as though you are all ready to fly at one another's throats! Señor Zorilla, I do not like you when you have that sneer on your lips. It makes you positively hideous!"

Zorilla smiled wanly.

"And you, Señor Nolan! Are you going to kill someone? Zorilla? Everybody? *De veras!* It appears the spirit of the pronunciamento is being violated!" She gazed at her father.

"What is it?" she asked.

Silently Don Pedro pointed, and as Juana followed his gaze she seemed for the first time to see the riflemen at the edge of the brush.

"*Madre de Dios!*" she exclaimed. "There are the red caps again!" She turned and faced Zorilla, her eyes blazing with simulated passion.

"Order them back to their tents, Señor Zorilla, or I shall also refuse to abide by the terms of the pronunciamento!"

Zorilla laughed with the air of a master.

"*Peste!* I am resolute. Señor Nolan has murdered one of my men, a fellow named Benico. Señor Nolan was seen this morning washing blood from his hands. I have appealed to Señor the Magnificent, and he professes to believe Señor Nolan innocent. Señor Nolan is guilty. He is to be shot for the crime. If Señor the Magnificent refuses to turn him over to us, we will shoot him where he stands!"

Zorilla met Juana's gaze with an evil smile. She was aware that she was helpless to avert the impending tragedy. She looked swiftly at Nolan and observed that he was intently watching Zorilla. She knew from Nolan's expression that at the instant the outlaw signalled his men to shoot Nolan would draw and kill him. Nolan would immediately be riddled by the bullets from the riflemen, and perhaps her father and Clelland would likewise be shot down.

Her cheeks paled. She looked again at Nolan and her father, deliberately walked to where her father stood and pushed him in front of Nolan, while she stood directly between them and the riflemen.

But now she observed that her father was strangely agitated. He was drawing his breath in great gasps and staring with distended eyes westward over the mesa. She followed his gaze and saw many horsemen coming toward them at a gallop. At the same instant a great blast of air rushed from Don Pedro's lungs and became articulate with the one resonant word:

"*Testera!*"

The cry was one of vast delight and relief. The sound was so sincere that Zorilla seemed to whiten with apprehension. He turned to see Testera and perhaps a hundred vaqueros not more than a hundred feet distant, moving rapidly toward them.

"*Diablos!*" gasped the outlaw; "how did he get away?"

Juana looked at Nolan.

Nolan was still watching the outlaw chief. Nolan had not looked toward the approaching vaqueros; he had kept his gaze upon Zorilla with a cold fixity that betrayed the deadliness of his intentions. Now, with relief in sight, the danger of a massacre past, when there was a chance of meeting the outlaw chief as man to man, he spoke coldly:

"Zorilla is a coyote!"

Zorilla's gaze was malignant, but he said nothing. He turned his back upon Nolan, held up the palms of his hands to his men, and turned again to face Testera and his vaqueros.

The outlaws slipped out of sight behind the bushes and escaped to their tents. Testera came on quickly. He was pale, his eyes were blazing. Behind him his men pressed him eagerly, as though anxious to avenge the indignity which had been put upon their leader.

Testera slid his horse to a halt and dropped out of the saddle directly in front of Don Pedro.

He opened his mouth to speak, but Don Pedro raised a fat hand for silence; so Testera bowed his head and stood respectfully before his master.

Tragedy had been averted. The solemnity which accompanies the imminence of death had been dispelled as though by magic. Faces that had been pale were now growing soft with colour. Incipient smiles appeared. From the doorway of the house Clelland laughed with sardonic guffaws. Nolan's eyes glistened with some secret emotion. Juana's smile was bright. Testera grinned mildly, knowing that he had arrived in time. Only Don Pedro was serious.

His eyes flashed dark lightnings at Zorilla. His lungs swelled and his cheeks puffed as he gazed at the now deserted brush where the outlaws had been. The paleness had left Don Pedro's face; it had grown ruddy with a flow of blood which had returned from the place where it had receded upon the Magnífico's comprehension of personal danger. In a word, Don Pedro was again El Magnífico.

"Zorilla!" he thundered, eyeing the outlaw fiercely. The latter said nothing, though he met Don Pedro's gaze steadily, with embarrassment and amused defiance in his eyes.

"You are listening to me, Zorilla?" roared Don Pedro.

"One must listen when El Magnífico speaks," conceded the outlaw. "His voice is like the braying of a jackass."

It appeared Don Pedro did not hear Zorilla's final words, for as they were spoken he appeared to be judicially observing Nolan, for he had placed his chin in his right hand and was gently stroking it. That he heard Zorilla was apparent to all, however, for all observed how new blood rushed into his cheeks and into his temples.

"Zorilla will observe how I set all his scheming at naught," he resumed. "Zorilla contrives to capture my Testera. Zorilla imagines that by capturing Testera he will be able to defy me. But behold! I call, and Testera appears! You ask me how it happens that Testera appears when last night you captured him. I answer that you have no knowledge of the extent of my power. Testera had not been a prisoner for an hour when my vaqueros, who had watched you, and who had permitted you to get yourself into this trap, appeared and released him! I have permitted you to betray yourself, Señor, that I might in the end confound you with proof of my omnipresence.

"But, señor, like all great men, I refuse to stoop to pettiness. I might have you shot for your impudence. I might have you flogged for presuming to attempt to set your authority above mine. I do neither. I set you an example of generosity and mercy. I am the last one to violate the spirit of my pronunciamento. You are free to go and come as you please. But beware how you stretch my patience, señor! Begone! The Señorita Juana will remain!"

Zorilla walked away, grinning. Juana smiled and curtsied to Nolan. Clelland laughed. Don Pedro looked at all of them with thunder in his gaze, as if to reprove them for levity upon an occasion so solemn.

Five minutes later, in the house with a bottle of wine between them, Don Pedro was looking across the table at Testera.

"Señor Testera," asked Don Pedro, "how did you escape Zorilla's men?"

"I was tied to a tree," answered Testera. "They left me there. Just before dawn, when the darkness is most dense, someone crept up to the tree and cut my bonds. My deliverer must be a man of violence, for though there was no wound upon me, when I looked at my hands—where the deliverer had touched them in freeing me—they were stained with blood!"

CHAPTER XIV

"Ai!" exclaimed Don Pedro.

He sat staring at Testera, wondering how he could convince his captain of vaqueros that he had been instrumental in causing the deliverance. He had no idea of the identity of the secret friend who had slain the red cap who had attempted to murder Nolan and who had freed Testera from his ropes in the forest. But he wanted to impress Testera with his power and prescience as he imagined he had impressed Zorilla, Nolan, Clelland, and all those who had listened to him there on the portico.

His stare at Testera became a mysterious smile. He deliberately closed an eye at his captain and drew a long breath, inflating his huge chest until it seemed that further expansion would burst it. Then he slowly exhaled and sent a gale of laughter into Testera's face.

"*Diablo!* Don't you see, Testera?"

Testera looked puzzled.

"My eyes are not as good as they were," apologized the captain.

"Nor your mind," suggested Don Pedro. "And yet you should know that I keep an all-seeing eye upon my men."

Testera started.

"Does Magnífico mean——"

"Ai! Go on, Testera."

"——That he sent my deliverer?"

"Testera thinks!" declared Don Pedro solemnly.

"You knew what was happening?"

"Testera, I know everything!"

"You sent the man to cut my bonds?"

Don Pedro smiled.

"You knew I had been captured?"

Don Pedro smiled.

"You knew I would suspect Zorilla and that I would come with my men as soon as I could?"

"I had faith in Testera."

The captain was amazed. He stared with open mouth at his master.

"You know who cut my bonds?" he asked.

"*De veras.*"

"You know who cut the red cap's throat?"

"Assuredly."

"*Diablo!*" breathed Testera. "Such knowledge is staggering! I am confounded!"

Don Pedro drank a huge goblet of wine.

"It is nothing, Testera," he beamed. "Those who rule must have greatness of mind."

Don Pedro was pleased with himself. His thinking of pretending to have been aware of everything that had happened during the night had been nothing less than an inspiration. And since none knew the identity of the secret friend he felt he was safe in thus turning the ignorance of his subjects to his own advantage.

And now he had another inspiration.

He got to his feet and smiled with ineffable gentleness at his captain of vaqueros.

"Behold how I shall calm my people!" he said. "Follow me! It will be well that all shall know that there was no accident about this!"

He strode to the portico, Testera following, still amazed.

The disturbance at the house, the sudden plunging of Testera's horsemen over the mesa, had aroused the guests. And when Don Pedro reached the edge of the portico he found that nearly all the feasters were gathered before him.

They were many. They were massed near the portico; they had surrounded the house; they were grouped far out under the trees. They were jabbering excitedly, for by this time word of what had happened had spread through them, and they were wondering what was to be done.

Near the edge of the portico Don Pedro saw Dean and Carey. The two were talking with Nolan and Clelland. At a little distance stood Galt and Simms, the train robbers, and close to them Belden and Colton, the detectives who had trailed the criminals.

Juana was not visible. Don Pedro thought she was in the house, for while he and Testera had been sitting at the table drinking and eating he had heard the swishing of a dress.

It was well that Juana was not there to listen to him. For he had found that it was difficult to lie with a straight face with his daughter watching him.

As he reached the edge of the portico he was aware that all were watching him, and he smiled at them with all the dignity he could muster.

"My people——" he began.

A silence had fallen; all were waiting.

But a voice had broken the silence, interrupting Don Pedro. An irritable voice, coming from a point near the edge of the portico; the voice of an American.

"Shay!" it said, "whaz all the rumpus about? We wanna know?"

Don Pedro reddened. Toward him from the fringe of the crowd came three men, arm in arm. The three were Manville, the moonshiner, and Pennel and Lathrop, the revenue agents. They lurched against one another as they staggered forward to the edge of the portico.

The voice was Pennel's. His face was scarlet, his hat off, his hair tousled, his eyes bleared. Lathrop was in worse condition; he had drunk so much that he was in a state of partial paralysis, so that his legs bent under him and his head was drooping forward.

Manville was drunk but could hold himself upright. And he seemed amused at the plight of his companions, for he grinned slyly at Don Pedro, and winked owlishly as the three halted in front of the huge figure of their host.

"Don't pay no 'tention to Pennel," he said. "He's drunk. Tasted my whisky. Liked it. Tasted some more. Can't stand nothin'. Lathrop, too. Quarrelsome. They wanna fight."

Dean and Carey drew the three away, Pennel protesting that he didn't want to fight, but that he wanted to know what the "rumpus" was about.

And now, after some laughter, there fell another silence, and Don Pedro went on:

"My people," he said, speaking loudly and clearly, "there has been trouble, and insubordination. A man named Benico was found this morning with his throat cut. The man was one of Zorilla's men. He had been prowling around Señor Nolan's camp, and someone stole up on him as he approached Señor Nolan, and killed him. His blood fell upon Señor Nolan's slicker. That is how blood came to be upon Señor Nolan's hands this morning. Señor Nolan is innocent. I know it. I also know who killed Benico, but I do not intend to tell you his name at this minute. It is sufficient to say that the man who killed Benico is the same man who last night cut Testera's bonds and released him after Zorilla and his men had captured him so that they might this morning dispute my authority without fear of encountering the opposition of Testera and my vaqueros. Zorilla thought to catch me unawares. Me! The goose tries to outwit the fox!"

There was vociferous applause, which Don Pedro did not attempt to quell. He stood there, his face beaming, leaning forward the better to catch the welcome sounds, his eyes glowing with pride.

"I know you love me," he went on. "That is easy to see. And I know also that you have respect for my power and my wisdom. That is as it should be. One greater than the others must rule. Zorilla would rule. Is Zorilla greater?"

Hoarse shouts of derision and anger greeted the reference to the outlaw chief.

Don Pedro held up a calming hand, and his smile grew broader.

"Zorilla is my sworn enemy! He is a dog! Yet mark how I treat him. I do not order him shot as I might do when his villainy is exposed. No! I merely stand here on this portico and smile pityingly at him. But, my people, Zorilla, in attempting to overthrow my rule, has violated the rules of the pronunciamento. He held the Señorita Juana as hostage. I have taken her away. She shall be seen no more at his tent. And now listen to my judgment of Zorilla!

"He and his men shall be held inviolate no longer. The protection of the pronunciamento does not apply to them. My vaqueros shall drive them from the mesa! I call for five hundred men with arms to help Testera! But there must be no killing unless Zorilla and his men provoke it. They will be taken out upon the plains ten miles and told to show their faces here no more. During the remaining days of the feast they may not again be seen under penalty of death at the hands of him who first sees them!"

He turned to Testera.

"Act immediately, my Testera!" he directed.

CHAPTER XV

And now, as Don Pedro ceased speaking, he heard the rustle of a silk dress behind him. He stood rigid. No need to tell him that his daughter was behind him, coming toward him. He paled, and wondered if she had heard him lying to his people!

He did not look around. Evidently there was something in Juana's manner that bade the people pause, for they and Testera and Nolan and all of them stood still, looking behind Don Pedro. And Don Pedro knew they were looking at his daughter.

Don Pedro heard a whisper at his shoulder. Juana's voice came softly into his ear:

"Do not send Zorilla away, Father. That would be a mistake. Hold him here as a hostage for the conduct of his men for the duration of the feast!"

Don Pedro's eyes flashed.

What a fool he had been for not thinking of that! He was elated. And yet he was slightly irritated. Given another minute and he, himself, would have had that inspiration. Why, it had been lying dormant in his mind all along; it had been ready to spring forth into speech. Only Juana's coming had prevented his announcing it. So elastic was Don Pedro's mind, and so quick his wit, that he took advantage of the thoughts of others so readily that they were sometimes half convinced that they had offered their suggestions too late.

So it was with Juana. She stepped back, looking wonderingly at her father. And there may have been a little awe in her glance at him.

"Silence!" thundered Don Pedro, not realizing that at the instant he spoke, save for his own voice, there was dead silence on the mesa.

He raised a ponderous hand and again inflated his chest so that it extended almost as far outward as his stomach.

"I have reconsidered. I did not speak of this before because I hesitated to be harsh. But Zorilla's crime was great. Zorilla is not to leave the mesa with his men. He is to remain as an assurance for the conduct of his men during the remainder of the feast! I have spoken! Testera, you will act accordingly!"

Don Pedro stood rigid at the edge of the portico while the captain of the vaqueros rode away at the head of his men, followed by numerous other men bearing implements of warfare, which they ran and procured while

Testera drew up his men and gave them instructions. Quickly the throng in front of Don Pedro's house dispersed to witness the greater scene that was to be enacted at Zorilla's tents.

Almost regretfully Don Pedro watched them go. He would have held them a little longer if he could have found occasion or excuse, for it pleased him much to stand where all his people might feast their eyes upon him.

But he observed that Nolan and Clelland did not follow the others, and he was convinced that Nolan, at least, wanted to stay in order to be near him. Nolan liked him. Also, Nolan was a brave man.

Don Pedro was flattered. When a brave man, such as Nolan had shown himself to be, wanted to be near one, it were foolishness to disappoint him. He did not observe that Nolan was exchanging fervent glances with Juana, nor that she, now standing near the doorway, was coquetting with Nolan.

"Señor Nolan," he said, "you will dine with me. It is almost midday. It has taken time to deal with Zorilla."

Ignored, Clelland glanced sidelong at his friend, with a glance which conveyed the intelligence that he knew how things were going and that he would not remain to interfere. Therefore, without a word to Don Pedro or a look at him, he moved southward, following the crowd, which was pressing toward Zorilla's tents.

Clelland grinned as he walked. He had decided to take no part in the banishing of Zorilla's men, but he wanted to be near the scene in case any trouble developed.

Zorilla's tents were erected near the southern edge of the mesa, at the crest of a three or four hundred foot sheer precipice which rose above the spreading plains.

Clelland anticipated trouble. He had not counted Zorilla's men, though he knew there were a great many of them, and that they were all well armed and accustomed to fighting. If Zorilla ordered them to fight they would fight, and there would be much to interest a spectator. So Clelland made his way rapidly through the trees for perhaps a mile, still following Testera and his vaqueros and the somewhat heterogeneous mass that trailed along.

Clelland halted close to a huge tree when he came in view of the outlaw camp, and he stepped behind it, thus safeguarding himself against stray bullets should Zorilla decide to fight.

When the vaqueros rode up there was no one visible near the tents, but Testera, knowing the outlaw method of fighting, did not approach too close before making known his intentions. He halted his horse at a little distance, observed that his men were close behind him, and called loudly for Zorilla.

After a few minutes had elapsed, Zorilla emerged from the canopied tent. He stood erect before Testera; there was a smile on his lips.

"Ai!" he exclaimed; "you come from the braggart! What new foolishness has he invented?"

"Your men are to leave the mesa!" said Testera.

Zorilla was quick to detect the omission of reference to himself.

"And me?" he asked, still smiling.

"You are to remain!" gruffly declared Testera. "El Magnífico will hold you so that if your men commit any crime against him he can the more readily shoot you."

"Pedro the glutton did not devise that scheme all by himself," declared Zorilla. "I suspect the Señorita Juana had something to do with it. It is she who provides the boaster with brains!"

"Have done!" growled Testera. "I did not come here to parley with you, but to order your men from the mesa!"

"Ai!" laughed Zorilla. "That may be another matter. My men do not care to leave. They anticipate great pleasure during the feast. Some of them may be reluctant. What then?"

Testera tapped the holster of his pistol. The significant action drew a broader smile to Zorilla's lips.

"Ai, Testera, my men play that game well. I warn you that at this minute they are watching you from the tents. If they are wise, a dozen of them will be aiming at you this instant!"

"And I warn you that if you meant that as an order you are signing your own death warrant!" said Testera. "For I no sooner go down than you will be riddled. You see, Zorilla, knowing you as I do, I gave that order before we started to come here. And I tell you this: If your men are not all out and facing us unarmed within one minute, my vaqueros will begin to shoot into the tents!"

Zorilla scowled, then smiled.

"You will wait a full minute, Testera?" he asked.

"Not longer!"

"It will be enough."

Zorilla turned, strode into his own tent. Testera heard his voice, though he could not distinguish the words. Instantly, Zorilla came out, strode to the opening of another tent, drew back the flap. Again Testera heard his voice, but as before he could gain no idea of what was being said. Zorilla duplicated his performance at the other tents. Then he sharply ordered his men to appear, and they came concertedly, without weapons, and stood grinning before the captain of the vaqueros and the others.

"We yield, Señor Testera," smiled Zorilla. "My men will leave the mesa as quickly as possible after getting their things together. As for myself, I shall also obey Don Pedro's wishes."

Zorilla continued to smile. Most of his men were smiling, and even those whose faces were sullen seemed to be repressing mirth.

"You have an hour," answered Testera. "I shall withdraw."

He gave an order, and his men wheeled their horses and rode away, Testera behind them. Testera was something of a soldier, and it might be expected that he would betray some satisfaction over the outcome of his visit to the outlaw chief. But as Testera rode away he scowled.

"That was too easy," he thought. "Now he will play some dog's trick or other! He was not angry enough."

CHAPTER XVI

Having implicit faith in Testera, Don Pedro did not worry over the probable outcome of Testera's visit to Zorilla. It seemed to Nolan that Don Pedro had already forgotten the incident, for instantly he had ascended to the portico and had seated himself at the big table.

He motioned Nolan and Juana to chairs opposite him, poured himself and Nolan flagons of wine, drank deeply from his own, set the flagon down, and began to select sweetmeats from the various platters and dishes in front of him.

Nolan was not hungry or thirsty, though he drank from the flagon out of respect to Don Pedro's feelings.

Nor did Juana drink, though she tasted some candied fruit from a silver dish near her.

She seemed to outward appearances perfectly at ease in Nolan's presence. She was calm, she appeared cool, while Don Pedro was sweating profusely, and even Nolan felt the heat. Likewise, Señorita Juana seemed to have become more beautiful than ever. She had been well trained to the courtly mannerisms of her station, and she bore herself as one accustomed to homage and admiration. In fact, there was that in her manner which told Nolan that admiration to her was no new thing; there was also an insinuating sophistication in the expression of her eyes that would effectually hold men at a distance. Watching her covertly, Nolan became convinced that it would be a rash man that would offer her an indignity.

Yet, through her sophistication Nolan detected embarrassment. Her quick blushes betrayed her, and there was a shyness in the depths of her eyes when she glanced at Nolan which told him what he wanted to know. He wanted to get her away where he could talk with her without listeners, but could not because he was Don Pedro's guest, and it appeared Don Pedro wanted him to stay where he was.

Don Pedro consumed a vast quantity of sweetmeats. There seemed to be no end to his appetite. And between mouthfuls he talked, always of himself and of his accomplishments. And after a while he drew Nolan into the house and showed him books that he had brought from the Rancho Paloma.

Nolan had read few of the books. There were Calderon's and Lope de Vega's dramas. A history of Rome. Voltaire. Volney's *Ruins*. A translation of *Gil Blas*. An algebra. Some English books. Pope, Smollett, Goldsmith, Defoe.

Juana stood in the open doorway, listening and watching, while Don Pedro talked of his books. She did not always look at her father; often her gaze rested upon Nolan. When Nolan was facing her she watched her father, but when Nolan turned his back or bent over the better to see the books that Don Pedro showed him, Juana's gaze went to Nolan's black hair, with its unruly ringlets, to his broad shoulders, his slim waist which so sharply contrasted with her father's portly stomach, and to his lithe, shapely legs.

"One must read," said Don Pedro. "It is only by reading that one discovers what the world is thinking about. Wisdom comes with reading. And even though there is nothing new, there is much to be learned by considering each writer's viewpoint. I haven't written, though I have felt the urge to write. I feel that I am cheating the world by not putting some of my more important thoughts on paper."

Nolan nodded, though he hardly heard Don Pedro. He was in the mood to assent to everything his host claimed, for by this time he had succeeded in exchanging several glances with Juana, and he divined that she knew of his love for her.

"*Soy purita Mejicana*," said Don Pedro, gazing at his flagon. "I have nothing Spanish about me. I am a descendant of *Itzcoatl*, who was the fourth king of Mexico."

Don Pedro drew an oddly shaped dagger from a sheath at his belt and held it in the palm of his left hand.

"Observe," he went on. "This dagger has been in the family for many generations. It was placed in my keeping by my father, who in turn had it from his own. The figure of the serpent on the handle is a symbol—*coatl*—meaning serpent. Its back is crested with knives and arrowheads of obsidian—*itzli*—Itzcoatl. In other forms, however, especially upon documents, it is written syllabically. There is the figure of an arrowhead, *itzli*, root *itz*; figure of a vase, *comitl*, root *co*, figure or sign of water, *atl*; the whole Itzcoatl. The documents of this class, in which the syllabic writing predominates, are generally land registers, tribute rolls, judgments of courts, genealogies; and were continued long after the conquest."

Don Pedro paused, drank deeply from his flagon, which was lidless; set the flagon down and puffed out his chest.

"So you can see from where my greatness comes," he said. "I have inherited it. But I do not pride myself upon my ancestry," he added. "I am great in my own right. You have seen how I rule my people. You have observed the nimbleness of my mind. That was plain in the case of Zorilla and the murdered Benico. Wisdom—nothing less. Prescience—an ability to feel in advance what is happening. Señor Nolan, you have observed that my people stand in awe of me. You see, they know that while I love them I am inflexible. When I tell a man to come, he comes; and when I say go to a man, he goes. When I pardon a man, I pardon him, and when I tell him his life is forfeit, so it is!"

Nolan said nothing; but Juana, looking down at the top of the table, fingered a square of candied cactus. Her lashes were drooped, but her eyes were glinting with mischief.

"Ai," she said gently, "Don Pedro is inflexible. There was that most excellent Roderuz, for example. He had flogged a peon until the man could not stand, and for no reason. Don Pedro ordered him shot for cruelty. And, quite mysteriously, Roderuz was released."

Don Pedro flushed.

"Roderuz would have left three children behind," he explained.

"And Lopez Ruiz," went on Juana softly; "he had stolen a horse. He was caught trying to escape toward the coast and was brought back and sentenced to be shot. But the sentence was never carried out. Ruiz lingered in the cuartel for many days. And one day he was gone."

"Ruiz escaped," explained Don Pedro.

"And his jailers were never punished."

"They were deprived of their wine for a month!" declared Don Pedro.

"Monstrous punishment for permitting a desperate criminal to escape," suggested Juana.

Don Pedro smiled wryly.

"If you drank you would know that deprivation *is* a punishment!" he declared.

"And that tall man—Meduza—who stole the *dinero* from the Franciscans! He was placed in a dungeon. One morning the door of the dungeon was found open. Meduza had escaped, and nobody knew how the door came to be left open."

"A few pesos," said Don Pedro. "It is my belief that the door was left open at the suggestion of the Franciscans themselves. Besides, the churchmen do not lack money, and their loss was replaced."

"Mysteriously," smiled Juana. "Yes, Don Pedro is just. He is merciless. He is inflexible. He is ruthless. Even Señor Valdez, who came right into the potrero of the Rancho Paloma and tried to steal a horse, was at liberty the next day. The door of his cell was found open, and there was none who could explain it."

Don Pedro's face turned a red-pepper hue. He hid it in a wine flagon and drank so deeply that it appeared the flagon had been drained a long time before it left his lips.

When he set the flagon down his face was stern.

"The end of the Valdez matter has not yet come!" he declared. "I shall discover who opened Valdez's cell door, and the wretch who did it shall pay dearly! I warn you that I am not to be trifled with!"

"Señor Valdez dined sumptuously before he left that night," Juana went on, still softly, though she still appeared to speak to the table. "I saw the remains of the feast in the morning. And Philippe told me he had served at your orders."

"For myself," gruffly said Don Pedro. "I felt the need of food and I had Philippe serve."

"But you did not partake of the food?"

"Alas! I was called to the garden. When I returned the food was gone."

"In the garden at midnight! Father, what were you doing there?"

"Did I not say that someone called me?"

"Who, Father?"

Don Pedro's cheeks were crimson; his gaze was furtive. He perceived that his daughter knew something. And yet he would not admit his guilt.

"I do not know. I heard a voice. When I reached the garden no one was there."

"Ai," said the girl, "that explains it."

"*Peste!* Explains what?"

"The sounds that Vittorio Cerros and myself heard that night."

Juana now glanced slyly at Nolan, and her lips curved into a smile when she saw his straighten.

"You were in the garden with Cerros?" gasped Don Pedro in amazement.

"We were seated upon the stone bench under the circle of palms," smiled the girl. "Vittorio had come with his guitar. He played under my window, and I went down into the garden with him. There was a beautiful moon, though we sat in the shadows where it could not reach us."

"Ai!" gasped Don Pedro.

Nolan's face was long.

"And as we sat there—Vittorio insisting that he loved me more than he was able to express—we heard sounds as of someone walking. We kept quiet, and pretty soon we observed my father walking in the garden. You were coming very slowly, as though deep thoughts engaged you; and you passed very close to us without seeing us."

"But just a minute ago you said my coming had explained a sound. One would infer from that that you had not seen me. And now——"

"One forgets," sighed Juana. "Perhaps there were other things that I saw. I remember very hazily, Señor my father."

Don Pedro drew a deep breath. He perceived that Juana knew more than she had revealed. His thoughts stopped, and he sat there looking at her, his eyes betraying stupefaction, his mouth open.

"We were speaking of death, Vittorio and I," resumed the girl. "Vittorio grew poetic. I remember his words. 'Thoughts of death and eternity are not pleasing,' he said. 'It is when we begin to realize that we shall wake to no more dawns that remorse and dread begin to annoy us. No more shall we thrill to the thought of a well-cooked dinner. No more eager looks at the wine flagons. No more of filling our eyes with pretty girls. No more of lying in the shade on some remote hillside enjoying the beauties of nature and wondering——' "

"*Diablos!*" growled Don Pedro, alarmed, for he perceived that Juana was quoting his own words to Valdez; "you have too good a memory! And yet——" he appeared to hesitate——"and yet in a girl that is a remarkable thing, and I have a mind to reward you for the—for not disturbing me that night."

"That *tendero* at Hermosillo still has that rope of pearls," said Juana quietly.

"*Peste!* Those shopkeepers are robbers. The necklace is too costly."

"Ai, it is valuable. But not as valuable as a good memory."

"Well," sighed Don Pedro, "you shall have it!"

Don Pedro refilled his flagon. He was so agitated that he neglected to serve his guest. But presently he smiled, for he saw Testera returning with his men. Evidently there had been no trouble.

He sat, receiving the report of his captain. And when Testera rode away he observed that a man and a woman stood near the edge of the portico. The man wore a look of guilt and the woman one of intense fury. And when Don Pedro told her to speak, words tumbled over one another getting out of her mouth.

"Your tongue trips, Señora!" reproved Don Pedro. "*Diablos!* My ears are ringing! Speak more slowly!"

"Ai, Magnífico," wailed the woman. "My man, here, Lallo Padillo, is unfaithful to me. *Ay de mi!* At his age! He is fifty, and he has always been a good man until now! We have nine children, too, Señor the Magnificent; and now that he has become enamoured of that hussy he will leave us. He has not said so, but I can tell that he does not love us any more. For this morning when I talked to him he did not answer, but just stood and gazed far away, as though his wife and children were dirt under his feet. He was thinking of his inamorata, Señor the Magnificent! He had been with her last night, the first of the feast. I saw them under the palms. He was holding her and she was laughing. Such laughter, Magnífico! It was brazen! And I have always been a good wife to him, Magnífico; a *good* wife! I have cooked for him and his brood; I have worked in the fields. I have been true to him.

I have obeyed him. And now, when I am growing old and have lost my beauty slaving for him, he takes up with this lewd woman! Ai, Señor the Magnificent, if you do not help me I am lost!"

The woman yielded to a fit of weeping, and a dark frown drew Don Pedro's brow.

"Peace, woman!" he commanded. He produced a huge handkerchief and blew his nose loudly. Then he wiped his eyes, which were suspiciously moist. Then he scowled at the man.

"Padillo, what have you to say?" he asked.

"She lies, Señor the Magnificent!" declared Padillo. "I have not changed, nor do I stand and gaze far away, as she claims. I love no other woman. *Ya se ve*, I talk to other women. But, *diablos!* a man is not in love with every woman he talks to! One burden is enough! I am no sighing fool. And yet, as she claims, I was talking last night with the Señora Balano. We were under the palms, and she was laughing. But my arms were not around her. She would not permit that, Señor Magnífico."

"Ai, you tried!" quickly charged Don Pedro.

The man flushed and grinned defiantly.

"Just once, Magnífico. I wanted to see if she would object."

"H'm," mused Don Pedro, his eyes alive with interest. "You say she objected. How did you go about it?"

"We were talking. We were very close. She looked into my eyes and seemed to dare me. And then I tried to draw her closer."

"What—without speaking to her?" roared Don Pedro.

"I meant nothing," explained Padillo. "It was friendliness!"

"And she would not permit it?"

"She drew away."

"*Peste!*" exclaimed Don Pedro. "That was clumsy. Padillo, you are a bungler!"

And now Don Pedro perceived that the wife was gazing at him with amazement and chagrin. Don Pedro changed colour and instantly swelled out his chest.

"I repeat you are a bungler, Padillo!" he said. "A bungler for attempting so vile a thing; a bungler for being under the palms with a woman not your wife! This estimable woman who calls herself your wife has borne much from you, I can see that. A married man has no business browsing."

Padillo's face grew long.

"I did but try to even a score with my wife," he said. "Yesterday morning I saw her standing close to the scoundrel Dominguiz, who has been casting sheep's eyes at her for months. He was trying to put his arms around her, and she was fighting him off, very playfully, Señor Magnífico. She was not trying hard enough to evade him. I do not know whether he succeeded or not, for they went out of sight among the trees. And they were there long enough."

"Ai!" gasped Don Pedro. He gazed sternly at the wife, whose cheeks were crimson.

"Woman, what have you to say? Did Dominguiz finally succeed in getting his arms around you?"

"If Padillo thought so why did he not come to see?" asked the woman. Don Pedro's eyes brightened.

"Certainly, Padillo, why didn't you? You say you were near enough to see what was going on. Then you were also near enough to slay Dominguiz for his misbehaviour."

"When a woman favours a man she favours him," answered Padillo. "If my wife seeks lovers and I kill Dominguiz, she will seek others."

"So she will!" agreed Don Pedro. "Woman," he added, "you evaded my question. I ask it again. Did Dominguiz succeed in getting his arms around you?"

"He did, Señor Magnífico. He is very strong. But I managed to pull away before he drew me close."

"Ai!" breathed Don Pedro, "then he was trying to embrace you, to kiss you?"

The woman became sullenly defiant. "I do not know what his intentions were!" she answered. "But at least he did not kiss me, and I did not have an appointment with him under the palms!"

"Dominguiz has been making eyes at you?" sternly asked Don Pedro.

"Perhaps. A woman cannot prevent that, Señor the Magnificent."

"No," assented Don Pedro; "she cannot. Yet she can make a man understand that his attentions are not welcome. Did you try to make Dominguiz understand that?"

"Yes."

"How?"

"By smiling at him derisively, Señor."

"Show me the smile?"

The woman smiled, and Don Pedro's eyes gleamed.

"*Maria purisima!* You are beautiful when you smile like that, woman! Is it any wonder that Dominguiz fell? Señora, you should smile like that at your husband, and then he will not be seeking the Señora Balanos of this world! *Diablos!* You say you smiled like that when you wanted to show Dominguiz that his attentions were not wanted! *Madre de Dios!* I shall never understand women!" He gazed meditatively at the wife. "Señora," he added, "show me how you smile when you are trying to attract men."

Señora Padillo demonstrated. So bewitching was the smile that Don Pedro appeared to expand under it. An answering smile reached his lips, grew slyly. Instantly it passed from slyness to boldness, and one of his eyes closed in an unmistakable wink!

"*Peste!*" grumbled Padillo. "Señor the Magnificent grows too earnest!"

Don Pedro instantly frowned.

"*Bastante!*" he exclaimed, "as a mediator I must see before I judge. I know little of women, having been in seclusion since the death of Señora Bazan."

"Bah!" thought Padillo, "if you knew more I should lose my wife!" Aloud he said: "You see what she did to Dominguiz!"

Don Pedro rubbed his fat palms together.

"It appears neither of you is circumspect," he said. "You should not appear too interesting to the opposites of the sex you represent. Señora, if you see a man looking at you, you should make a face at him—like this—" he grimaced hideously—"and, Padillo, if a woman gaze amorously at you, you should bid her begone!

"Yet it appears neither of you has done wrong. It also appears that if any crime has been done, one crime will equal the other. So begone, and let me hear no more of your attempts at philandering! But hear me!" he added when they were about to turn away. "Send to me Dominguiz and Señora Balano that I may warn them!"

CHAPTER XVII

"You observe my greatness," said Don Pedro after Padillo and his wife had gone. He sat pompously erect, looking at Nolan and Juana, who had been watching and listening. "A man of less wisdom would have taken sides in that difference, and by doing so would have earned the enmity of either the man or the woman. But by convincing both that they were equally culpable, I have sent them away marvelling. They will think of me so often that they will forget to quarrel. And what is more important, neither will think hereafter that one can deceive the other. That game will have no further attraction, for it is only when we attempt to deceive that we enjoy ourselves."

"The woman may transgress again," suggested Juana. "She has a sly smile."

"*Por Dios!*" said Don Pedro, "did you hear Padillo accuse me of being engaged by it?" He frowned. "The smile of a coquetting woman never interests me. I am impervious to all amorous glances!"

Juana looked mischievously at Nolan.

"A pretty woman does not interest Father," she said. "You have seen that." She glanced at Don Pedro. "Have you seen Señora Balano? No? It is no wonder that poor Padillo lost his senses!"

"Men like Padillo lose their senses easily," asserted Don Pedro. "A pretty woman looks at them and—puf!—they are snared. It is because they are primitive and have no self-control. You will have observed that I am not like that. My self-control is marvellous! I do not say that I am unaffected at sight of a pretty face. I am stirred! I respond to beauty! But it is only the enthusiasm of an artist that I feel. No base passions rule me."

Juana wagged her pretty head at the table.

"Don Pedro feels no passions," she said. "He is the personification of cold, proud virtue. He is calm, aloof. His wisdom rules him. He is inflexible."

Don Pedro gazed sharply at his daughter. Perhaps he thought she was poking fun at him, and he was tortured by indecision. For he knew that her acute vision—which had more than once dragged his pretensions out to view—might have caused her to perceive his duplicity. And yet at this minute he felt that he was sincere. What had happened to him when Señora Padillo had smiled at him had nothing to do with the matter. Perhaps just then he had felt a surge of passion. But that was over, and perhaps would not occur again. At any rate, he had confidence in himself, confidence that though he might tremble on the verge, he would never fall. Yet he knew from past experience that it was not well to banter words with Juana. She was too nimble-minded an antagonist.

And now, observing a woman coming toward the house, and thinking that the woman might be Señora Balano, he was beset with a terrible impatience to be rid of his daughter and Nolan. So he got up from the table and began to walk ponderously back and forth on the portico, screwing his brows together, frowning and trying his best to appear lost in thought. He did not look at Juana or Nolan, though he stole covert glances at the approaching woman.

Juana smiled and looked at Nolan under drooping lashes. She knew what was troubling Don Pedro.

"Señor Nolan," she said, "Father is thoughtful. We disturb him. Undoubtedly his mind is troubled. Let us leave him with his meditations."

She had spoken loudly enough for Don Pedro to hear. And he did hear. But he did not look at them, thinking that if he spoke at all they would find some excuse to linger. And the woman was nearer and coming directly toward the portico.

Juana and Nolan stepped off the portico and vanished around a corner of the house. They had no more than disappeared when Don Pedro ceased frowning, smiled, smoothed his dove-coloured waistcoat, brushed a crumb from his pearl-gray satin knee breeches, cast a glance at his bulging calves, encased in pale blue silk stockings, adjusted his scarlet capote, and walked to the edge of the portico, where he stood erect and rigid, gazing with seeming absorption at the tops of some palm trees under which the woman was walking.

He appeared so engrossed that the woman was certain he had no knowledge that she was standing at the edge of the portico watching him; and it was not until she spoke that he seemed to become aware of her.

"Ai, Señor the Magnificent," she said softly; "I was told to appear before you."

Don Pedro looked at the woman.

Yes, she was just what Juana had described her to be! Not that Juana had told him in so many words that the woman was beautiful; but she had said that it was no wonder that Padillo had lost his senses.

Don Pedro's first sensation was a tingling delight. The next was jealousy, aroused over the thought that Padillo had dared to put his arms around the woman. And he knew Padillo had lied when he had denied embracing her. The man's manner had betrayed him.

His next emotion was rage against the woman herself for having permitted Padillo to take liberties with her. She was frivolous or she would not have permitted that.

Yet she was beautiful, and when she smiled at him after speaking, he was aware of a surge of pity and sympathy. Padillo must have forced his attentions upon her. A woman like this would not coquette with a man like Padillo!

"You are the Señora Balano?" asked Don Pedro.

"*Si*, Señor the Magnificent."

Her eyes were soft and expressive, and they were watching Don Pedro so intently that he felt a wave of strange exaltation swelling his chest. His cheeks grew crimson, and he observed that Señora Balano, divining what was happening to him, smiled serenely.

Don Pedro bowed Señora Balano into the house, for he was fearful that at any minute his daughter and Nolan might appear; his daughter to confuse him with her knowing glances.

He bowed Señora Balano to a chair beside a small table and sank into another opposite her. He observed that Señora Balano had become demurely quiet, and that her lashes were on her cheeks as she gazed at the table top. They were long lashes, he decided, and they rested caressingly against the satiny cheeks.

The chair under him creaked when his weight came upon it, but not until after the creaking ceased did Señora Balano lift her gaze to him. She did this just at the instant Don Pedro settled himself in the chair and looked at her. Thus it happened that their eyes met fully.

Don Pedro's pulses leaped. He drew a long breath which became a sigh before he could halt it, and he was a trifle dizzy. Yet he succeeded in speaking gruffly:

"So you are Señora Balano!"

There was dire accusation in his voice, but Señora Balano did not cringe under it. Instead, she smiled shyly.

"*Si*, Señor the Magnificent."

Don Pedro was aware of the subtle accent she had placed on the "Magnificent."

"*Que es eso?*" he asked softly, eager to hear her pronounce the word again.

She repeated it, and again Don Pedro experienced a delightful thrill. The way she spoke the word made him feel that she really thought him magnificent; she put some spirit into it.

"Señora," he said, "the Señora Padillo accuses you of—er—having permitted her husband to—to fondle you. She says she saw Padillo with his arms around you!"

"*Si*, Señor the Magnificent; that is true. But I could not prevent it. Señor Padillo is so ver-y, ver-y strong. I—I could not escape!"

"You tried?" asked Don Pedro. His resentment against Padillo was growing. Certainly he would find a way to punish the man!

"But, yes, Señor the Magnificent! I tried, to no avail. I was helpless in his hands. He is so ver-ee strong!"

Don Pedro wondered. Padillo to him appeared to be a rather impotent-looking fellow. However, the way Señora Balano described him he seemed of monstrous size and virility. Don Pedro wondered if he had really noticed Padillo, after all. Certainly, before he devised punishment for the man, he would take another look at him.

But curiously, although Señora Balano was a rather plump woman and rather taller than the average, she seemed at this minute to him a frail little being whom Padillo might have crushed in his embrace.

"*Peste!*" he exclaimed. "I had no idea that Padillo was so strong!"

"*Maria purisima!*" said Señora Balano, "he nearly squeezed the life out of me!"

"Ai!" said Don Pedro, frowning. "How did it come that you were alone with him in the palm grove?"

"I was there, Señor the Magnificent, and he came."

"You had an appointment?"

"Señor, he just came."

"Why did he embrace you?"

"I do not know how it happened. We were standing there, and suddenly his arms were around me."

"*Diablo!* I perceive that this Padillo is dangerous! You had no warning?"

"None whatever."

"He said nothing to you?"

"He assured me I was beautiful."

Don Pedro writhed mentally. He now hated Padillo.

"When he told you you were beautiful, he spoke the truth," he said.

"Ah, Señor the Magnificent."

"But are you sure you did not provoke the embrace? You are aware that women have a maddening habit of looking at a man with certain expressions."

"I looked at Padillo as I am looking at you, Señor the Magnificent." She gave Don Pedro a glance that made him tingle all over.

"*De veras!*" he gasped, "it is not difficult to understand what happened to Padillo! Señora, do you always look at men in that manner?"

"Señor, what is it? I am looking as I always look."

Don Pedro sighed. He saw one of Señora Balano's hands lying on the table. He gazed at it, observing the smooth, satiny skin, the shapely fingers. It was a small hand. Tentatively Don Pedro stretched forth his own right hand and reverently touched it. The contact intoxicated him. His touch became a caress, and his gaze grew eloquent as it met Señora Balano's.

He felt her hand move. The muscles fluttered, were still.

"Poor Padillo!" murmured Don Pedro. "He is not to blame. But still, his wife has complained, and I must therefore determine the degree of his guilt so that his punishment may be proportioned."

"Ah, Señor, he did so little!"

"Little?" demanded Don Pedro. "Do you say it is little for a man to embrace a woman when he has a wife upon which to bestow his affections? Señora, I perceive I must go further. You will rise and show me just how Padillo put his arms around you!"

Señora Balano instantly got up and moved around the table until she stood close to Don Pedro. Don Pedro trembled and paled.

"We were standing like this," she said as she looked up into his eyes. Her own were glowing softly, with mischief and with challenge, so combined as to confuse Don Pedro.

"Ai," he exclaimed softly.

"And then he put his arms around me."

"*Pero mas!* I don't see how he could help it!" said Don Pedro. He put one ponderous arm over her shoulder and the other around her waist, merely, he assured himself, to be certain as to how Padillo had done it. And then, enchanted, he drew Señora Balano closer.

"You did nothing?" he asked.

He felt her arms around his neck.

"*Ay de mi!*" she whispered. "What could I do? I was powerless. He is so big, so strong; so veree strong."

Don Pedro drew her closer.

"He held you like this?" he asked.

"Tighter, Señor the Magnificent," she answered in a low voice; "much tighter!"

Don Pedro heaved a sigh of delight. The woman was finding his embraces to her liking, or she would not be provoking him to a closer one. He was tightening his arms around her when through the rear doorway of the house floated a voice—Juana's voice.

"No, Señor Nolan," she was saying; "Father does not care for pretty women. You have observed that. He is cold, calm. Like a flawless jewel he glitters most brilliantly when the lights shine upon him. That is to say, señor, that his virtues will bear examination!"

"You are right, Señorita Juana," came Nolan's voice. "I have observed him. He's all wool and a yard wide!"

Señora Balano and Don Pedro had drawn apart at the sound of Juana's voice. The Señora dropped into her chair at the table; Don Pedro stood facing the doorway, for he expected Juana and Nolan would enter.

Don Pedro had flushed. He had thought Juana had seen him embracing Señora Balano. But when Juana stayed discreetly outside and did not again speak of him, he decided that the embrace had not been witnessed. Yet he was aware that Juana and Nolan were standing just outside the door, for he could hear their voices, speaking lowly.

And yet there had been something in Juana's voice which had sounded like mockery, like laughter, like derision. He flushed again. He must take no chances with Juana. She was observant, she was wise; and there were many things of value besides necklaces which she desired.

Don Pedro drew himself up haughtily before Señora Balano. He puffed out his chest, assumed an expression of disapproval, and scowled at her.

"Woman," he said loudly, "I perceive you are guilty of an indiscretion. Be thankful that it is nothing worse. For if you embraced Padillo as you were embracing me just now—when I desired you to demonstrate just how you had embraced Padillo, I do not wonder that the Señora Padillo grew jealous! Señora Balano, I do not believe that you are a wicked woman, but it is certain that you are a frivolous woman! Therefore go back to your husband and do not permit yourself to be seen again with Padillo!"

Señora Balano rose. She made a mock curtsy to Don Pedro, while her brilliant eyes flashed scornfully.

Drawing her mantilla close, so that it disclosed the shapely lines of her lissom figure, she walked close to him. Swaying a little, holding her head well back, so that she could look up into Don Pedro's eyes, she leaned closer.

"Señor the Magnificent," she whispered, "is *valiente*. Puf!"

An instant she lingered, looking up into his eyes. Then she deliberately reached up, tweaked his nose, and swayed out through the front door, laughing.

Don Pedro stared after her. But he did not move until he observed that she had no intention of returning. Then he settled his capote about his shoulders, frowned, smiled, and strode to the doorway.

He was convinced that he would find Juana and Nolan seated upon a bench which he knew was close beside the rear doorway, for he had no doubt that after seeing him and Señora Balano embracing they had sat upon the bench to laugh at him.

His amazement was great when he observed that they were not on the bench at all. For at a little distance and in such a position that she could not see into the doorway of the house no matter how she tried, was Juana lying in a hammock. It was evident to Don Pedro that Juana had been lying there for some time. Certainly she would not have had time, after looking in the doorway, to return to the hammock and surround herself with the things that were piled about her. A book, open in her hands; a silver platter of candy which was lying in her lap; a half-smoked cigarette between her lips with long ash upon it! And beside her, slowly swinging the hammock, was Nolan, so attentive to Juana that he seemed unaware of anything else.

"*Peste!*" growled Don Pedro. His imagination had played a trick upon him. They had not seen him. Their voices had sounded close, to be sure, but they would be just as clear from the hammock as from a position near the doorway. He had wasted virtue!

He turned, he would have followed Señora Balano. But just at that instant Juana saw him and called:

"Did the siren come, Father? And what did she say when you reproved her?"

CHAPTER XVIII

Don Pedro beamed upon his daughter.

"Ai," he replied, "she was repentant, my Juana. At first she thought to sway me with amorous glances, but when she observed my inflexibility she became contrite and begged me to forgive her for just this once. She promised never to meet Padillo again, nor to let any man other than her husband place his arms around her. I am satisfied that it was merely an impulse that moved her. She is not really a bad woman, my dear; she is just foolish."

"And so you let her go without punishing her?"

"After my lecture she will find her own conscience punishment enough," said Don Pedro.

Juana's eyes were reflective. Her voice was soft.

"The Señora Balano is not a tall woman, Father?" she asked.

"Tall?" he questioned, staring at her. He observed a gleam of mischief in her reflective eyes. "No, she is not tall. Yet I hardly looked at her. It is impossible for me to say. Yet it seems, now that you speak of it, that when she was standing before me I was able to look over her head."

"Would her head reach your shoulder, Father?"

Don Pedro flushed. His cheeks swelled. A pout appeared upon his lips.

What was Juana's meaning? Why was she questioning him about the Señora Balano's height? He stared at her; he glanced at Señor Nolan.

Nolan was watching Juana; his back was toward Don Pedro. He appeared not to be interested in the conversation; it seemed he was merely politely waiting for it to end that he might have Juana for himself.

And now, becoming aware that Juana's gaze had dropped and that it appeared to be centred upon his scarlet capote, Don Pedro glanced down at the garment. Instantly his cheeks grew as red as the garment. For upon the scarlet cloth where it bulged over his chest was an oval spot of white about the size and shape of a woman's cheek. Moreover, running at an angle over his right shoulder was a white streak, and at his waist on the left side ran another streak.

The spot on his chest was where Señora Balano had rested her cheek against him; the streaks were where her arms had been!

Rice powder! He had observed it on her face while she had been seated opposite him. The foolish woman had dusted her arms with it!

Don Pedro sagged. His mouth opened. If his brain could have formed words, his lips would not have been able to utter them. Flush after flush surged into his face.

But quickly his self-control returned. He straightened, swelled out his chest, smiled expansively, with a queer mingling of condescension and deprecation.

"I perceive that you have sharp eyes, Juana," he said. "At first I did not grasp your meaning. I did not tell you all.

"At first I was adamant. I had named a punishment for Señora Balano from which I would not deviate. I admit the punishment was more severe than seemed to be called for. And yet I was determined that such foolishness among women must cease!"

"What was the nature of the punishment, Father?"

"*Que es eso?*" (What is it?) "It was—er—that the Señora Balano should be publicly flogged!"

"Father! Such punishment for merely permitting a man to hold her in his arms! Why, Father!"

"Nevertheless, that was the punishment I named. You can imagine how the Señora Balano received the sentence. I thought she would lose her senses. She was stunned! She stared at me in amazement, for she had no doubt heard from others that I am merciful on occasion. But she observed no mercy in my eyes, for I had determined to stamp out that evil. And when she saw that I was unrelenting, she threw herself upon my breast and pleaded with me!"

"And you permitted her to go her way? Father, I am proud of you!"

"I felt that sort of punishment would be too great for her," said Don Pedro. "She is so slight, so little. And think of the humiliation!"

"So slight," said Juana solemnly, "so little. And yet, though you did not see her, you are able to say something about her size. Could you see over her head when her arms were around you?"

Don Pedro gazed with level eyes at his daughter. He suspected that there was another pitfall behind her gentle words, and he did not intend to be led into it. Therefore he grandly waved a hand, as though dismissing the subject altogether, and moved toward Juana and Nolan.

But he had not taken three steps when he saw Juana sit erect in the hammock and gaze past him with dilated eyes.

"*A la derecha! A la izquierda! Detras!*" (To the right! To the left! Behind!) "The red caps, Father! They are coming!"

Don Pedro turned swiftly. Swarming toward him from all directions—from around both corners of the house near him, from the brush that surrounded the grove in which the hammock was swung—came Zorilla's men, armed with rifles.

Zorilla himself was among the foremost!

The outlaws had appeared magically. It seemed that they had predetermined the method of assault, for not one of them paid any attention to Don Pedro. They swept past him in a flash and fell upon Nolan.

Nolan had turned at the frightened accents of Juana's voice, and his guns were just coming from their holsters when a dozen of the outlaws seized him.

The guns could not be drawn. Nolan's arms were seized; he was thrown, and half a dozen of the outlaws fell on top of him, burying him from sight. At almost the same instant half a dozen more of the outlaws seized Juana by the simple expedient of rolling her in the hammock, cutting the supports, and permitting her to swing helplessly in the stout meshes while they carried her away.

Zorilla had halted near Don Pedro. He stood with the muzzle of his revolver menacing his foe while his men, having bound Nolan's hands and feet, picked him up and carried him away, following Juana.

It had seemed to Don Pedro that there had been a hundred outlaws when they had first burst upon his vision. But as quickly as they had come they had vanished, leaving only Zorilla and half a dozen others near him. The half dozen, though, were armed with rifles, and these, tipped with glittering bayonets, were all pointing at Don Pedro. Therefore, observing that he was outnumbered, Don Pedro offered no resistance.

Don Pedro had paled at first, but now he was calm and deliberate. He glanced around.

"Testera will not save you this time, Magnífico," laughed Zorilla. "And you will not call for him. If you do I will let the air out of you, and, puf! there will be nothing left for Testera to find!"

"Very well, pulque eater," said Don Pedro. "I shall make no sound. See that you do as well when at last my vaqueros are beating you to death!"

"Save your breath, windbag!" sneered Zorilla. "You will follow my men to our tents. If there is any interference I shall put a hole in the middle of your back. Vamos!"

Don Pedro went in the direction taken by the outlaws who had carried Juana and Nolan away. Don Pedro observed that there were some guests of the feast about, but they stood as though dazed at what they saw, evidently awed by the outlaws.

Don Pedro stalked majestically under the trees, showing his contempt of Zorilla by not looking at him.

The distance to the outlaw camp was covered in silence; in a short time Don Pedro stood before Zorilla's tents surrounded by dozens of the outlaws, who scowled at him and criticized his appearance.

"Behold," said one, "we are honoured. This monstrous oaf who would have everyone believe he is magnificent, is in reality nothing but an appetite. He eats and sleeps and drinks and boasts. Nothing more. And because he does all these things well he would have us believe that he has the right to rule us!"

"*Diablo!*" exclaimed another; "half the ox teams in the country would be required to haul food for him. We cannot attempt to hold him; he would eat us out of all our supplies in one day. Therefore, that we may not starve, let us knock him on the head and be done with him!"

"I have a yearning for that capote," whispered another, in a voice that was loud enough for Don Pedro to hear. "If I thought there would not be a scramble for the capote afterward, I would slip my knife between his ribs!"

Don Pedro fixed the speaker with a contemptuous eye.

"You dogs do not use your knives when a man is looking at you!" he declared. "You, señor the outlaw, are not particularly courageous. I doubt that you have sufficient courage to draw your knife and permit me to have a look at it."

The outlaw grinned, drew his knife, and held it grasped firmly in his right hand. He crouched, and amid the laughter of his companions began to approach Don Pedro. He scowled ferociously, so that no one knew whether or not he really meditated violence. His companions appeared to think he was joking, for their laughter grew louder, and some of them urged him on.

Zorilla had vanished into one of the tents.

The outlaws crowded closer to Don Pedro, making an irregular circle around him and the outlaw with the knife.

If the man with the knife was joking he was making his joke appear a very earnest one, for when he approached within a pace of Don Pedro he lunged with the knife, and the stroke was straight at Don Pedro's ponderous stomach.

If the outlaw's stroke had gone home he would have succeeded in his desire to slip his knife between Don Pedro's ribs. But somehow Don Pedro's left hand warded off the knife, and his left hand gripped the outlaw's wrist.

Don Pedro twisted mightily with his arm. There was a snap that was heard by all the other outlaws, and a howl of pain from the knife wielder which might have been heard for nearly the entire length of the mesa. The knife dropped from his hand. He was drawn toward Don Pedro so swiftly that his heels clacked together in the air. The watchers clearly observed Don Pedro lift him bodily with both hands for an instant while he kicked and squirmed and howled. Then, with as much ease as an ordinary man would handle a child, Don Pedro hurled the knife wielder through the circle of men, bringing down half a dozen of them into a cursing, screaming mass.

"The devil!" exclaimed Zorilla, who had at that instant come out of one of the tents. "What has happened?"

Don Pedro had folded his arms. He now stood looking at Zorilla.

"Bah!" he said, "these dogs do not know magnificence when they see it. Having been accustomed to using knives they think to use one on Pedro Bazan! Observe! The man has a broken wrist! And I used only a very little of my amazing strength. You may send them all at me, Señor Zorilla. *De veras!* That will be as good a way as any to end our differences. Order them to attack me all at once and together, and presently you will have no men at all!"

CHAPTER XIX

Zorilla looked angrily at his men.

"Fools!" he accused. "Will you spoil my plans? Seize him but do not kill him!"

Don Pedro fought mightily against the great numbers of men that threw themselves upon him. He tried to draw the sword at his side but was prevented by a dozen hands that gripped it and wrenched it away from him. When the encounter was finished, half a dozen outlaws were stretched out on the grass, groaning; but Don Pedro himself was helpless in the grasp of others who were tying his hands against a recurrence of his anger. They had attempted to throw him to the ground, but had not succeeded, and in the end they desisted, while Don Pedro stood with his big legs braced like huge posts, mocking them.

"Pigmies!" he said. "Little boys. You learn at last why I am called Magnificent!"

They got Don Pedro into one of the tents after half a dozen more of the outlaws were crippled by vicious kicks from his boots. Two more were injured while lashing his feet together. But at last he was secured, though his voice could still be heard as he railed at them, mocking them.

There were a dozen tents in Zorilla's camp, and soon after Don Pedro had been drawn into one of them Zorilla ordered his men to conceal themselves. Nolan and Juana were in separate tents, both bound and helpless. In both tents, watching the prisoners, were outlaws.

The hour which Testera had given Zorilla was drawing to a close. Zorilla, smiling and confident, threw himself into the hammock under the canopy—the hammock in which Nolan had found Juana when he had sought her out the day before—lighted a cigarette and calmly smoked.

Already at a distance he could see Testera's men coming, their horses in a slow trot as they moved here and there among the trees.

Zorilla had wondered about the horses; he wondered how Testera had got them to the mesa top. To Zorilla's knowledge, there was no trail that could be utilized for the passage of horses, though many times he had searched for one.

Testera was clever. Also, Testera was brave. Zorilla knew it. And yet, for all his cleverness, Testera had been outwitted.

With outward calmness, though with covert interest, Zorilla watched the movements of Testera's men. He observed them come to a halt in front of Don Pedro's house; he saw one rider, which he supposed was Testera himself, dismount and walk to the portico. Later he went into the house and was gone for some minutes. Then he emerged and was met at the edge of the portico by several men, who gesticulated excitedly.

"They are telling him how I abducted Don Pedro," thought Zorilla. "Now Testera will come thundering here in a fine rage. But he shall see that Zorilla is not to be trifled with."

Zorilla swung around in the hammock and sat up when he heard Testera's troop approach. When he observed that to all appearances Testera meant to run his horses straight into the tents, he got out of the hammock and advanced several paces toward the troop, holding up a warning hand.

Instantly the troop halted, though Testera, who was riding in advance, was not more than twenty or thirty feet distant.

Testera's face was flaming with rage.

"Speak quickly or I order my men to fire!" threatened Testera. "Where are Don Pedro and the Señorita Juana?"

"Safe in my tents," replied Zorilla. "They have not been harmed, and will not be unless through some rash act of yours."

"*Diablos!*" raged Testera. "I shall have you riddled with bullets for defying me!"

"Testera will change his mind when he knows more," smiled the outlaw. "Don Pedro is in one of my tents. He is bound and helpless. Sitting close to him are several of my men, watching him with drawn weapons. I have given those men orders that if a shot is fired or if I shout *muertos!* they are to shoot Don Pedro. Testera, I suggest that you go back to your camp to await Don Pedro's orders. It appears we are not to be disposed of so easily."

Testera flung himself off his horse and advanced toward Zorilla.

"*Peste!*" exclaimed the outlaw. "Stop, or I shall give the signal!" He drew a breath and prepared to shout.

It appeared that inside the tent Don Pedro had been listening, for now his voice was heard.

"Don't be rash at my expense, Testera!" he called. "Half a dozen guns are pointed at my stomach. I have just finished breaking the heads of a dozen of these scoundrels, and I can tell by their eyes that they are eager to shoot me. Retire and prepare for a siege. They have food, but not enough to last very long. You know my appetite, Testera. By this time to-morrow, if they feed me as I require, there will not be a morsel of food left in this camp. And they dare not starve me, for they know that without food I would not last a day. And when I am dead you will no longer be concerned over their shooting me."

"Bah!" exclaimed Zorilla. "Puf! The wind bloweth!"

There was a silence. Then Don Pedro's voice came again.

"Follow me, Testera," he said.

A pause.

"You will retire, as I have said," went on Don Pedro. "To-morrow at this time you will return. You will come and stand where you are now standing. You will speak to me. If I answer you will know that they have fed me and that there is no more food in camp. I shall have eaten all of it. On the other hand, if I do not answer, you will know that they have killed me or that I have starved to death. And then you will attack the camp just as though nothing had happened. You will exterminate these vermin without mercy!"

Zorilla tried to smile, but the effort resulted in a mere grimace. His face had paled. There were groans from the tents, imprecations, mutterings, curses.

"Let us understand," said Testera. "I am to appear in this place at this time to-morrow. I am to call to you. If you do not answer and tell me that you have been well fed I shall attack immediately and kill without quarter. If you answer me I shall know that there is no food left in Zorilla's camp, and thus we can be certain that within a few hours afterward Zorilla will surrender?"

"That is right, Testera."

"Good!" said Testera.

"And, Testera——"

"*Si*, Señor the Magnificent."

"I make very bad business of eating when I have no wine. Wine puts an edge on my appetite, so that I enjoy the flavour of food. I eat best when I drink moderately. Therefore do you bring me three gallons of my dark Benicarlo, and two gallons of the thick white Mendoza, together with the lidless flagon that you will find on my table."

"*Diablo!*" breathed Zorilla. "If that much wine is brought here, my men will get the greater part of it!"

"Pay no attention to Zorilla," called Don Pedro. "He knows better. His men will not touch the wine. For I have ordered just enough for myself, and if I am deprived of any of it I shall not be able to eat properly. And if I do not eat you will make Zorilla and his men regret it!"

Zorilla was now looking dazed. He ran his fingers through his hair.

"*Madre de Dios!*" he gasped. "Five gallons of wine! The man is a tun. If he eats in proportion he will bring famine to the camp in an hour!"

Don Pedro laughed triumphantly.

"You observe my greatness, eh, Testera? You see how my mind works!"

"Ai!" groaned Zorilla, "his mind works fast, but not as fast as his stomach!"

Testera glanced sternly at Zorilla.

"You have heard?" he asked. "I think, in your position, I should feed him. To-morrow at this time I shall appear with every man on the mesa able to bear arms behind me. If Don Pedro does not speak to me instantly when I call, I shall open fire!"

"But what of the Señorita Juana?" asked Zorilla, a new light in his eyes.

"If my father dies I die also!" came Juana's voice through the side of a tent.

"So be it!" said Testera.

He wheeled his horse, gave a command to his vaqueros, and rode away.

Zorilla dropped to the hammock. Though the day was not hot, he mopped his forehead with a handkerchief. He foresaw defeat. After a time he got up.

"At least I shall do as I please with that dog Nolan," he thought.

He went to the tent in which Nolan had silently listened to what had been said. He found Nolan sitting on the ground with several of the outlaws squatting near, watching.

Nolan was grinning, and when he saw Zorilla's face the grin widened.

"You heard?" sneered Zorilla.

"Magnífico spoke loud enough," answered Nolan. "You'd better feed him."

Zorilla's face reddened with anger.

"And what shall I do with you, dog of a gringo?" he snarled.

"I'm not makin' your plans," replied Nolan.

Zorilla's face whitened at the contempt in his prisoner's voice. He aimed a kick at Nolan's face, which the latter avoided by moving his head quickly.

The icy gleam in Nolan's eyes dissuaded the outlaw from kicking at him again. There was something in Nolan's gaze which gave Zorilla the thought that there was a possibility of his meeting Nolan again, at a time when the latter would not be bound and defenseless. And if such a time ever came, Nolan, he was convinced, would repay him for the kick.

And yet he felt reasonably certain that Nolan was fated to die to-day. For in the next tent was Waldron, who had told Zorilla of his hatred of Nolan and of his yearning to be revenged for a certain indignity at Nolan's hands.

Waldron had sought out the outlaw soon after appearing upon the mesa, telling Zorilla that through association with him he would find opportunity of paying his score with his ancient enemy.

In Zorilla's jealous hatred of Nolan was a longing to kill his rival. Yet he was aware that he himself dared not kill Nolan; he must not even be suspected of conniving at Nolan's death lest Juana blame him and hate him.

No; Zorilla must hold aloof. It was well enough to capture Nolan, as he had captured Juana and her father. That had been cleverness, and cleverness is everywhere commendable. As a matter of fact, Juana had felt the romance of the action, for though she had been bound like the others she had several times smiled at Zorilla.

She would smile at him as long as he did not harm Nolan or her father or herself. And there was a chance that after a while she would admire him. And after admiration there was no telling what might develop.

Yet at this minute Juana was in another tent and out of sight of Nolan, and she could not tell what was happening.

Zorilla ordered his men out of the tent. After they had gone he leaned over Nolan, seized his nose between a forefinger and a thumb and tweaked it viciously.

"You love Señorita Juana," he said.

"I'll kill you for that, Zorilla," declared Nolan.

"I think not," answered the outlaw, showing his teeth in a wide smile. "You are aware that I also am in love with Señorita Juana. And when I love I permit no one to interfere. Much I would like to kneel upon you, take your throat in my hands, and slowly choke the life out of you. But I cannot do that, since the Señorita would suspect. You must be killed, Señor Nolan, but it must be done so that I will not be suspected of having had a hand in it."

Nolan did not look at Zorilla; he turned his head and gazed out through the flap of the tent, where he could see two men carrying tankards.

Don Pedro's wine.

Zorilla sat down in front of Nolan, leaned toward him, and spoke softly: "Do you know Señor Waldron?"

Nolan was again looking at Zorilla, and the latter saw his eyes chill.

"That is one thing you gringo dogs never learn," laughed the outlaw. "You cannot dissemble. You hate, and one can see it in your eyes. You love, and you become jackasses. So you know Señor Waldron? And he is not your friend. Very well. He has told me of your enmity. Once you humbled him before some men in one of your foolish cantinas. You shot his gun from his hand. Is that so?"

Nolan turned his head.

"Bah!" exclaimed Zorilla. "You think self-control is a virtue! Perhaps it is when it is masked with a smiling face. If you were one of my race, Señor Nolan, you would not turn your head away like that, but would look straight at me and smile. And therefore I would not be able to read your thoughts. But now I would know, even if Señor Waldron had not told me."

"Hell!" smiled Nolan. "You make me sick!"

"You will be sicker, Señor Nolan!" snapped Zorilla. "And I am telling you something now that will entertain you during the day. You will have time to meditate upon it. To-night your legs will be unbound. But not your arms. After dark two of my men will come for you. They will lead you northward on the mesa to a place where the three of you will be met by a fourth man.

"The fourth man will be Señor Waldron! After my men have given you into the custody of Señor Waldron they will return. You will be alone on the edge of the mesa with Señor Waldron. At your feet will be a precipice three hundred feet high! Do you know what will happen?"

Nolan's lips curved with derision.

"Ai! I see that you do!" smiled Zorilla. "Well, you will have the day to meditate upon what will befall you when, with your arms bound, you stand at the edge of the precipice facing Señor Waldron! Señor Nolan," he smiled, "I leave you to your reflections."

CHAPTER XX

Jim Nolan's reflections would not have provoked enjoyment in Zorilla because they were derisive. Nolan was not a coward, and he was aware that there is a time for every man to die. If he had any emotion in the matter at all, it was that before dying he would not have a chance to kill Zorilla for tweaking his nose and for having the temerity to love Juana.

He was tightly bound, and there was no hope of escaping. For as soon as Zorilla disappeared several outlaws sauntered into the tent and squatted near him, to watch him. Once in a while one of them would address him in broken English, using the broad profanity that they had picked up through association with American cowboys, but most of the time they conversed in their own language.

For Nolan the time passed slowly. Once in a while he could hear Don Pedro's voice rising above the mutterings of the outlaws. It seemed Don Pedro was being fed. Once Nolan heard him roar at someone who must have been appointed to attend him:

"*Diablos!* More of that boiled pigeon! And another helping of *carne con cuero! Peste!* Do you think I am a child? What? The *bacalao* is all gone? Well, then, bring me some red herring and some sardines in oil and vinegar! The herring are gone also? Olla? No! Keep that for the hungry dogs that will nose around after the scraps I leave! You will bring me some anchovies, some shrimps, and the rest of that toasted bacon! And more wine! I don't half drink!"

There followed a half-hour interval of silence during which the outlaws in Nolan's tent talked in awed whispers regarding Don Pedro's enormous appetite.

"*Muy Dios!*" growled one; "he will keep his threat to eat everything. We shall go hungry to sleep!"

"There is no end to him," said another. "When you think now surely he will have had enough, he begins all over again. It appears that the taking of food merely excites his craving for more!"

"I have heard that once at a feast in Hermosillo he ate a quarter of beef, a dozen fowls, a pot of podrida, enough frijoles to feed a dozen families, besides maize, a table full of sweetmeats, and a hand of cheese. In addition they tell me he drank nearly a cask of wine."

"Yet he does not particularly like frijoles," said still another. "So that, if he ate them at Hermosillo, he must have felt that there was a lack of food."

"*Peste!*" grumbled one of the outlaws, "a pint of frijoles and I am filled for a week!"

They again became silent, for Don Pedro's voice was raised again. The tent in which he was feasting could not have been far away, for his voice was heard with great distinctness.

"What! No more partridge? The devil! I am disappointed, for I liked the taste of that last one. When I see the cook of the fiesta again I shall have to compliment him. Meantime, I will console myself with some of that excellent kid meat and stuffed olives. No more? *Sus!* Then some more of that lamb! No? I remember; I finished it. It was the lamb I remarked about because of its tenderness and the sauce you poured over it. You were trying to secrete some!

"More wine!"

A silence. Then—

"That is all? Señor the waiter, I am but half fed. If you do not bring me more food I shall not open my lips when Testera comes to-morrow. No, not if Zorilla orders me shot!"

"There is no more," said a voice, evidently that of the waiter.

"I hunger!" roared Don Pedro; "you are starving me! I famish! If you do not at once set food before me, I shall cry out that you are killing me! And then Testera will come!"

"*Madre de Dios*, be quiet!" admonished the waiter. "I will see if there is any food left."

Evidently food still remained to be eaten, for again Don Pedro's voice was heard.

"Ai!" he cried, "you lied! A roast chicken and a platter of new cheese!"

"It is the last, El Magnífico," said the waiter in a hollow voice. "You are indeed leaving us nothing with which to withstand a siege. A day or two and we shall have to surrender to Testera."

"Wine!" roared Don Pedro. "Men with no appetites need no food. Whereas, I must have much, having a glorious desire for food!"

Nolan heard the waiter groan. After that there was another long silence, which was broken by Don Pedro's voice calling for wine. Half an hour later a man stuck his head in the flap of Nolan's tent. He was wiping his glistening forehead with a sleeve of his calico shirt. His visage was dolorous. And when he spoke Nolan knew him for the waiter.

"The Holy Padre protect me!" he wailed to the other outlaws. "We are cleaned out! There is not a morsel of food left in the camp! Even the sweetmeats have gone down his marvellous gullet! The wine has vanished—all but a flagon or so that he said he meant to have when he awakened!"

"He is sleeping?" asked one of the outlaws.

"Like a child," answered the waiter. "But in his sleep he murmurs '*Bueno*'! and smacks his lips! Never have I seen a man who loves food more!"

The waiter withdrew, muttering unintelligibly. There was nothing unintelligible about the remarks of the outlaws who remained with Nolan. Again they drew upon their stock of American oaths, no doubt intended for Nolan's ears. But Nolan grinned at them, stretched out on his right side, and went to sleep.

The outlaws were still in the tent when he awakened; their sour visages told him that they still resented Don Pedro's assault upon the food stores.

"The Señorita Juana," asked one outlaw, "has she been fed?"

"It seems El Magnífico saved something from the ruin for her. A roast chicken and a portion of wine. He was careful that she alone received any of it, for he required that she call to him to tell him that she had dined. *De veras!* El Magnífico knows a thing or two!"

Through the flap of the tent Nolan could see the dusk coming. The day had been hot, and he was suffering from the strain of his bonds. Twice during the day he had been given water, but no food. For that matter, none of the outlaws had received food, and so Nolan's hunger was not so keen as it might have been. Only once—when he had overheard Don Pedro devouring his repast—had he experienced any craving for food.

The outlaws in the tent with Nolan were restless. After the dusk came, they no longer attempted to speak in English, but confined their talk to whispers in their own tongue.

Nolan could not tell what they were talking about, and he cared little. He was aware of what was in prospect for him, and he was little interested in other things.

After dark Zorilla entered the tent. He stood for some minutes in front of Nolan, looking down at him.

Nolan did not look up after the first glance.

"You are impatient, Señor Nolan?" asked the outlaw chief. "This has been a hot day and your bonds have irked you. Be patient yet a little longer and you will be taken for that walk I promised you!"

Zorilla laughed.

Nolan whistled several bars from the "Cowboy's Lament," and the outlaw's lips whitened with rage.

"You will not be buried, though, Señor Nolan," he said. "Some day, perhaps several years from now, some wanderer will find your bones at the foot of the precipice I was telling you about. At any rate, it is certain that the Señorita Juana will never see you again. She will think that you ran away, and she will always think of you as a coward who deserted her, who fled from danger. She will think that, Señor Nolan, because I shall tell her!"

There came no answer from Nolan. For an instant longer Zorilla stood, then he muttered a "Puf!" of contempt, turned, and went out of the tent.

The darkness inside the tent increased in intensity. Yet sometimes, when a slight breeze stirred the flap of the tent, Nolan caught glimpses of lanterns which he knew were hung beneath the trees on the mesa. And of course, despite the fact that by this time everyone on the mesa must know that Don Pedro and his daughter had been abducted by the outlaws, the feasting and the drinking would be going on as usual. There would not perhaps be quite as much hilarity, but people must drink and eat no matter what was happening to those who were less fortunate.

Nolan had been wondering about Clelland. Did his friend know of his extremity? Nolan thought not. Clelland might know he was captured, but certainly Zorilla would not let anyone know of his intention to permit Waldron to kill him.

Nolan was convinced that Clelland would find means to free him, if given time. But the point was that there was little time. And being aware of Clelland's appetite for strong drink, Nolan felt that it was quite likely that at this moment his friend might be sleeping off the effects of wine that he had drunk, which could be so easily obtained anywhere upon the mesa.

From a near-by tent Nolan could hear Don Pedro calling for more food and threatening to call for Testera if food were not given him. Someone was expostulating with him, attempting to calm him, and assuring him that, as he had already eaten all the food in the camp, it was impossible to provide more unless Don Pedro gave an order upon the cook of the fiesta.

This, of course, Don Pedro would not do. And as no more food was brought Don Pedro continued to shout and threaten.

Later, while Don Pedro was still creating a commotion, someone entered Nolan's tent. The darkness had grown so deep that Nolan could not even distinguish the form of the visitor, yet he felt a new presence, and he had heard the rustle of the canvas.

Nolan heard whispering, and an instant later felt hands at his ankles, loosening the ropes that were tied about them. Other hands seized him and he was lifted to his feet, where he stood for a time swaying back and forth in pain while the blood resumed circulating in his legs. Then, abruptly, before the numbness had gone, he was led and shoved through the tent opening into the cool night air.

At a distance he observed the many lights on the mesa; he heard laughter, voices raised in light talk, some music. But it was evident that Testera had withdrawn his vaqueros as Don Pedro had ordered, for it appeared there was no one within a quarter of a mile of the outlaws' tents except the outlaws themselves, and they were invisible.

There was no moon. Zorilla had chosen the time wisely, for later the moon would rise.

Nolan could not tell how many men were near him, though he was certain there were several. Zorilla, possibly, the two men he had mentioned, and Waldron. Waldron, of course, was certain to be near, for it was Waldron who had been appointed to kill him.

The halt outside the tent was brief. Nolan was again shoved forward. His legs were so numbed that they functioned only partially, and he fell, face down.

He was lifted roughly. This time he was partially supported by a man on each side of him, who led him forward by gripping his elbows.

They went forward in silence. Nolan was aware that he was being taken to the northern section of the mesa, where there were countless hills and gullies, a maze of wild growth, and a forest of low-growing trees.

There were no lights at all in that direction, for the guests of the feast had obeyed the human instinct to mass together near the base of supply, where they would have the companionship and the ease they sought.

There was no word spoken by the men who were leading Nolan away from the outlaw camp. The trail grew rougher as Nolan and his captors continued northward; the sound of voices ceased, the music died away, the lights of the feasters grew dimmer and at last vanished altogether. Nolan and the outlaws who were leading him had entered the broken section of the mesa.

Nolan felt they must have been walking for about an hour when a voice, sepulchral in its hollowness, came from one of the members of Nolan's escort.

"Here!" it said.

The hands upon Nolan's elbows jerked him to a halt. He stood, the hands still gripping him, waiting.

He had no means of knowing the character of the land around him. Was he standing at the edge of the precipice Zorilla had told him about? Were his arms to be unbound before he received the shove that would send him into eternity? Or would Waldron make his presence known and torture him with delay to punish him for what he had done?

He didn't know much about Waldron, though at this instant he reflected that he had been somewhat astonished when Zorilla had told him what Waldron was to be permitted to do. He knew now that he had not judged Waldron to be that kind of a man. In spite of their enmity, he had respected Waldron.

But his feelings at this moment would make little difference. He must have misjudged Waldron, or the latter would not be with him, contemplating this kind of revenge.

There was whispering near Nolan. The voices grew louder, and there was passion in them.

"We were told to stay and see it done!" declared one voice. "You will shove him off now or we shall do it!"

The words were spoken in Mexican. Nolan understood them. He had thought that he had himself well under control, that he had nerved himself for this ordeal until there was no danger of his weakening in any manner. He was amazed at the swift pulse of hope that shot through him at the possibility that there might be a violent disagreement and that he would have a chance to escape.

There were more passionate words; then came the violent action Nolan had hoped for.

The hands holding his arms were swiftly withdrawn. The instant Nolan was released he turned and leaped toward the point from which he had heard the voices, knowing that the edge of the precipice could not be in that direction.

He ran half a dozen steps when he stumbled over an obstruction and fell headlong. He had felt himself going and had twisted his body so that he struck the ground upon one shoulder, but the force of the fall was so great that the breath was knocked out of him, and he rolled over on his back, unable to rise.

There was no more talking. Near him in the darkness he heard sounds of scuffling, the thudding of blows, heavy breathing, grunts, curses. A knife must have gone home, for a man's voice screamed in agony. Later came a gurgle—a sound resembling that which Nolan had heard when the prowler on the mesa had been murdered the night before.

Nolan knew another murder had been done, perhaps two.

He had now got to his feet, but the fall had caused him to lose his sense of direction, so that he was reluctant to step in any direction until he felt certain he would not walk off the edge of the precipice.

As he stood near where he had fallen the scuffling continued. Then came a shrill cry of terror and the sound of something falling. One of the fighters had gone over the edge of the precipice!

Nolan could hear the body falling, could hear it crashing through brush; heard a thud as it struck a rock or a ledge; heard a hideous scraping and slithering as it slid down the precipitous slope, with boulders and gravel and loosened earth following after it.

Followed a flat, dead silence.

Then another scream, and again the sound as of a body crashing through brush. Again the scraping, slithering sound, again the rain of earth and gravel and rocks, and again the dead, heavy silence.

And now Nolan knew which way to go. He turned from the sounds he had heard and began to run blindly away from the edge of the precipice.

But he made slow progress and a great noise. For the ground was uneven and rocky, and every step he made his boot heels struck obstructions and sent up clacking sounds. His spurs jangled musically. Twice within a short space he fell because, as his arms were still bound, he could not keep his balance.

He heard someone clattering after him. Whoever it was was having as much trouble as he. Yet the sounds were directly behind him, and were very close.

Nolan stopped. Instantly the sounds of pursuit ceased. Nolan went on again, moving as quietly as possible. Yet he hadn't taken three steps when he heard someone again moving behind him. And this time he felt certain there were two men following him.

He stumbled against a jagged spire of rock and struck his head against it. He stood there, partly stunned, reeling: though even in this condition he was aware that silence had come again.

The silence was broken by a voice.

"Nolan!" it said sharply.

The voice was Waldron's!

Nolan did not answer. He did not intend to reveal his position to his enemy so that the latter might shoot him. It seemed to him that Waldron had lost track of him and was playing this trick in order to locate him that he might shoot him and thus end the pursuit.

"Nolan!" came Waldron's voice again, more insistent.

Nolan remained silent. Again and again Waldron called.

Waldron's voice seemed to come from the right of Nolan, at a distance which Nolan judged to be about a hundred feet. And now, during an interval in which Waldron did not call, there came a rattle of stones, a clacking as of someone walking, and the jingling of spurs from Nolan's left.

The sound ceased. Whoever had been walking there had stopped and was evidently listening.

"Nolan!" came Waldron's voice again.

A voice came from Nolan's left. The sound of it sent the blood surging through his veins in leaps.

Clelland's voice!

"Hell!" it said. "He must be somewhere around here. I heard him fannin' it!"

His friend and his enemy together, searching for him!

What did that mean?

Of one thing Nolan was certain: that Clelland was his friend and was not searching for him in order to kill him. But he knew just as positively that Waldron had been appointed to execute him, and he could not understand why the two should be together in this quest.

Only one solution occurred to him. It was that Waldron was somehow deceiving Clelland until such a time as he would be able to secure his revenge without great personal risk. If Waldron could contrive to get Nolan and Clelland together without either of them being suspicious of him he might——

"He ain't far," said Waldron, interrupting his thoughts. "I heard him a minute ago not very far ahead."

"He'd likely fall an' bust his head—him tryin' to run with his hands tied that way," grumbled Clelland. "I told you back a piece that we'd ought to yell at him an' stop him!"

"I wanted to let him get away from that cliff," answered Waldron. "He might have tumbled over it. An' there might have been more of them greasers around. I wouldn't trust Zorilla."

"Nolan!"

This time it was Clelland who called.

"Why, that's Bill Clelland!" answered Nolan. His voice was cold, deliberate.

"Whoop!" yelled Clelland.

"And Nolan asks Bill Clelland to stay right where he is until he explains how it comes that he is on my trail with a man who was appointed by Zorilla to kill me!"

"Why, you old horse thief!" laughed Clelland. "You're on the peck! You're spittin' poison with that politeness! An' usin' a tone of voice to me! Haw, haw, haw! Waldron, you stay where you are until this thing is settled. For if he's got his hands loose an' you're close enough, he'll tie into you!

"Jim," Clelland went on, "I reckon it sure does look fishy to you, an' I ain't blamin' you. But you ain't doubtin' Bill Clelland, are you?"

"I'll admit I'm sort of puzzled," conceded Nolan.

"Sure! You would be. But I reckon I can straighten this all out in a jiffy. Here she goes:

"I was dead drunk this afternoon when I woke up to find someone sittin' on top of me an' dousin' me with water. It was Waldron. 'Clelland,' he says to me, 'Zorilla's got Nolan, an' to-night he's turnin' Nolan over to me. I'm to take him to the north wall of the mesa and shove him over. Before I do that I can shoot him or knife him—whichever I seem to think is the best way of killin' him!'

"I was shocked sober. I rose up with Waldron hangin' onto me. An' after I'd choked him so that his tongue was hangin' out I says to him that if he was figgerin' to kill you he was goin' to make a bungle of it.

"When he got his breath back he told me that if he'd have intended to do any killin' he wouldn't have come to tell me about it before doin' it, an' after I got over my anger I seen that was a fact.

"Well, then Waldron asked me to come along to the mesa edge where the killin' was to be done. They was to be two of Zorilla's men along to see that the thing was done proper. Well, when Waldron an' you an' Zorilla's men got there I was close. I'd been followin' them from the time they left the camp. I was right close when they give Waldron the word to stick a knife into you an' shove you over. Then Waldron an' me went into them. Both them hombres is layin' at the foot of the mesa busted wide open. An' you're here, safe an' sound, an' Waldron's here, wantin' to be your friend. An' I'm here, stayin' your friend, no matter how much you jaw me!"

There was a long silence, and the blackness between the three men was a shade lighter from a faint tinge of yellow in the eastern sky, which was heralding the rising moon.

Nolan broke the silence.

"Boys," he said, "I reckon I ain't half as smart as I thought I was. An' if you'll come over here an' cut these ropes around my wrists, I'll be proud to shake hands with both of you."

They found Nolan. And standing there in the darkness, with the golden flood in the east ever rising, they performed the rites of friendship.

CHAPTER XXI

The three travelled southward, bearing a little west so that they would not strike Zorilla's camp. Nolan was silent while Waldron, his voice betraying his pride in at last being able to claim the friendship of the man who had once humbled him, related to Clelland the incident of Don Pedro's gastronomic feat. From time to time during the recital Clelland chuckled hilariously.

"Don Pedro could do it, too!" he declared. "You say it took a dozen of them to tie him?"

"And there were four or five of them badly injured," added Waldron. "He cracked one man's wrist as you or I would crack a pipe stem!"

When the three friends reached the southern end of the mesa they were encompassed by a heavy silence. There were no lights anywhere. Farther northward on the mesa the moon was bathing the treetops and filtering down through the branches into the grass of the clearings, and still farther northward the rugged section was glowing with a phosphorescent light; but the southern end of the mesa was dark, for eastward a mountain peak stuck its dark silhouette between.

Nowhere was there visible evidence that any person of all the vast number of guests of the feast was awake. It appeared that all were asleep. The three friends paused under a dimly burning lantern to consult with one another. Waldron looked at the watch he carried.

"No wonder!" he said: "it's two o'clock!"

The lantern in whose light they stood was one of a festoon which drooped over a rough wooden table about which were scattered remnants of food, bottles which had been drained of their contents, and several jugs, which were empty. The other lanterns had burned out, and they hung limply in the dew that had fallen. Near by was a low tent from which issued the heavy snoring of a sleeper.

Nolan seemed to be familiar with the section; he felt that he had seen it in the daylight, though Waldron and Clelland confessed that they had no knowledge of their thereabouts.

"We are near the mess camp," declared Nolan. "I've an idea it's over this way." He turned and led the others northward, toward a clearing, and when Clelland came to a certain spot he exclaimed shortly.

"Sure! You're right, Jim. This is where we made our camp!"

The cooks, Nolan felt, would not be hard to find. And yet, when the three reached the place where Nolan had seen the food supplies piled high in tiers and rows and mounds, he stopped and scratched his head in bewilderment.

For the huge piles and mounds of supplies had vanished!

Here and there were a few crates and boxes and barrels and sacks, but these formed only a fraction of the vast store that had been there previously!

Nolan felt that perhaps he was mistaken about the location of the mess camp. But in the dim light of the moon that was now filtering down through the trees he observed the small stream from which he had washed the blood from his hands on the morning after the murder had been committed, and of which he had later been accused. The stream was there, and the tables at which he had seen the cooks at work. Scattered all around was the débris of a large culinary department—empty crates from which fowls had been taken to be slaughtered, accumulated piles of food scraps and bones, chunks of manioc and maize, rinds of melons, feathers, and all the rest of the unappetizing miscellany of cast-off edibles.

Near by also were the tents which he had observed upon former visits, occupied, he knew, by the cooks of the feast themselves. Several of the tents were now demolished, and a few of them were wrecked and piled in heaps. Also, nearly all of the wagons which had been standing around were gone.

"Looks like somethin' has happened here!" declared Nolan.

He ran to an upright tent. Just as he was about to reach out to open the flap he straightened. In the shadow of the tent he saw a huddled object—the body of a man.

Clelland reached the body first and leaned over it. He stood erect, his face betraying amazement.

"Knifed!" he exclaimed.

He went into the tent and came out again, his lips in straight lines.

"Two more in there!" he said. "Their throats cut!"

However, there was none to hear him, for Nolan and Waldron were running toward the wreck of a tent around which other bodies were huddled in grotesque positions.

Silently now, for they knew they had stumbled upon the proof of a massacre, they ran from tent to tent, peering here and there in the faint moonlight at the hideous and ghastly faces of the murdered.

"This is Zorilla's work!" declared Nolan, when after a time they drew together for a conference. "We've got to find Testera!"

They separated. Clelland ran south, Waldron north, while Nolan plunged westward through the brush and under the low-growing trees around which were grouped the tents of the guests of the feast.

And now there were sounds all around the three men. They had been heard. Guttural voices, pitched high in alarm, greeted Nolan as after a time he plunged through some brush almost at the entrance to a tent. Half a dozen men arrayed in their night garments appeared around him. A knife glittered. The moonlight glinted upon a rifle barrel which was aimed at him.

"*Apresura!*" he shouted in the only Mexican term he knew to apprise them that he was in a hurry. "Hustle!" he adjured them, relapsing instantly into the idioms of his own tongue. "Where is Testera? There has been a clean-up! The cooks! They have been murdered! Quick! Where is Testera?"

Half a dozen hands pointed westward.

"*Alli, alla!*" gesticulated one, pointing to an aisle through the trees, where Nolan could dimly make out the form of a man walking back and forth.

Nolan ran toward the man. He spoke to the man, who was acting as sentry, and at once he was surrounded by other men, who appeared quickly out of the surrounding darkness. Then came Testera's voice, and the vaquero chief himself came forward and peered at Nolan in the moonlight.

"Nolan!" he exclaimed. "The devil! I thought Zorilla had you!"

Quickly Nolan explained the circumstances of his escape. Then he told Testera of the massacre of the cooks.

A concerted groan rose from the vaqueros assembled in the semi-darkness around Nolan and Testera.

The vaquero chief exclaimed hoarsely:

"*Peste!*"

He shouted an order in Mexican, and within a few minutes, with all his men running behind him, he made his way to the mess camp. There in the moonlight, which had now become so bright that the men could distinctly see one another's faces, he gave voice to picturesque profanity.

"This is what comes of Don Pedro's generosity!" he declared. "If he had listened to me, his pronunciamento would not have included Zorilla and his hounds! This is their work! They have stolen the supplies, they have killed the cooks, and now they are in Diablo Cache, laughing at us! And they have the Señorita Bazan and Don Pedro himself!"

"Let's get goin'!" said Nolan. "We've got enough men to herd ride Zorilla. He can't have more than a hundred!"

Testera's eyes gleamed.

"Does Señor Nolan know Diablo Cache?" he asked. "You do not, of course, or you would not have spoken so confidently. Diablo Cache is impregnable. It can be reached from only one direction, and that by crossing a crevasse which is spanned in only one place by a natural bridge only just wide enough for an ox cart to pass. And this bridge, Señor Nolan, is in plain view of those who will always be watching it. You may be sure that whoever starts across the bridge will be shot down before he goes very far!"

"Well, we'll have a look at it, anyway!" declared Nolan.

"*Ya se ve*" (to be sure), said Testera grimly, without enthusiasm.

By this time it seemed that all the guests on the mesa had assembled around Testera. Clelland and Waldron had come back and were standing near Nolan. Men and women in various states of undress were running excitedly about, scurrying back and forth, arming themselves, calling to each other. Women were screeching, children were crying.

Testera was a deliberate commander. He ordered one of his lieutenants to take charge of the people, instructing him to arm them and follow him as quickly as they could. Then he looked at Nolan.

"Let us go forward to the cache, Señor," he said.

He shouted an order to his vaqueros, and the entire company moved forward as one unit, Testera ahead, with Nolan and Waldron and Clelland close beside him.

CHAPTER XXII

His hunger completely satisfied and his thirst quenched by all the wine that had been brought to him, except a flagon that he had sent to Señorita Juana, Don Pedro had stretched out in his tent and was fast asleep when some time after dark he was awakened by something touching his hands and feet. Startled and resentful, he tried to sit up, to discover that his hands and feet were securely bound and that a number of men seemed to be sitting on him.

"Pigs!" he shouted. "What now? Do you not permit a man to rest after eating? Remove your carcasses before I slay you!"

"Bah!" came Zorilla's voice from the darkness of the tent; "the wind-bag bloweth again. If he raises his voice I bid you stuff a gunny sack into his mouth!"

Don Pedro essayed to reply to his enemy, but the men close to him appeared to interpret the sound of his voice as sufficient excuse to obey Zorilla's order, so that instantly a foul, greasy rag was stuffed into His Excellency's mouth and immediately drawn tight by another rag which was tied at the back of his neck.

Groans and threshing from the corner of the tent where Don Pedro was lying gave evidence of the gigantic effort the captive was making to inflict injury upon his tormentors. But presently many men bore him through the tent opening and vanished into the surrounding darkness.

Somewhere outside the tent Don Pedro was thrown into the bed of an ox cart, and with a strong guard walking at the side of the vehicle he was carried slowly and joltingly across the face of the mesa into the mysterious distance.

He was stifled by the rank odour that came from the floor of the cart, but he kept very still, because he was fearful that his clothing would be ruined by useless effort to escape.

But this indignity had definitely changed Don Pedro's feelings toward Zorilla and his men. He was aflame with a rage against them, and he knew that hereafter his pronunciamento would not protect them from his wrath.

It seemed to him that, as the cart went forward, fewer and fewer men accompanied it. At first he had heard many voices accompanying the progress of the cart; now he was aware of only three or four.

He listened as well as he could above the jolting and rattling of the wagon.

"The Chief will get food," confidently said one of the walking men. "He will get all of it, if possible. That will repay us for what we have had to feed the big stomach in the cart!"

"Let us hope that Zorilla brings wine, also!" said another fervently. "My tongue is so dry that it clacks against the roof of my mouth."

"Zorilla will play no longer," said still another voice. "By this time Nolan is dead. His enemy, Señor Waldron, has thrown him from the edge of the mesa, at Serpent Cañon. The fat oaf in the cart is helpless. The Señorita Juana is by this time safely at Diablo Cache. Once we reach there, and we have food enough, we will be able to stand off ten thousand men!"

Don Pedro mumbled profanely through the foul cloth upon his lips. Yet the men had spoken the truth about his condition. He was helpless, for they had tied him down upon the floor of the cart, and though he strained at his bonds they did not yield at all.

The men continued to converse in their own language. Don Pedro was now too enraged to listen to them. Meanwhile the cart rumbled on, going farther and farther away from the section of the camp which was most thickly populated; encountering rougher ground, at times careening violently; often striking obstructions that brought the bottom of the cart thudding against Don Pedro's head.

When the moon rose Don Pedro could tell in which direction he was moving, though the sides of the cart were so high that he could not look over them to determine the character of the land through which he was passing. But he knew something about Diablo Cache, for he had visited the place more than once to inspect it.

When the cart at last came to a stop and the men accompanying it gathered around the oxen and talked in whispers to one of their number who had evidently been leading the beasts, Don Pedro realized that they had reached the narrow, natural bridge that led from the main body of the mesa over a deep and wide crevasse to the grotesque rock and lava formations that composed Diablo Cache.

And now the flesh on Don Pedro's body began to creep and grow cold. For he knew that the crest of the bridge was barely wide enough for the wheels of the cart to pass. If there should be a stumble or a slip, cart, oxen, and himself would tumble to instant destruction.

"*Madre de Dios!*" growled one of the men. "It is bad enough to cross this place in the daylight. At night it looks like the abode of Satan. It is deep. If a man should fall it would take him minutes to reach the bottom!"

The voice of the man was sepulchral; a wave of dank air assailed Don Pedro in the cart. The vehicle moved forward again, this time at a creeping pace, as though men and oxen were crawling. Don Pedro could not see outward, but he had a feeling as of balancing himself upon the edge of a vast precipice, with the utter darkness of a great void swimming below him. He held himself rigid as the rumbling wheels of the cart crunched and slid under him. Twice he heard cries of alarm from the men as the cart slid perilously sideways. Once the cart stopped while a voice ahead of the oxen cursed the lack of light.

"If Zorilla proposed to cross here to-night he should have provided more moonlight," said one of the men, feebly attempting levity.

"Yet crossing even now is not worse than would happen if we had stayed on the mesa," answered another man. "Once we are over, we are safe. For from behind the barricades we can pick off any who attempt to cross the bridge."

There was a pause, while a heavy silence enveloped cart and men. Then the cart moved on again, the stolid oxen plodding slowly, the cart swaying behind them; the men silent, following.

When one of the men broke the silence, Don Pedro knew they had reached the broader land of the cache, for the man's voice had a lilt in it.

"*Maria purisima!*" he exclaimed. "We have that to be thankful for! And when I leave here it shall be in the daylight!"

His fellows laughed. A lash snapped, and the oxen went forward at a faster pace, while the men spoke again in their normal voices.

The cart was drawn on some distance, and when it came to a stop Don Pedro felt that the ropes which bound him were being loosened. He had a hope that they would untie his arms, or at least his legs. But they wisely left those bonds untouched as they dragged him from the cart and carried him bodily into a place where no light from the moon penetrated. They had laid him down upon a litter of small branches of trees—at least, it seemed so to him—which were covered with a blanket. They removed the cloth which they had tied over his mouth, but Don Pedro had nothing to say to them. What they had said about Waldron pushing Nolan off the cliff at Serpent's Cañon worried him. He had grown to like Nolan. If they had killed Nolan the action could mean only one thing, which was that Zorilla had indeed ceased "playing," and from now on meant to continue in earnest the depredations which had made him feared and dreaded throughout the section.

CHAPTER XXIII

Señorita Juana had also divined a change in Zorilla. A captive, like her father, she had held in the beginning a humorous contempt for the outlaw chief. Not since she had been captured on her way back to the Rancho Paloma from a visit to her *padrino* had she entertained the slightest fear of Zorilla.

Whether this was because as a woman she had a deeper insight of the man's real character, or whether she had from the first considered him merely as a man, to be trifled with as she had trifled with others of his sex, she was not now able to tell. Certainly, at any rate there had come a visible change in him.

At first he had had a habit of regarding her with contemplative amusement, which had seemed to recognize her contempt of him, and which had appeared to tell her to wait.

What she was to wait for she did not know, though she had assumed that he was convinced that finally she would fall in love with him. She had observed that conceit in his manner. Zorilla was a handsome fellow, to be sure, but she was certain that she would never fall in love with any man whose knowledge of his attractions was so great that he betrayed it. She knew how to treat a man of that type.

However, she was now uncertain, because Zorilla had changed. His glances at her were no longer glances of amusement. There was passion in them, a fierce intentness, a consciousness of power that startled her.

Yet even now she did not fear him, though she was confined to his tent, under guard, and she was aware that since he had violated the pronunciamento, he was certain to continue his aggressions. She also knew that she could expect no help from Testera and his vaqueros until they had demonstrated their superiority in the battle that was sure to come. And in the event that a battle might go against him Zorilla might have her removed to a place where Testera and her father would never find her. Zorilla knew of such places, she was certain, for no one had been able to discover his secret camps.

The afternoon following the capture of her father, Nolan, and herself had been hot, though to her, because of her father's insistence upon being fed continuously, the hours had not seemed long. She had been amused by the way the outlaws had responded to Don Pedro's demands. Upon every face she saw was concern mingled with awe and amazement. It appeared to her that the outlaws were aware that Don Pedro's appetite was not to be appeased.

She drank some of the wine that he had ordered sent in to her; she ate a portion of the roast chicken he had thoughtfully saved for her. And when he had yelled through the walls of the tents to her asking her if she had been given all he had sent, she was able to reply that she had, and to respond with a word of encouragement.

Zorilla had overheard that word, for when, toward dusk, he entered her tent, he smiled grimly at her.

"The Señorita laughs," he said. "It is well, perhaps, to laugh when one can. For later you will need something to amuse you!"

"*Si*, Señor the outlaw," she replied; "that is true. Yet I never lack amusement when you are near."

Zorilla bowed and smiled.

"Then you will be amused all the rest of your days, *caro mi*; for the remainder of your days will be spent at my side."

"Then I promise that Zorilla will not be amused!" she answered.

"You will have different views before long," he smiled.

"You will be prepared to change yours, also, Señor Zorilla. For I warn you that each day I shall hate you more!"

His eyes gleamed.

"At least you will not give your affection to the gringo dog," he snarled, losing his temper, "for to-night he dies!"

She smiled at him with cool insolence.

"I have heard," she said, "Señor Nolan is to be pushed off a cliff. He will die knowing I love him, and afterward I shall never look at another man!"

Zorilla paled.

"*Peste!*" he growled.

He left her.

Some hours later, when the inside of the tent was black with the darkness which had descended, Juana heard men entering. She was seized, bound, and carried outside into a faint star haze.

She could dimly discern objects around her. She saw numbers of the outlaws moving here and there; she felt that they were striking their tents, rolling them into bundles and loading them upon ox carts that she could observe when they passed between her and distant festoons of lanterns.

She no longer heard her father's voice, and so she concluded that he had been taken away. Zorilla was not waiting for Testera to come on the morrow; he was breaking camp in the middle of the night and stealing away.

When she had been seized and bound inside the tent a gag had been forced into her mouth and a handkerchief drawn tightly over it and tied at the back of her neck, so that she was not able to make a sound.

Nor was she permitted to remain for long watching the men and the ox carts, for one of the carts drew up beside her, and she was lifted and placed into it. Instantly the vehicle moved forward into the darkness, and in a short time the blackness of distance had swallowed her.

She heard voices which appeared to follow the progress of the cart. There were halts, conferences. Came a time where there was no sound except the dry creaking of the wheels, the crunching of stone and earth, the scuffling of the hoofs of the oxen. Then, as if a tension had been broken, came voices again. Then another halt, and Juana was lifted from the cart and set down on a level.

Around her rose towering walls of granite in grotesque shapes. She felt she had been brought to Diablo Cache, and though she had often heard of the place she had never visited it. She was standing on a level which seemed to be composed of lava or basalt, for it was corrugated, porous, flaky. The moonlight had grown strong, and she could distinguish the faces of men grouped around her—the dark visages of the outlaws composing Zorilla's band. There were a dozen of them, and most of them were grinning at her as though amused.

Two other men were leading the oxen away. Gazing backward over the trail which had brought her here, she could see a narrow bridge spanning the crevasse. It was long, slender, and she shivered as she observed the black emptiness on each side of it. It was a perilous path to travel even on foot, and when she realized that she had crossed it in the ox cart she swayed dizzily.

The moon touched various weirdly shaped rock formations around her. Directly ahead—eastward—was a wall which had the appearance of a battlement or a parapet wall, in which were fissures which seemed to have been arranged for defense. Upon a corner of the wall near her was a sort of bartizan with holes knocked in it. All about were other oddly formed rocks—minarets, spires, towers. In the moonlight the place seemed like an ancient castle in ruins, although she knew better. Yet, though her knowledge of fighting was limited to what she had heard in conversations among the men of her acquaintance, she was aware of the strategic importance of the spot Zorilla had chosen. Testera was a brave man, and among his vaqueros were many men of high courage; but she knew that courage alone would not win this place from Zorilla.

For a few minutes she was not molested by any of the men who had brought her to the place. She was somewhat amazed to observe that they were giving her very little attention. All were facing the back trail; and as she stared in that direction she saw what interested them.

Coming toward her, and moving as rapidly as they could under the cracking lashes of heavy whips wielded by men who walked beside them, were oxen drawing heavily loaded carts. There was a long line of them; and as she watched they gingerly crossed the narrow bridge over the crevasse and were guided across the level upon which she stood. One by one they crossed the bridge and the level and vanished behind a low wall of rock, eastward.

Behind the ox carts came a band of the outlaws on foot. They were laughing, shouting, brandishing their rifles.

In single file they crossed the bridge. They came toward her, peered closely at her, and went on following the ox carts out of sight behind the low wall.

Last to cross the bridge was Zorilla.

The outlaw chief came toward her, and in the moonlight she observed that he was smiling.

He approached her, stopped, bowed suavely.

"Señorita," he said, "it is now time for Zorilla to laugh!"

Before she could speak the hot words that were on her tongue he stepped swiftly forward, swept her into his arms, and carried her through an aperture in the big wall.

It was evident that she had been taken into a large cave or cavern. She could not tell, for she was engulfed in darkness. Nor could she defend herself, for her hands and feet were bound.

The gag and cloth were removed from her mouth by Zorilla's hands. She could hear him laughing as he accomplished the task. And then, though she fought him as best she could, his arms were around her, holding her tightly to him, while his lips were pressed to her cheeks, her throat, her hair.

CHAPTER XXIV

Dawn was breaking when Testera and his men, together with Nolan, Clelland, Dean, Carey, Waldron; Galt and Simms, the train robbers; Abe Pennel, the revenue agent, and his friend Ben Lathrop; Belden and Colton, who had pursued the train robbers to the mesa; and Vittorio Cerros, one of Juana's admirers who had arrived late at the feast, reached a point on the mesa from where they could command a view of the bridge over the crevasse.

Accompanying Testera and the others were hundreds of the males of the feasters, armed with weapons, and crowding behind the vaqueros. Farther back, and out of range should there be shooting, were clusters of women and children who were to be helpless witnesses to what must occur.

Testera's men were unmounted, for there would be no need of horses should there come an opportunity to advance upon the cache.

At Testera's command, his men approached the bridge over the crevasse by keeping in the shelter of the huge boulders that were conveniently strewn over the face of the mesa at that point. Nolan, Clelland, Dean, and the others, not less mindful of the danger of exposing themselves to view from the cache, were also careful to keep in concealment as much as possible.

At a distance of perhaps two hundred feet from the bridge was a gully which was almost large enough for the whole of Testera's troop and the volunteers who had come with Testera. The entire force, with the exception of a few of the more reckless, quickly dropped into the shelter.

Fringing the edge of the gully, upon the side facing the bridge, was an irregular line of rocks and queerly shaped chunks of lava, which made a fairly effective line of breastworks for Testera and the others. The enemies of Zorilla could not see the outlaws, nor, unless a reckless besieger exposed himself, could any of Zorilla's men get a view of Testera's men.

Yet whatever plan of action Testera contemplated, he must act quickly. Zorilla's men had seized all of the food supply except a few odds and ends which they had evidently overlooked, and though Testera had already dispatched some men to various ranches for supplies, he knew days would elapse before they could return with food in a quantity sufficient to feed the vast number of men and women with him. Testera was also aware that Zorilla had taken possession of food enough to last him for many days. The vaquero chief was also aware of the fact that there was water available to the cache, for he knew of a small stream that trickled down a gorge well back from the bridge that spanned the crevasse, where the outlaw and his men could drink and be safe from the danger of a well-aimed shot. Also, though Testera had not yet succeeded in finding such a place, there was a possibility that there might exist a secret exit from the cache which would permit Zorilla and his men to escape him if by any chance the cache got too hot for him or his food supply was in danger of becoming exhausted.

Peering at the cache from between two huge boulders, Testera considered the situation.

So far as he could discover there was no evidence of life or of movement in the cache. The level extending from the bridge to the base of the low, grim-appearing battlement which had drawn Juana's attention the night before was deserted. There appeared to be no one near the openings of the minarets; the crags of the granite cliffs with which the cache was dotted gave no evidence of men being concealed behind them. The low wall behind which Juana had observed the ox carts disappear was as destitute of life as the distant peaks of some mountains far behind it.

But Testera was not deceived. He knew that the outlaws were concealed and waiting, that they were watching the bridge, and that their rifle fire would sweep away any man who attempted to cross.

"What you theenk, Señor Nolan?" he asked.

Nolan was crouching behind a rock adjoining Testera's. He scowled at the vaquero's question.

"I think I've been a fool!" declared Nolan.

"Some time we all have that thought, Señor Nolan," grimly smiled Testera. "Have you a parteekular time in mind?"

"I was a fool for not shootin' Zorilla when I had a chance!"

"Et ees strange that we have the same thought, Señor Nolan. I have had the opportuneety more than once. I have let him slip—puf! He is gone. Mabbe he return. Zen—— *Peste!*"

A bullet droned past Testera's head, which he had wagged when he had talked, and which he had evidently slightly exposed to the enemy.

Testera smiled grimly. The smile grew as a shot from one of the vaqueros answered the bullet which had been sent at Testera. A cry of pain floated to the ears of the vaqueros, and Testera called a compliment to the man who had answered the shot.

"That bridge will not be crossed at once," said Testera.

Nolan made his way down into the gully to where Dean, Carey, Waldron, and Clelland were waiting.

The prospect of a siege was not attractive to Nolan. Waiting while he knew the Señorita Juana was Zorilla's captive would be intolerable to him.

He had always been accustomed to swift, direct action, and he was consumed with impatience when he joined his friends.

"I reckon it would be cussed foolishness to try to cross that bridge to get at the outlaws," he said. "There'll be a moon to-night, same as last night. But even if there wasn't a moon that bridge is right on the skyline, an' a roadrunner couldn't get across there without Zorilla's men seein' it. Testera says there ain't any other way to get across. But I reckon there is. Brains ought to do it. You've got 'em, Dean. I'm askin' you to go projectin' around with me to try to find a way to get over there."

"We'll look," answered Dean noncommittally.

Later Nolan and Dean and Carey, accompanied by Waldron and Clelland, slipped out of the gully and crossed a section featured by low, ragged hills through which they could pass without fear of being exposed to the rifle fire of Zorilla's men.

They went northward along the deep gorge that separated the main section of the mesa from the cache, and for hours they examined the gorge and estimated distances.

The gorge was so deep that in certain places the bottom could not be seen; and where the bottom was discernible it was almost covered by a wild and impenetrable tangle of trees and brush. There were places where the wall of the gorge sloped down from the edge of the main mesa, where a descent might be possible; but the cache side of the gorge was featured by sheer, smooth walls of rock.

At one spot, which was far north of the bridge, the gorge narrowed until it was not more than twenty or thirty feet wide. Nolan was hopeful when he and his friends reached the place, and he suggested throwing a bridge of tree trunks across the chasm to a narrow rock ledge on the opposite side.

Dean mutely pointed to the perpendicular wall which rose hundreds of feet above the ledge. The face of the rock was worn so smooth by the elements that it glistened and gleamed like polished marble.

Nolan frowned.

It was late in the afternoon when they finally reached another narrow section of the gorge. That, too, was surmounted by a sheer, smooth wall. But Dean pointed out a narrow ledge that ran irregularly upward along the face of the wall to a deep recess in the face of the rock. For a long time Dean stood contemplating the wall, the ledge, and the slight cavern. He studied the formation of the rock near the recess in the wall; he gazed long at some rotted rock that formed the roof and part of one side, and he gravely regarded some fissures that seemed wide enough to permit the passage of a human body through them.

The fissures appeared to lead upward to the crest of the rock wall; but Dean would venture no opinion until after moving far down the edge of the gorge he again scrutinized the spot. Then he turned to Nolan.

"The wall can be scaled at that point," he said.

They went back to a point opposite the wall, and Dean indicated how the feat might be accomplished.

But Nolan looked blankly at the deep chasm that yawned between the spot where they stood and the ledge from which the climbing would have to be done.

"How will we get to the ledge?" he asked.

"Over a rope bridge," answered Dean. "It is a primitive method, but we are impatient and we have no time to waste. There is plenty of rope back at the cook camp. The distance to that spire of rock near the ledge is not more than fifty feet." He smiled. "There ought to be a man among the vaqueros who can throw a loop that far. By tying two ropes together, we will get one long enough to reach. Then a light man can work his way over there, taking a heavier rope with him. After that the job will be simple."

The party went back to the cook camp, where they found plenty of heavy rope which under Dean's instructions was woven into a rather heavy cable. To the cable Dean attached smaller ropes, cutting them all off at a length of about three feet and tying them to another heavy rope which he ran parallel with the other heavy one. The arrangement when completed resembled a rope ladder when it was laid out on the ground. This was duplicated, and when both were complete short branches of trees were lashed about six inches apart to the lower rope, thus completing the construction of what would be a sort of suspension bridge when its ends were finally secured.

Darkness had come by the time the rope bridge was completed. Dean counselled waiting until morning to throw the bridge across the chasm, but Nolan was too impatient to wait, and Dean agreed to go ahead with the affair.

The bridge was loaded into an ox cart and taken to the point in the gorge where it was to be erected.

Testera had left his vaqueros in charge of a subordinate and had joined the others at the gorge.

The task of throwing a loop over the spire of rock on the farther side of the gorge was simple: Nolan accomplished it at the second attempt. Nolan was preparing to work his way hand over hand across the rope to the spire when Dean halted him.

"We'll have a lighter man for that, Nolan," he said. "The rope is strong, and yet it will chafe some on the edges of that rock over there."

Testera suggested a man from among his vaqueros, and the others waited while the vaquero chief returned to the gully and came back with a young, agile-appearing vaquero who was little more than a medium-sized boy in stature. The vaquero had big white teeth, which flashed in a smile as he observed the rope, which was now stretched tightly from the rock spire on the farther side of the chasm to a tree trunk upon the side where the group of men stood.

The end of another rope was tied to the vaquero's belt, with which he would later pull across a heavier one, and then finally the rope bridge itself. With a grin he swung out upon the tightly stretched rope and began with amazing rapidity to work his way across the chasm.

He was about halfway over when Nolan crouched, drew the heavy pistol at his hip, and snapped a shot toward the crest of the rock wall on the opposite side of the chasm. Dean, Carey, Clelland, and the others were startled, yet their concerted gaze went instantly to Nolan's target.

Lying face down on the crest of the ridge was one of the outlaws. His red liberty cap was clearly visible in the dusk, and all could observe the rifle in his hands, which had evidently been trained upon the figure of the vaquero suspended above the chasm.

But now the rifle had drooped. One of the man's hands still grasped it, but the weapon dangled in his loosening fingers. The man himself appeared to have relaxed, and he was leaning perilously over the edge of the wall.

Nolan did not fire again. Grimly, while the others stood rigid, Nolan watched the red-capped man.

"Dam' good shot!" declared Clelland. "I swear I can see a hole right in the top of his head!"

At that instant the red cap's rifle dropped from his grasp. The weapon slid for a little distance down the smooth rock wall, until its stock struck a jutting knob of rock which momentarily broke its fall. Then it toppled outward and fell far down into the tangle of brush at the bottom of the crevasse.

The man's body jerked convulsively. The movement caused his body to topple at the brink of the wall, and he began to slide over the edge.

Dean gasped; Carey muttered. But Nolan, Clelland, Waldron, and Testera, accustomed to grim scenes, grimly watched, their faces expressionless, giving no sign that the impending horror was affecting them.

Another convulsive movement of the man's body sent it sliding over the edge of the cliff. Nolan, gun in hand, was searching for other targets, it seemed, for as the man's body began to slip over the edge of the wall, Nolan's gaze was roving along the crest.

Limply the red cap's body slid down the smooth surface of the wall. It struck the jutting knob which had momentarily retarded the descent of the rifle; it appeared to catch there for an instant, slipped off, and fell with a hideous crashing through the tops of some trees and down through the heavy tangle of brush.

A silence followed the fall.

Then came Nolan's voice.

"I reckon he was alone," he said. "A sentinel. There ain't no signs of any more."

He grinned across the chasm at the little vaquero, who was now seated on the ledge near the rock spire, calmly pulling the heavy rope across.

CHAPTER XXV

Behind the wall of rock where the ox carts had been hidden the major portion of Zorilla's men were gathered. They had not partaken of food in many hours, and their throats were athirst for the contents of the many casks they had brought from the cook camp. Therefore in the hours before dawn there was much activity behind the rock wall. Crates were being ripped open, boxes were unpacked, bales were torn apart and their contents seized by eager hands; the casks were tapped and huge flagons filled.

Zorilla had vanished into one of the caverns with the Señorita Juana, and there were few of the outlaws who cared whether he emerged again or not. They ran hither and yon seeking such delicacies as they might find in the crates, the boxes, and the bales; they drank heavily of the liquors they found in the casks.

Yet though they feasted and drank as they had not feasted in days, they were not unmindful of the menace of Testera's vaqueros. They knew Testera, and they expected he would be after them as soon as he discovered what had been done at the cook camp.

For that reason—though they did not cease feasting—they kept an eye on the bridge that spanned the crevasse. A red cap might be tearing mouthfuls from a slab of manioc upon which was perched half a roast chicken. He might be drinking a quart of wine from one of the stone flagons they had stolen; but frequently he would stick his head around the rock wall—which was in reality a low, long escarpment—to scan the bridge.

There were times when a dozen of the red caps were peering around the escarpment at one time. They watched the bridge from both ends of the escarpment; and after they had drunk for a time there were several of the more reckless who climbed to the top of the wall and sat there, flagons in hand, dangling their legs and singing.

However, even the reckless ones knew Testera. And when the dawn began to break they slid down from the escarpment and showed themselves no more.

When daylight came, there were few of the outlaws sober. The few, realizing what impended, kept a careful watch of the bridge. At various points they stationed riflemen, whom they gave instructions to shoot at the first sign of movement beyond the bridge.

It was not long after dawn when a red cap's rifle cracked. Instantly a thin, dry report answered the red cap's fire. The red cap screamed and slid down the escarpment, badly wounded.

Testera was at the other end of the bridge!

Thereafter there was not so much drinking.

Zorilla appeared.

The chief reached the shelter of the escarpment by making his way along the bottom of a narrow gulch through which flowed a stream of water.

Zorilla was in an ill humour, and yet with his first glance at the faces of his men he was aware that he must mask his real feelings. More than once they had shown him that there was more of tolerance than of respect in their acceptance of him as their leader. When they were in the mood that they now were in slight provocation would throw them into violent mutiny. Mutiny now would mean that he would lose Juana. And though he was now bitter against her, remembering a dagger she had tried to use on him not more than two hours ago, he was resolved to conquer her.

Therefore he grinned at his men when he drew near, and joined them in their attempts to empty one of the wine casks.

Testera was at the other end of the bridge, they told him.

"He will come no farther!" he declared. "Yet Testera's men will be sober, while if we continue to drink there will come a time when there will be no men to defend the bridge."

"*Pero mas*, we will drink in relays," grinned the outlaw to whom Zorilla had spoken. He was a fat fellow with long, flowing mustachios, and already so drunk that he swayed as he talked with his chief.

"The more sober will guard the wall," he added. "And when thirst comes upon them they shall come down and drink."

"*Peste!*" grumbled Zorilla. "Testera will cut all our throats!"

The fat outlaw laughed.

"We shall see that it does not happen until the wine has been drunk, at any rate!" he declared.

He tried to press another flagon of wine upon Zorilla, but the latter refused it. Thereupon the fat outlaw laughed again and thrust his face close to his chief's.

"You will drink no more!" he said. "Ai, then, the Señorita——!"

"Diablos!" growled Zorilla. He shoved the fat man violently. The latter, unable to keep his equilibrium, staggered and fell, landing under an ox cart and lying there with face upturned, grinning foolishly.

A roar of mirth came from a number of the outlaws who had witnessed the encounter. With a pulse of trepidation Zorilla realized that they were all so drunk that they were not even quarrelsome. As for guarding the bridge, there was not one of them on guard.

In fact, there were few of them still able to drink. Zorilla had more than eighty men, and it now seemed to him that more than half that number were stretched out asleep in various places. Some were under the carts, others were in them, still others were lying in the shade cast by the overhang of the escarpment; some were stretched out under trees that were scattered here and there; half a dozen were unconscious at the edge of the gulch through which Zorilla had come to reach them. But not one was standing guard at the wall, not one was even looking toward the bridge.

"The devil!" exclaimed Zorilla.

He seized a rifle from one of the sleeping men and crept to the escarpment, where he crouched at a slight break in the rock, through which he could observe the bridge.

There was no visible sign of Testera or of any of his men. Zorilla had heard the exchange of shots that had taken place previously, and he was aware that Testera and his men were somewhere at the edge of the mesa, possibly in the gully just beyond the approach to the bridge. If they knew what he knew, there would be one great rush of men across the bridge, and the outlaw band would be killed or taken.

While the sun mounted higher, Zorilla grew aware that the silence behind him had deepened. For a long time there had been little sound except for an occasional voice of one of the drinkers, but now even the drinkers had ceased talking.

Zorilla's gaze searched among the carts. All his men were stretched out with the exception of one who was sitting on the ground leaning against a wheel of one of the carts, waving a flagon back and forth and lowly singing "La Paloma."

Zorilla knew he was doomed to do what guarding there was to be done until his men recovered from the effects of what they had drunk, and so with a sigh he returned to his vigil.

The sun climbed higher. A great peace seemed to reign. Nowhere was there any evidence that any living thing breathed or moved. As far back on the mesa as Zorilla could see, there had seemed to settle the serenity of a great calm. No breeze stirred the leaves of the trees on the mesa; there was not even a little swirling dust cloud such as one could often observe leisurely travelling in its eccentric curves across the face of the land.

Far beyond the mesa, clear over to the north where the plains stretched in silent majesty, there was not a suspicion of life or movement. In all the vast arch of white, shimmering sky there was no cloud. All around him were silence and inanimation.

Zorilla had drunk two flagons of wine, and he had not tasted food in about twenty-four hours. The wine had filled him with a strange exhilaration, which was growing each minute. He began to feel that he was immune to harm, even if it should happen that he should carelessly expose himself. He was Zorilla! Many men had trembled at the sound of his name. Should he hide from Testera and his vaqueros? Should he lie there not daring to show himself above the crest of the wall?

Almost he yielded to an impulse to stand erect and shout defiance at his enemies, but a recollection of what had happened to one of his men a few hours ago dissuaded him, and he sank down again, grimacing.

Ai! He hoped one of Testera's men would show himself! They would see that he, too, was a marksman!

He grew calmer, almost nonchalant. At any rate, if he dared now show himself above the wall, he was convinced that none of Testera's men would be rash enough to attempt to cross the bridge.

There was humour in this situation. On the other side of the bridge were hundreds of men lying in concealment, waiting for an opportunity to cross the bridge. They supposed there were a great many of his men lying in ambush. They did not know that he alone was on guard, that his was the magic hand which was staying the progress of a multitude.

Zorilla smiled. A conviction of omnipotence stole over him; a feeling of ease and security took possession of his senses, lulling him to an entrancing lethargy.

The sun grew hotter, but still Zorilla was not uncomfortable. As a pleasant inner warmth grew upon him he smiled peacefully and rested his head against the rock. The face of the rock was cool to his cheek. He relaxed and went to sleep.

The bridge was now unguarded, and if Testera had but known, he might now have advanced without danger to himself or his men. But while Zorilla slept there was still no sound or movement. The sun reached the zenith and began to descend the western arch of the sky.

Zorilla and his men slept on.

CHAPTER XXVI

However, Zorilla had not been asleep more than two or three minutes when there was movement behind him.

In one of the ox carts there came a stir among what seemed to be a bundle of rags between two casks in the bed of the cart.

The bundle of rags became animate, seemed to be rising from the bed of the cart. But quickly the bundle of rags took shape, finally evolving into the figure of a man.

The man stood up between the casks and stared around him in hazy bewilderment. His gaze took in the reclining figures of the outlaws who were lying among the carts and along the base of the rock escarpment; he stared long and hard at Zorilla, half lying against the side of the escarpment, rifle in hand.

The man grinned foolishly and with one hand reached up and shoved his hat back from his forehead so that the blinding glare of the sun shone full into his face.

The man was Manville, the moonshiner.

Manville was trying to remember the occurrences of the night before. He had a hazy recollection of prowling around among the wine casks at the cook camp. He had been thirsty. With a long reed in hand he had climbed between the two casks and had tapped one of them. Then, with the aid of the reed, he had drunk wine until he had toppled over between the casks. Now, the effects of the liquor having worn off, he was just beginning to realize dimly that he was no longer in the cook camp.

Everything around him was unfamiliar. There were no long wooden tables, no perspiring cooks, no mounds of miscellaneous débris, no scent of cooking. He could see no tents, no festoons of vari-coloured lanterns, no guests of the feast moving about. And the silence oppressed him.

With a foolishly judicial gaze he stared about him at the red caps. He remembered to have seen them before, but he couldn't clearly recollect where. Anyway, what did it matter? Not one red cap was standing. Therefore they were harmless. They were probably dead, for they seemed to lie in grotesque positions.

He wasn't concerned about them. He was merely thirsty. He observed that the reed he had previously used was still sticking out of the bunghole of one of the casks. He had a glimmer of remembrance about the reed, and he leaned over, placed one end of it in his mouth and began to draw upon it.

The result was satisfying, and he relaxed to a reclining position.

He stayed there long, but presently he dropped the reed and heaved a deep sigh.

He could now only dimly see the red caps lying around him. They made a blur of colour on the landscape, and for a time he sat on the end gate of one of the carts trying to fix at least one of them clearly in his vision. Curiously, they appeared to have become more numerous.

"They ain't no use crowdin' round thish way," he admonished them, waving a hand at them. "There's plenty of wine for all of us."

He tried to climb down from the cart and fell headlong.

Sitting up, he grinned foolishly at the cart.

It had tilted with him; that was it! Otherwise he would not have fallen. To prove to all the assembled red caps that he was not as drunk as they probably thought him, he swayed to his feet and stood reeling, grinning.

With some difficulty he singled out a red cap huddled against a wheel of the cart.

"Why don't yuh shay somethin'?" he asked. His gaze caught a glitter of metal, and he stooped and drew out the red cap's revolver.

Standing erect again he stared at the weapon. Steadying himself, he threw it over the edge of a near-by cliff.

"Tryin' to shoot me when I ain't lookin', eh?" he said. He laughed. "Nobody's got no business packin' a gun, anyway!"

A grotesque idea seized him. There were "scads" of red caps lying all around him. He went from one to another, drawing their guns from their holsters and throwing them over the edge of the cliff. The sun was hot, and the continual bending to reach the weapons was physical exertion that brought the perspiration from him in streams, and yet he got a malicious enjoyment out of the task. What did they want guns for, anyway? There was nobody to shoot. Besides, there was the pronunciamento. Nobody dared to shoot. Then why carry a gun? Somewhere he had heard that Don Pedro was having trouble with these red caps; and if he could help Don Pedro out, he intended to do so.

There was a man—Don Pedro! Don Pedro had stood with him against Pennel and Lathrop; and now he'd do a good turn for Don Pedro.

With some of the red caps he had difficulty. Half a dozen he had to roll over before he could get at their guns. Some of them he used roughly. But not one of them awakened.

Manville was very thorough. His mind was in such a state that he could think clearly of only one thing at a time. It seemed to him that right now the most important thing in the world was to get possession of the guns worn by the red caps, and he kept searching them out and finding them. Two he came upon lying under a tree halfway down the side of the gulch. Several others were in ox carts. He found them and took their revolvers. Some were lying under the carts. Many were stretched out at the base of the escarpment. One red cap, not so drunk as the others, resisted. Manville at first argued with him, then struck him heavily on the head with the butt of the weapon he had taken from the man's holster.

Resist him, eh? He'd show them! Didn't they know that Don Pedro didn't want any of them to carry guns?

At last he seemed to have obtained all the revolvers. And then, remembering one man he had seen curled up on the side of the escarpment, he clambered to where Zorilla lay and drew the latter's revolver from its holster. He held the weapon in his hands and grinned at the sleeping outlaw chief. And when his gaze rested upon the rifle lying at Zorilla's side, he picked it up.

It seemed he had forgotten about rifles. And now there filtered through his brain the conviction that a red cap had no more right to a rifle than he had to a revolver. At any rate, he meant to take the rifles away from them, now that he thought of them; and so he half slid and half fell down the side of the escarpment with Zorilla's. Immediately he tossed the weapon over the edge of the cliff, and he stood reeling, a smile of malice on his lips, as he heard it clatter and crash against the rocks on its way down.

His brain was getting clearer, though his thoughts were still definitely centred upon depriving the red caps of their weapons; and so he shambled here and there, gathering them up and tossing them over the edge of the cliff.

In half an hour the work was complete, though he was still imbued with a spirit of thoroughness and searched again and again among the wagons and around and in them, for other rifles.

He found no more. He felt of his own holster, and hesitated. Then his eyes grew sly, and he tapped the holster significantly, as though to say that he had better keep the gun there.

And now, his work done, he stood, swaying, mopping the sweat from his face. When upon him dawned the conviction that he was thirsty, he scrambled to the bed of the cart, again sought his reed, and spent a long time drawing the wine over his eager lips.

When he again dropped the reed he was about ready to collapse. Yet he did not. He stood, swaying back and forth, gazing around him at the red caps.

He had a feeling that he should not linger in the vicinity. He had done something he shouldn't have done. But he could not remember what the something was. Yet the instinct to avert a threatened danger was strong in him, and so at last he got out of the cart and went staggering away toward the gulch. He lost his footing at the crest and fell down the sloping side of the place, landing near the stream of water at the bottom.

He might have stayed there had he not been still troubled with an urge to get away from the scene of his adventure; so he got to his feet again and made his way down the gulch until he came to a wash. He went up the wash to a level where there were no trees, and where the sun beat down upon him with a blinding brilliance.

For some minutes he stood, blinking, undecided.

He had come out upon the level that led to the bridge. And at that instant Testera's vaqueros were watching him, and a hundred rifles were levelled at him.

Yet not one of the rifles were discharged. Testera's voice, raised in sharp warning, had prevented Manville from being killed. He was so obviously drunk that the vaqueros would not have shot him at once, perhaps, if their chief had not spoken.

Manville stood, staring wonderingly about him. He was lost. He was in an unfamiliar section, and he did not know which direction to take to return to familiar surroundings.

The mesa beyond the bridge looked inviting, and yet there seemed to be no way to get to it. A chasm yawned at his feet. He saw the narrow bridge, but shook his head at it as if to decide that he would not attempt to cross it. After a time he swayed over to the base of a high rock wall. He leaned against it, settled one of his shoulders into a convenient crack, and stood, dizzily surveying the world that swam around him.

Everything looked strange to him. Without doubt, somebody had moved the mesa. Yet perhaps the mesa had been merely turned around. Anyway, it didn't matter. Nothing mattered. No use to worry. When he sobered up—if he ever did—he'd try to find his way back to the mesa. Right now, however, his only concern was the heat. Where he stood the sun beat down directly upon his head. He staggered away from the place, made his way around a huge projection, and followed the rock wall until it opened into a recess of cavernlike proportions. A wave of cool air blew into his face.

That was better. He kept moving against the breeze. The sunlight no longer struck him; shadows began to envelop him. He continued to stagger forward, meeting a dense darkness that presently engulfed him. He stood, after a while, swaying uncertainly. Turning around, he looked back. Somewhere a ray of light danced in his vision. He moved a little to one side. It seemed to him that his feet struck on an obstruction, for he lost his balance and fell upon something that crackled under his weight. Whatever the something was it yielded to his weight. He was too weary to get up, and so he stretched out and went to sleep.

CHAPTER XXVII

When Zorilla awakened it seemed to him that he had slept several hours. He had opened his eyes suddenly, for he had been dreaming that Testera and the vaqueros were charging across the bridge.

Peering through the crack in the rock wall, he observed that nothing was happening. The bridge was empty; there was no sign of his enemies anywhere. The level beyond the bridge still looked peaceful; the level on the cache side held no menace.

Zorilla was filled with a self-accusing anger. He had done the very thing that his men had done. He glanced cautiously around to observe if any of his men had witnessed his carelessness; and when he perceived that none had seen him he was immediately decided that he would punish them for failing to keep watch.

He was amazed when, reaching for his rifle, he discovered that it was no longer beside him. Evidently the weapon had slid down the face of the wall. He looked for it, but could not see it. Then he reached for his revolver. He felt foolish and stupefied when his fingers encountered the empty holster.

Furious, though there was a pulse of fear in his rage, he jumped down from the ledge and landed, wild-eyed, in the level near the ox carts.

He saw his men lying around him. Some were under the carts; some were reclining in sitting positions against the wheels; others were stretched out at the base of the escarpment. Not one was in an erect position; all were sleeping.

Zorilla felt helpless without a pistol. He leaped to the side of the sleeper nearest him and was amazed to find an empty holster. He ran to the next man. No gun. He ran to the next and the next, his apprehension growing. By the time he had examined the holsters of all the men he was trembling with a conviction that had gradually been assailing him—that there had been treachery while he had slept; that some enemy had stolen upon his band and himself and disarmed them.

Finding no revolvers, he ran here and there searching for rifles. He found none on the level. But happening to pause at a certain point at the edge of the cliff that descended sheer from the level upon which he stood, he saw a litter of rifles and revolvers on the plain below.

Although the sun was hot, a cold perspiration bathed Zorilla. He stood for an instant at the edge of the cliff, his mouth open, his knees shaking. Obeying a sudden impulse, he ran to the crest of the gulch, leaped down its sloping side and dove headlong into some concealing brush. He had a feeling that someone was watching him, that there were rifles pointing at him. Even while lying hidden in the brush, the flesh of his back rippled and crawled and shrank.

He heard no sound, observed no movement. Somewhat reassured, he cautiously raised his head and looked about him. Nothing happened. With a little more confidence he stepped out from behind the brush and moved some distance down the gulch.

Still nothing happened.

He ran down the gulch to the wash through which Manville had travelled, and walked up it, knowing that by pressing close to the battlement wall he could not be observed by Testera's men on the other side of the bridge.

Keeping in the shelter of the wall, he reached the mouth of a cave. There, for some minutes, he stood listening and watching.

Nothing happened. Yet Zorilla knew that treachery was in the atmosphere around him. The silence was impregnated with it. His flesh was again creeping; he seemed to feel an all-pervading menace, as if all about him were concealed foes waiting for him to reach a certain position or do a certain thing.

He had left Juana in this cave. With her, to guard her, he had left one of his men. He had taken off the girl's bonds before he had tried to make love to her. With the help of his men he had rebound her when she had repulsed him. The knife she had shown him he had taken from her.

He loved Juana, there was no doubt of that. He might have taken her by force, for he could have escaped from the mesa as easily as he had escaped to the cache. But he did not want Juana unless she wanted him, and so he had chosen the cache with the idea of holding her until she should at last fall in love with him. Don Pedro he would also hold, merely as a hostage to insure his safety. He felt reasonably certain of his ultimate success.

That confidence, he now realized, had been born of the advantage he had held over Testera. The advantage gone, he was fearful, suspicious.

Trouble was imminent. His men—those he had left on the level—were drunk and unarmed. They would be of no service to him. But the night before, soon after he had reached the cache, he had sent ten men, fully armed, to scale the battlement wall and to patrol the higher levels, with orders to keep a sharp lookout for Testera's vaqueros.

He felt that he, too, must reach the higher levels; he had an uncomfortable conviction that at any instant he might see Testera's vaqueros rushing toward him.

He entered the cave and made his way in the darkness to the bed of branches where he had left Juana and her guard.

"Mendez!" he called sharply.

There was no answer.

Zorilla called again, and felt a chill racing along his spine when only a hollow echo came back to him.

"*Peste!*" he exclaimed aloud.

His thought was that Mendez had also deserted him, or had gone out to join the other men, who had been so busy at the wine casks. Perhaps Mendez had succumbed to the traitor who had disarmed the other men; it was just possible that Testera's vaqueros were already in the cache! They might be all around him, watching him! They might even be in the cave, close to him, waiting to pounce upon him!

For a time he stood motionless, staring toward the front of the cave at the faint beams of light that hovered there. In the darkness that surrounded him he was almost certain that he detected the vague outlines of the forms of crouching men. The feeling grew so strong that he grew panic-stricken and began to run toward the mouth of the cave.

He ran until he reached a point where the light from outside shone on him. There, not having heard any sounds behind him, he paused and listened.

The silence of the cave had not been broken. He stood, and could not even hear the echo of his own hurrying footsteps.

A damp sweat broke out on his forehead. There had come no shots, no movement, no sound of any kind to strengthen his previous premonition of the presence in the cave of his enemies.

Still his vague apprehension persisted.

He was afraid. Still, was he not Zorilla? Zorilla, whom everybody feared? It was strange that a brave man, such as he had shown himself to be, should hesitate and tremble as he was trembling.

Mentally stiffening himself he began to retrace his steps toward the rear of the cave. He assured himself that he was now boldly going back, but in truth his steps were amazingly short and jerky, and his muscles seemed paralyzed.

He would have felt better if there had been a gun in his holster. Until now, he had never been without a gun. Sleeping or waking he had always kept a gun at his side. Strange it was how helpless one felt without a gun after having been accustomed to wearing one. He felt almost as if he had been stripped of his clothing. He had nothing to rely upon now but his mind and body, and these felt inadequate.

True, in a leg-sheath was his knife. Yet at a distance a knife was useless.

He went back about fifty feet. The light from the entrance went no farther than that. He stood, surrounded by a semi-gloom, facing the utter blackness of the depths of the cave.

There, for many minutes, he stood, lacking the physical strength to go farther.

Again a cold sweat broke out on him; and again the panicky feeling seized him. He was about to retreat again when a voice, dry and taunting, reached him.

"Are you playing a game, Señor Zorilla?"

The voice was Juana's.

"*Diablos!*" Zorilla almost shrieked. "Why didn't you speak before?"

"I was amused by your actions, Señor," she laughed. "You seemed so—so afraid that someone was about to say 'Boo' to you. And I wanted to see how fast you could run."

Zorilla did not move.

"Where are you?" he asked.

"You should know that. I am where you left me. Why, once you came and stood very near me. I could have touched you if my hands had been untied."

"Are you alone?" questioned the outlaw, still half convinced that some of Testera's men were in the cave.

"Alone and hungry," answered Juana. "And very thirsty. You have an odd way of making love, señor the outlaw. Go right this minute and get food and water!"

"Presently," said Zorilla. He was convinced that she was alone in the cave. If any of her friends were with her, she would be trying to urge him to come to her.

He laughed.

"You shall have food and drink. But you will have to go with me to the level above to get them. I shall have to untie you. But I will not untie you unless you promise you will not attempt to escape."

"It seems I shall not eat nor drink, after all," she said.

"What! You mean you will not give your promise?"

"I shall not. Untie me and I shall escape."

"The devil!" was Zorilla's thought. "I shall have to carry her. And that is a job! Yet she must go with me, for without her I will be like a hunted coyote."

Aloud he said:

"I ask nothing better. It will be your own fault if while I carry you I will seem to hold you too tightly."

"I shall know how you should carry me, Zorilla; and I promise you that if you hold me too tightly I shall bite you!"

Zorilla laughed. Juana's terrible threats merely amused him. He saw her again as a supplicant—a supplicant who made futile gestures. To him she was never more attractive than when she was defying him. If she had been silent he would have suspected that she contemplated some mischief.

He moved closer to her, guided by her voice. When his investigating hands reached her he discovered that she was sitting on the edge of the bed of branches.

She was motionless as he stooped to grasp her around the waist in order to carry her. She made no sound when he swung her free of the bed of branches and held her in his arms.

He was taking the first step toward the light at the entrance of the cave when there came a terrifying crashing among the branches upon which Juana had been sitting. The branches seemed to erupt; Zorilla heard them crackling and scraping upon the floor of the cave, as if someone, half buried in them, was throwing them off. Then there was a heavy thud as of someone falling; then a voice, hollow and hoarse, and vibrant with rage:

"You won't hold nothin', you mangy son of a gun!"

Zorilla shrieked in sudden terror. He dropped Juana, leaped over her, and ran toward the entrance. For an instant he was framed in the light; then he fell headlong and vanished.

CHAPTER XXVIII

The task of drawing the rope bridge across the chasm had taken longer than had been anticipated, for there were long intervals when no work could be done at all because of rifle fire from various points along the summit of the wall.

The man Nolan had shot had not been the only sentinel; for while Nolan and the others were grouped on the mesa straightening out the bridge so that it could be pulled over by the Mexican vaquero on the other side, there came another report from the top of the wall, and a Mexican stooping near Nolan grunted and pitched forward. A bullet had struck him between the shoulder blades; Nolan had seen the dust fly from his shirt.

There were other shots, but Nolan and his party were running for shelter, and no one was hit.

But the killing of one man increased the caution of the others. There was a long wait, while Nolan's men, in various places of concealment, sought to discover where the shots had come from.

Darkness came while they waited. The high wall on the farther side of the chasm was black and towering, and its top was obscured by jagged shoulders that projected from its sides. For a time there was no moon, and the star-dotted vault of sky did not provide light enough to disclose any of the outlaw riflemen who might have been moving about up there. And when after a while the moon came out, it shone directly down through the trees upon the spot where the bridge was to be thrown across.

Nolan and his men did not dare to expose themselves.

The little vaquero, however, safe under a projecting ledge, was pulling the heavy rope toward him. He advised Nolan to wait until a cloud passed over the moon. Meanwhile he lighted and smoked innumerable cigarettes. The concealed men could see his smiling face by the light of the matches.

Waiting for the moon to darken was a task requiring patience. Clouds swam majestically in the sky, but most of them were white and fleecy, and the moon shone through them almost as brilliantly as if they had not been there. But toward midnight a black cloud sailed out of the west and passed across the face of the glowing orb, darkening the world until the men of Nolan's party could not see one another.

Instantly a dozen hands were working at the rope bridge. They straightened it out; they felt the little vaquero on the other side tugging at it. It slid over the edge of the chasm slowly, like a great serpent slithering down over a ridge. After a time it stopped. Nolan and Clelland ran back with two of the rope ends and lashed them to trees.

They waited.

Presently there came a low whistle from the other side of the chasm. It was answered by Nolan. Then came the voice of the little vaquero.

"*Bueno!*" he said.

But the black cloud passed over the face of the moon, and again the land was flooded by a brilliant white light.

Nolan and his men again scattered and concealed themselves.

The moon sailed down into the western sky until, far away, it seemed to become impaled upon the peak of a mountain. More swiftly now it appeared to sink, and at last darkness came again.

It was now in that hour between night and dawn when the darkness is deepest. Swiftly the rope ends were pulled taut and lashed; the rope braces were stretched and the bridge was completed.

Nolan, carrying his rifle, thought he was first on the bridge, but he hadn't taken half a dozen steps forward between the swaying guide ropes when he became aware that someone was ahead of him.

"Clelland?" he asked.

"Yep."

On the mesa side were a number of Testera's vaqueros. Testera himself was not to cross, for he had decided to remain on the mesa to direct an assault at the other bridge. At intervals of two or three minutes he sent his vaqueros after Nolan and Clelland. Dean and Carey and Waldron and the other Americans were to remain with Testera.

When about twenty of the vaqueros had crossed, Nolan called.

"That's plenty. The ledge is packed. It will be slow work getting up. Wait."

The darkness was now so dense that Nolan and the Mexicans on the ledge could not see one another. Nolan knew Clelland was beside him because Clelland occasionally spoke. They could not see the wall towering above them, the abyss below, or the level of the mesa where they had left Testera and the others.

There was nothing to do but to wait until the darkness lifted, for though there were other ledges above them, and a fissure with ragged edges up which they might climb, they could not locate them in the blackness.

The sky was a heavy velvet blue, and though the stars created a softly luminous haze, their light did not penetrate to the pitch blackness that reigned above the chasm.

The high rock wall against which they were crouched was not exactly perpendicular. It bulged outward near the top, where a strata of granite projected because it had yielded less readily to erosion. The strata of granite formed a sort of ledge on the face of the wall, thus making it impossible for a rifleman on the crest to shoot downward at Nolan and his friends. For many feet on their climb upward they would be protected by the ledge; and Testera's riflemen, concealed on the mesa, would make certain that no red cap would gain a position from which he could fire upon them. They would be in no danger from the red caps until they reached the top of the wall.

In an hour the darkness began to lift and presently Nolan could distinguish the faces of the men on the ledge with him. A little later he could discern a smaller ledge but a few feet above him. Intervening were jutting knobs of rock upon which he could step in the climb to the second ledge.

Nolan began to climb. He had no difficulty in reaching the second ledge, and by the time he was standing upright upon it Clelland was ascending. By this time it was light enough for Nolan to read the expression of Clelland's face, and he was not surprised to observe that there was a smile on his friend's lips and an eager light in his eyes.

Clelland was never more satisfied than when fighting! And never yet had Nolan seen fighting serious enough to keep Clelland from smiling.

Nolan made another ledge. A fourth brought him to a broad, ragged crack in the face of the wall which provided projections enough for climbing. He mounted the fissure to the wider ledge that Dean had pointed out to him; and once upon it he was surprised and delighted to observe that a section of the wall, invisible from the mesa at the point where he and Dean had stood when the latter had been examining the place, was traversed by a ledge that ran at an angle up its face and into a greater fissure which was large enough for a man to climb in comfort.

Nolan glanced back the way he had come. Clelland had reached the ledge below him; strung out behind Clelland were the Mexicans, stolidly making their way upward.

Nolan grinned down into Clelland's face.

"Not so bad, eh?" he said.

He dodged at the flash of Clelland's rifle, and felt the powder burn his face. The bullet from the weapon had passed so close to him that he had felt the heat of it.

Quickly he glanced up the fissure. At a bend he saw an outlaw standing rigid. A rifle was at his right shoulder and at the instant Clelland's bullet had struck him he had been aiming, apparently, at Nolan, because Nolan had been first in line.

Clelland's bullet must have entered his chest, for as Nolan looked at him he dropped the rifle he had been carrying and pressed both hands low on his breast. His knees doubled under him and he toppled into the fissure, sliding far down, head first, so that Nolan could see only his legs and the soles of his *potro* boots.

There was shooting from the mesa. Evidently Testera's men had caught sight of some of the outlaws at the edge of the wall. Clelland was grinning grimly.

"You go on up," he told Nolan. "Testera is coverin' us. If any more of the scum stick their heads over the edge I'll take care of them. But it ain't likely there'll be any more."

He waited, his rifle ready, as Nolan continued his ascent. Nolan reached a projection near the top of the wall and boldly peered over. Then he climbed over the edge and disappeared.

Instantly Clelland was after him, with the Mexicans crowding him closely.

When Clelland clambered over the top of the wall he found Nolan crouching behind a ridge of lava. There were no red caps in sight.

"There's seven or eight of them," Nolan informed his friend. "They were fannin' it when I sighted them. They're over behind that ridge. It's likely there's a trail down that side somewheres."

Nearly all of the vaqueros were now beside Nolan and Clelland in the shelter of the lava ridge; the others were rapidly ascending.

Day was already far advanced, and the clear white light of the morning disclosed the character of the high land on the top of the cache.

Stretching away from the lava ridge behind which Nolan and the others were concealed was a level perhaps a quarter of a mile wide. The level was composed of smooth rock covered in spots with sandy earth in which were growing nondescript weeds and grasses. Here and there was some sparse brush. A ridge of rock at the southern edge of the level seemed to surmount a slope that ran down the southern side, probably to the lower level of the cache near the bridge that stretched over the chasm, where Testera had first placed his men.

The cache was really a mountain. Eastward and southward its sides sloped. Far down on the eastern side the slope was broken by a deep gorge. Beyond the gorge were the plains. The gorge appeared to run entirely around the mountain with no land connection except the narrow bridge over which Zorilla and his men had brought the ox carts.

The mesa itself was about three hundred feet above the plains that stretched westward from its base. East and south the plains were farther, for at the eastern end of the mesa the land sloped sharply downward, forming one side of a mighty valley.

It was a lofty eminence upon which Nolan and his friends found themselves; a wild, virgin spot so high that the surrounding country was dwarfed to toylike proportions.

The mountain top was circular with the exception of a promontory that projected eastward; and the lava ridge behind which Nolan and his friends were concealed followed the general outline of the top clear around on both sides until it almost touched the ridge where Nolan felt the red caps were hiding.

"We'll chase them out of there right fast!" declared Nolan. He divided his force, sending some of them west behind the ridge and others eastward. He and Clelland held the first position.

As Nolan anticipated, the flanking parties he had sent out soon caught sight of the outlaws, and from behind their barricades they opened fire.

There was some desultory firing in response, which did no damage. The vaquero fire was more effective. From behind the ridge where the outlaws were concealed came screams of rage and pain. A red cap ran, crouching, toward a great boulder behind the ridge. He pitched forward and rolled into a depression as Nolan's bullet hit him. Through a break in the ridge Nolan could see him stretched out, motionless.

Half an hour after the first shot had been fired by one of the vaqueros of the flanking party, a vaquero leaped over the lava ridge and began to run toward the spot where the outlaws were concealed. Instantly the other vaqueros clambered over the ridge and followed him.

Nolan and Clelland followed, and when they reached the other ridge they saw half a dozen red caps leaping from ledge to ledge down the sloping side of the mountain. They were panic-stricken, and the vaquero fire was deadly. One by one the outlaws dropped until there remained only one far down the mountain side.

He was an agile fellow, and he leaped from rock to rock, with amazing rapidity and sureness. Dozens of bullets struck around him, richochetting past him, sending up little puffs of sand around and in front of him. He seemed, however, to escape being hit. And when at last he vanished behind a jutting shoulder and the men on the mountain top could no longer see him, Nolan felt like applauding him.

Nolan stood at the crest of the slope looking down, grimly laughing.

"Glad he got away," he said to Clelland, who was standing near him. "He earned his life."

At that instant a bullet droned past Nolan's head. He dropped quickly behind a boulder.

"Uh-huh!" grinned Clelland. "Seems he thinks yours ain't no account!"

The progress of Nolan's party was halted until they could dislodge the concealed outlaw.

They could now see a portion of the level at the cache, though the natural bridge over which Zorilla had reached the stronghold was shielded from view by the battlement wall on the west. It seemed to Nolan that the wall ran around to the south also, though he could not be certain from where he was crouching. At any rate, he and his friends would not be able to look down upon the entire level of the cache until they were able to reach the point where the solitary outlaw was hidden.

They were aware that in making the descent they must not expose themselves to the outlaw's fire, and so they spent several hours creeping from rock to rock down the big slope in an effort to locate the man and finish him.

Noon came, and they were still moving slowly down the face of the slope. The sun began to descend the western sky, and still they had not located the outlaw. Nor had he fired another shot at them, for they had been careful to keep in concealment.

Toward the middle of the afternoon they had succeeded in getting close to the point from which the last shot had been fired. Their progress might have been more rapid had they known that most of Zorilla's men were at that moment lying asleep on the level near the escarpment; but they had no doubt that Zorilla had heard the firing and had sent reinforcements to his sentinels.

It was the little vaquero who had drawn the rope bridge over the chasm who first sighted the solitary outlaw. From a distance Nolan saw the little vaquero stand erect and wave a hand.

The vaquero was standing upon a ledge near the edge of the battlement wall, and as Nolan watched him he aimed his rifle downward over the edge of the ledge and fired.

Then he turned and grinned at Nolan, calling out that he had killed the outlaw and that there were no others about.

Ten minutes later Nolan and his friends stood at a spot on the slope from where they could look down upon the level of the cache. They were not more than a hundred feet above the level of the cache, and they saw that below them a terrible battle was raging. It appeared to them that all the remaining members of Zorilla's band were milling about on the level, near the rock escarpment. There were shouts, blows, and the clanging of metal. So terrific was the mêlée that they could not distinguish the character of the combatants, whether they were all Zorilla's men or whether Testera's vaqueros were mixed with them. They were looking down, and it was difficult to recognize any of the fighters.

But now they observed other men swarming over the natural bridge spanning the chasms, and they knew that those who were crossing the bridge were Testera's vaqueros.

The voice of the little vaquero rose, freighted with concern. Apparently he had singled out one man in the group of fighting men below, for he repeated over and over:

"*Diablos! Madre de Dios! Valga me Dios! Muertos!* They will kill him!"

Then he started to run down the slope, careless of possible injury, recklessly jumping from rock to rock, sometimes rolling and sliding in his eagerness to reach the level.

And after him, equally reckless, went Nolan, Clelland, and the others.

CHAPTER XXIX

Zorilla had placed Don Pedro far back in a cave which was as dark as a dungeon. Still bound and helpless, Don Pedro had strained at the ropes until he had grown tired, and then, aware that he was merely exhausting himself uselessly, he became quiet and tried to listen to what was going on outside.

He could hear faint sounds, but he could not distinguish their character. After a while the sounds ceased. There was a period of complete quiet, during which Don Pedro must have slept; for when he again became aware of his surroundings he felt better.

Yet with the feeling of physical improvement came the realization that he was hungry and thirsty. With an effort he struggled and sat erect on the edge of the heap of branches which had been his bed.

He raised his voice.

"Dogs!" he shouted. "Bring me food and drink!"

There was no answer.

He called again and again. Only the echo of his own voice came back to him.

For a time he was quiet, listening, trying to determine if there was anyone in the cave with him. Once when he thought he overheard someone breathing not a great distance from him, he called:

"Who is there?"

No answer, though Don Pedro was certain he could still hear someone breathing.

"Come closer, weak knees!" he commanded. "Declare yourself, faint-hearted loiterer! Are you of that thieving band which has trussed me like a fowl ready for the spit? If so and you come within reach of my blade, you shall not trouble Pedro the Magnificent again!"

Don Pedro knew they had not taken his sword from him. He had felt the hand guard during the night, when it had pressed into his left hip; and he was aware that it had been lashed to his leg. His efforts to reach it had been futile, but he expected that his threat would be respected.

Yet there was no answer. Don Pedro was positive he still heard breathing other than his own.

"*Peste!*" he grumbled; "you are either a coward or a fool! It is quite likely you are both! Do you not know that if you come and release me you will be handsomely rewarded? You shall have what you ask for."

"I ask for nothing," suddenly came a voice.

Don Pedro started. Though he had suspected a presence in the cave with him, he had not expected anyone to answer, for whoever was in the cave with him was very likely one of Zorilla's men. And he had no expectation that such a man would talk with him.

"If you ask for nothing, you are a fool!" declared Don Pedro. "At any rate, once I am out of here and at the head of my men, you will get something. I promise you that!"

"A meal, perhaps?" suggested the man.

"*Valga me Dios!*" roared Don Pedro. "A meal? Yes, I promise you a meal. Yes, a meal. And I will have your neck stretched so far that you will taste your food long while it goes down!"

"You mean to have me hanged?"

"You are keen, my friend. And it seems you know how Don Pedro treats his enemies!"

"*Si*, Señor the Magnificent. I know. Señor the Magnificent roars and blusters and fills the air with dire threats, but when the time comes to punish, his courage runs out at the tips of his fingers!"

"*Diablos!*" roared Don Pedro. "If I were near enough I would choke that lie back into your throat!"

"Or you would feed me and send me forth with your blessing," laughed the other.

"Bah!" growled Don Pedro.

"Ai!" sighed the man; "this is different."

"Different from what, fool?" asked Don Pedro.

"From another time," said the man. "A time when Señor the Magnificent was host. It is said that once you tortured a fellow named Valdez with words."

"Ai!" exclaimed Don Pedro. For an instant he was silent. Then he again spoke. "What do you know about my words to Valdez?"

"What everyone knows—that you tortured him with words."

"You speak of that low fellow who stole my horses and left only the *grullas*?"

"The same."

"Bah! I see that I was a fool to let him off. He has squealed like the javelinas!"

"Why not, Señor the Magnificent? Do you remember how, when you interrogated him, you sat at your table and consumed enough food for a dozen men, while he stood near, famishing?"

"Bah!"

"And how you talked to him of death? How he was to be led out and shot?"

"*Peste!*"

"And how you drew word pictures for him to make him regret the life he was leaving?"

"*Diablos!* What was his life that he should regret to leave it?"

"Life is sweet to all, Señor the Magnificent."

"Bah! Your life is sweet to you, eh? You prowl around at night, stealing and murdering. You spend your days in secret fastnesses, drinking vile liquor and eating offal. You dare not venture abroad in the daylight lest you be taken. And yet your life to you is sweet. Tush!"

Silence. It continued so long that Don Pedro felt that he had angered the man and that there would be no more conversation—and therefore no chance of his prevailing upon the man to help him to escape.

"Bah!" he said again tauntingly; "you say life is sweet. Yet you have never lived. You have only existed. There is a difference. You do not know what freedom means. You have never known the joys of eating a well-cooked meal. You subsist upon maize and manioc and pulque and calabash and such things. You do not know roast beef, carne con cuero, olla, lamb, fish, ham, garlic, bacalao, sardines, anchovies, shrimp, bacon, roast fowl, hash. You might steal a melon; you may kill a fowl occasionally. But once you get a fowl you do not know how to prepare it for eating. You never touch tarts, sweetmeats, candied fruit, honey, cheese, panales. You do not know the dulces. You do not know good tobacco. You drink wine that swine will not touch. A flagon of the white wine of Mendoza would befuddle you. The dark Benicarlo would turn your sluggish blood into a sparkling fluid that would race in your veins like fire! Aguardiente would kill you. And you sleep like dogs—with the chigoes! Bah! You live! Cut my bonds and you shall have all these things!"

"It is too late, Señor the Magnificent."

"Too late! Why is that?"

"Zorilla has condemned you. To-morrow you are to be taken out and shot!"

"*Peste!*" growled Don Pedro. "I shall not be shot if you loose my bonds."

"It cannot be changed," said the man firmly. "Zorilla's word is final. Don Pedro, you are unfortunate."

Don Pedro laughed. Yet there was uneasiness in the sound.

"It is afternoon of the second day of your confinement here," the man went on. "You speak of food. But in a few hours you will have no further use for food!"

"Bah!"

"You had hopes that I would release you?"

"Pish!"

"Thoughts of death and eternity are not pleasing, eh, Señor the Magnificent? It is when we begin to realize that we shall wake to no more dawns that remorse and dread begin to annoy us! No more shall we thrill to the thought of a well-cooked dinner, eh, Señor the Magnificent? No more eager looks at the wine flagons! No more of filling our eyes with pretty girls? No more of lying in the shade on some remote hillside enjoying the beauties of nature and wondering about ourselves—where we shall go when death overtakes us—why we were put here in the first place—what is the basis for the scheme of things? No more of anything! That is the thought that awes us, eh, Señor the Magnificent?"

"Cease your maundering, señor!"

Don Pedro's voice was thick with emotion. He was now sitting on the very edge of his bed of branches endeavouring to gaze through the gloom of the cave at the face of the man who was speaking. He was perspiring; he was trembling with eagerness and hope. For somewhere in his memory words such as he had just heard were stored. He could not remember whether he himself had spoken them or whether they had been spoken to him. For once in his life he regretted having talked so much that he could not remember what he had said. He blamed himself for not having listened more faithfully when others had talked. The words were familiar; they were insinuatingly significant; they brought upon him a great breathlessness.

"That *is* a picture, eh?" the man went on. "At any rate, it is the only one we are able to see. And after to-morrow's dawn comes you will not even be able to see that. Do you know why, Señor the Magnificent? It is because you are able to comprehend only the material things. You drink, you eat, you sleep, you love, you hate, you envy, you steal."

"What?" shouted Don Pedro. "I steal!"

"Wait!" commanded the man. "Let me finish. You attempt to satisfy appetite. I eat, Señor the Magnificent, and likewise I drink. Yet I thrill to thoughts of the mysteries beyond this life. I do not fear to die. I am wise and powerful, and yet I observe the work of the Infinite Being in the petals of a flower!"

The man's voice ceased. A silence fell.

Don Pedro's voice seemed to choke him.

"Ai!" he said, "I know you now! You have been using the words I used to you when I gave you your life! Is this the way you reward me, Señor Valdez?"

The man came closer. He was at Don Pedro's side, and working at his bonds, loosening them. And his voice was full of emotion.

"Your words, Señor the Magnificent; your words. I used them so that you might feel as I felt when I heard them coming from your lips. You now know how greatly Valdez appreciated your action!"

Don Pedro's bonds dropped from him. He seized Valdez and embraced him. Then he would have rushed toward the mouth of the cave, but Valdez halted him.

"Wait, Señor the Magnificent," he said. "All morning on the top of the mountain there has been firing. Testera is coming. There is no need for you to risk your life."

"Bah!" roared Don Pedro. "You counsel waiting when the Señorita Juana is in danger!"

He broke away from Valdez and ran toward the entrance, his long sword rasping as he drew it from its sheath.

CHAPTER XXX

When Don Pedro reached the mouth of the cave the bright sunlight dazzled him, and he stood for some seconds shielding his eyes with his hands until they grew accustomed to the glare. Then he stared out upon the level of the cache, which was deserted. Far away, though seeming to come from a point above him, he heard the intermittent cracking of rifles.

He ran out on the level, his long sword in hand, looking about him for his enemies. Seeing none on the level, he ran down the gulch where some ox carts were grouped, and as he rounded a sharp bend he saw, at the crest of the slope of the gulch, a number of red caps grouped around the wine casks they had stolen.

He clambered up the slope and confronted them. His eyes were glaring with the passion that had come upon him, and when he observed what they were doing he roared:

"Dogs! Drinking while I am dying of thirst! *Peste!* I shall spit you like so many ortolans!"

With another roar he was among them.

Zorilla's men had feasted heartily. For two days and a night they had never ceased drinking from the casks. So intent were they with their drinking that they had paid no attention to the firing on the mountain top, if indeed they had heard it. They had not even discovered that their pistols and rifles were missing.

Now, confronted by the terrible apparition appearing so suddenly from the gulch, they fled from the casks and ran here and there searching for their weapons. Finding none, they began to retreat from Don Pedro.

The ox carts were scattered about the level behind the escarpment. There had been no method in their arrangement, no definite formation. The carts had been left wherever the whims of the drivers had impelled them to stop. The oxen had not even been released from their yokes. The thirsty beasts stood, wild-eyed, tugging and straining to escape. A few, having discovered the uselessness of effort, had lain down with their yokes still on, and were watching with brooding eyes.

There were about twenty carts on the level. Some casks, having been emptied, had been dumped upon the ground. Other casks, tapped, were dripping wine upon the parched sand. All about was scattered the débris of the feasting. Crates, broken, littered the level. Boxes, bales, ripped open and smashed, their contents partly consumed and the remainder wasted, had been thrown here and there among the empty casks. Torn gunny sacks, the carcasses of fowls, half-eaten slabs of maize and manioc, had been crushed in the sand under the *potro* boots of the outlaws. Portions of fish were lying here and there. The odour of garlic permeated the atmosphere. Here was a box of onions, broken open and scattered. Half buried in the sand were cabbages, lettuce.

Fear of Don Pedro was apparent in the faces of the outlaws who retreated from him. They remembered what had happened to several of their fellows when the giant had been captured. He had then not resorted to the sword he had carried; with his bare hands he had crippled those who had sought to lay hands upon him.

Now, themselves without weapons, there was not one who dared face Don Pedro. Many of them ran back until they were at the base of the escarpment. They could not scale the rock and slide down the other side of it, because they knew they would fall by the rifle fire of Testera's men, who were concealed in the gully on the other side of the natural bridge. They could not go forward, for to do so would be to come within reach of Don Pedro's sword. There was nothing to do but to dodge here and there among the ox carts in the hope of slipping past Don Pedro and getting into the gully behind him.

For some minutes chaos reigned. Red caps were seen under the carts, in them, behind them. The outlaws fought with one another for whatever concealment they found. Their imprecations, their curses, their shrill cries of terror filled the level. They were powerless without their weapons; there was none with courage enough to attack Don Pedro bare-handed, as he had previously attacked them.

Three of the red caps, cornered at a wheel of one of the carts, and rendered desperate by the prospect of dying at the point of the sword, made a concerted rush toward the gully.

The first was laid flat by a blow of the terrible sword, which caught him upon the back of the neck as he tried to run past. Don Pedro had used the flat side of the weapon, but the blow was so savage that the other outlaws, hearing the loud smack of the steel against the man's neck, groaned aloud.

The second man felt the point of the weapon. He screamed and fell, rolling down into the gully, crying out that he was killed. But Don Pedro had stayed the blade, and he knew the man was not even badly wounded. Yet he would no longer take part in the fight.

The third man had almost got by when the point of Don Pedro's blade, swishing in a furious arch after him, struck his shoulder. The steel did not penetrate his flesh, but the force of the blow was so great that it knocked him over and he went rolling and shrieking down the slope of the gully.

Don Pedro paused and glared ferociously at the other outlaws, who, pale and shaken because they thought their fellows had been killed, were beseeching him for mercy.

"Dogs!" he shouted at them. "Take me to my daughter or I shall slaughter you like swine! Where is the coward Zorilla? Speak quickly!"

Their cries were unintelligible; yet by their actions and gestures he divined that they did not know. Yet though he was furious with rage against them, he already regretted striking the three who had tried to escape. While the outlaws on the level chattered and cursed, and begged him to desist in his work of destruction, and assured him that they would surrender, he glanced sidelong at the men he had struck, fearful that he had killed them. When he perceived that none was badly injured, he drew a great breath of relief.

But his relief merely served to increase the ferocity of his appearance. Tortured by the knowledge that he had really killed the men, his face would have revealed his concern, whereas, knowing they were not badly injured, he could now with grim amusement pretend to further murderous designs upon the unarmed wretches who retreated from him.

He pressed them closely, darting here and there at them, flourishing his big sword, making wide sweeps at them; the blade hissing shrilly as it clove the air.

He was a terrible spectacle to the red caps. They had thought him ponderous and slow of movement, and in the past they had been somewhat disposed to ridicule him because of his supposed unwieldiness of body. His movements now were in the nature of a revelation. He darted after them swiftly, and they needed all their physical agility to escape him. More than once a cornered red cap was forced to leap over one of the carts to evade the blade that darted at him. Several, casting aside any dignity they might have had, scrambled on hands and knees under the carts, only to be compelled to turn suddenly and go in another direction when they observed that Don Pedro had leaped to the other side of the cart before they could cross under it.

Don Pedro seemed to be endowed with superhuman energy. He was awkward and ponderous, to be sure, and yet in some amazing fashion he appeared to be always close enough to a fleeing man to make the man realize that if he made a false move the menacing blade would overtake him.

There was no escape for them. There was not one with courage enough to attempt to escape by way of the gully. So great was their respect for Don Pedro's swiftness of movement that they finally began to herd together along the base of the escarpment, perhaps with the instinct that overtakes a herd of cattle sorely beset by wolves. Even those who had concealed themselves in and under the carts dashed toward the others and crowded among them until all were standing, paralyzed with fear, each wondering if he was to be the unfortunate upon whom Don Pedro would concentrate his attack.

After they had ceased running and had grouped together, Don Pedro strode to a point about twenty feet from them and stood scowling at them. To the red caps he appeared a huge and malignant agent of death and destruction. His eyes were ablaze with the fires of wrath; he was breathing fast and heavily, and appeared to be in the throes of a mighty, destroying passion.

And yet his thought as he stood there facing them was far from warlike. Now that he had them together and properly respectful of his prowess, what was he to do with them? He was reluctant to kill any of them, and as they were merely underlings, serving a master, he really held no very deep resentment against them. His first rage had been dissipated with his upsetting of the three men who had rolled into the gully. What he really wanted was to find Zorilla.

And yet, standing there, he was not unaware of his complete mastery of the situation; nor could he entirely suppress the thrill of pride that seized him.

"Dogs!" he said to them. "You observe the greatness of the man who has conquered you! You know now how useless it is to fight against me! I have been patient with you. I have spared you when I might easily have killed all of you. What have you to say?"

"Mercy, Magnífico!"

A number of voices in concert uttered the plea. Others of the red caps were vociferous in their protestations of innocence of intended villainy. Many cursed their chief for what had been done. All were eager to assure Don Pedro that they were his friends.

While the voices came to him Don Pedro folded his cape about him and walked majestically along the edge of the precipice near by. His long sword was lying with its blade in the crook of his left elbow; his right hand was still grasping the hilt, as though he was not yet satisfied with the subjugation of the petitioners.

At a certain point near the edge of the cliff he paused and stared downward. He had caught the glitter of sunlight on metal at the base of the cliff, far below.

Several glitters. Shapes that were familiar. Rifles, revolvers, lying in heaps in the sand, with the sun shining upon them.

"Ai!" he exclaimed, at last partially realizing how it happened that the outlaws were unarmed.

A traitor was among them, perhaps.

Valdez? Not Valdez, certainly; for Valdez had been in the cave with him. And Valdez, though a friend, would not dare do such a deed. Only a man of great stealth, or a man whose passions were very much aroused, or one whose——

He ceased to speculate. He again confronted the red caps.

"If you know where to look for your arms, go and get them!" he roared at them. "Then I shall fight you all together! *Peste!*" he added, with a great assumption of impatience. "I am thirsting for your blood!"

"Ai!" exclaimed one of the red caps, "we know not where our weapons went!"

"What? You do not know where they went?" roared Don Pedro. "You lie! I swear you lie!"

"It is the truth, Magnífico," said another. He flushed and gazed guiltily downward. "We had not eaten or drunk in two days. If you will remember, Your Excellency ate all of the food at the camp on the mesa—and drank all the wine." He now gazed at Don Pedro with some reproach in his eyes. "We were hungry and thirsty. *Diablos!* Food and wine were here, brought from the mesa. We ate and drank. It would appear that we ate more than—I should say that we drank more than we ate. In fact, we drank too much, Magnífico. It must be that we drank oceans. At any rate, we drank until we could no longer stand, when we went to sleep. I do not know how long we slept. There is none here who remembers, or who kept track of the hours. But when we awakened—Miguel Languez I think it was who awakened first and aroused the others—our rifles were gone!"

"Your rifles only?" asked Don Pedro with a start, looking sharply at their holsters.

"Our rifles and our pistols, Magnífico," added the man. "They had evidently been stolen from us in our sleep."

"What?" roared Don Pedro. "Stolen in your sleep! And you do not know who took them?"

"We do not know, Magnífico. They were near us when we were drinking and just before we went to sleep. Now they are gone and we do not know where they went."

Don Pedro fondled his long sword and scowled at the red caps.

"Dogs!" he growled. "I think I know what has happened. You saw me coming. I would be visible as I made my way down the gulch. You saw me and, being frightened, you hid your weapons so that you would not have to fight me. S'death! Get them and fight like men!"

Knowing that they were helpless, and not having lied to Don Pedro, the red caps could do nothing but acquiesce.

"*Si*, Señor the Magnificent," said the one who had spoken first. "We admit that we do not care to fight with you. We know too well what would happen."

"Ai! Then you know what a terrible fighter I am?"

"It is well known, Magnífico. There is not a more terrible fighter in Mexico."

"You all know that?"

Came a chorus of fervent "*si's.*"

Don Pedro's chest began to expand. He frowned at the red caps, he fondled the long sword; he marched up and down before the huddled men, turning around and making sure that they viewed him from all sides.

"It is well that you recognize my greatness!" he said at length. "Otherwise, I should spit you in spite of the fact that you have no weapons. But now, since you yield to me, you will get the oxen going. You will take the carts back to where you found them! Vamos! *Apresura!* If you loiter I shall split your ears!"

The red caps sprang to obey. Almost instantly, it seemed, the first ox cart was headed back the way it had come. But by the time there were half a dozen of the carts in line and moving, there came a shout from the foremost of the drivers, and Don Pedro glanced in that direction to see Testera and his vaqueros swarming over the bridge to the level of the cache.

Also, Don Pedro saw something else. Down the slope of the mountain came Nolan, Clelland, and a score of men bearing rifles. Nolan and his followers reached the level almost simultaneously with Testera's vaqueros. The whole company halted, amazed, when they observed what was happening. They stood, silently watching, as the red caps, driving the ox teams, continued on toward the bridge with their train, Don Pedro at their rear, marching very erect and brandishing his long sword.

The head of the ox train reached the bridge, crossed it. One by one the other carts followed. Presently the last one rumbled across. The progress of the train had now brought Don Pedro opposite the point where Testera stood.

Don Pedro halted, faced the vaquero captain. The magnificent one was rigid as a ramrod.

"Testera," he said, "I deliver my prisoners to you!"

Awed, yet with eyes glowing his admiration for the deed that had been done by Don Pedro, Testera bowed. He called sharply to his men, and the vaqueros swarmed behind the ox train and escorted it over the bridge and out upon the mesa.

But after the train reached a point well back from the chasm, Testera brought the cavalcade to a halt. He was filled with curiosity to see what Don Pedro intended to do next.

The feasters, who had taken no part in the affair except to view it from a distance, had now pressed forward. There seemed to be thousands of them. They filled the space between the gully and the edge of the chasm;

they were perched upon rocks; they were in near-by trees; they were everywhere. They were chattering, shouting, laughing, and screaming praises.

Don Pedro caught one note from the multitude which seemed to dominate all other sounds.

"El Magnífico!" it came; "El Magnífico! Viva! Viva! *Ay de mi. Hola!* El Magnífico!"

A great man. They were acclaiming him for his deed in single-handedly capturing the outlaws. He hoped that the traitor who had stolen the guns and dropped them at the base of the precipice would not step forth to rob him of this credit, which he felt was rightfully his. Of a truth, he had not known that the outlaws were unarmed, and he would have attacked them in any case. Yet he was perspiring with dread lest someone step forward and claim the honour.

Grandly he waved his sword.

"It was nothing, my children!" he declared. "Take them away!"

Yet Testera and his men did not move. Testera's gaze was upon the slope of the mountain. He was now waving his hands and pointing.

The whole company—vaqueros, red caps, Nolan, and Clelland, and even Don Pedro—was now looking at the mountain side.

Some friars—Franciscans in brown; black-cloaked Dominicans; Recoletanos in gray; and a tall, slender priest with a thin, ascetic face and long black hair upon which was set a flat-crowned, roll-brimmed shovel hat—had come forward, pressing through the throng that surrounded Don Pedro.

They, too, turned their glances up the mountain side, where a gaudily attired figure was leaping from rock to rock toward the summit.

Everyone on the level of the cache recognized the figure as Zorilla. He was in plain sight; there was no place on the mountain side where he could conceal himself from the view of those who watched him. Near Nolan and Clelland stood a score of men with rifles. On the mesa were Testera's men. They could have brought the outlaw chief tumbling down the mountain.

But there was no shot fired. After looking at the outlaw chief, all eyes were turned to Don Pedro as though their owners wondered what he would do.

Don Pedro's eyes flamed; he stood rigid. And at that instant, in the dead silence which had fallen, there came a cry of delight, and the Señorita Juana appeared from the mouth of a cave in the battlement wall and ran toward Don Pedro.

Seeing her, Don Pedro lumbered to meet her. He opened his arms, and she ran into them. She was held tightly for a moment, and then Don Pedro held her from him and looked searchingly into her eyes.

"You are unharmed, my sweet?" he asked.

Her laugh rang clear.

"Zorilla is like Popocatepetl, Señor the Magnificent!" she said. "He is big. He rumbles and roars. But when he is alone with a woman! *Ay de mi! Lo hare mañana!*" (I will do it to-morrow!)

Don Pedro laughed and looked at the tall, slender priest—his parish counsellor. Their eyes met.

Don Pedro laughed.

"Let him go!" he said, nodding toward the outlaw chief. "He cannot escape. I will send Testera after him to bring him to the trial! Before me—all of you!"

They obeyed him. Presently across the mesa they went—the prisoners ahead, driving the ox carts, Testera's men next, escorting them; the feasters flanking the outlaws and the vaqueros, and hurling taunts at the former. Nolan and his friends joined the press just in front of Don Pedro and his daughter. As Nolan passed Juana she looked at him steadily, speculatively, with the ghost of a derisive smile on her lips.

"*Mañana*," she whispered. "Señor, you also are like Popocatepetl!"

CHAPTER XXXI

Don Pedro was speaking to the feasters, who were assembled on the level before his house on the mesa.

Zorilla's men had been led away by the vaqueros. They had left late in the afternoon, to be taken to the cuartel at Pezon, where they would be confined until they were tried for the murders they had committed. Zorilla had not yet been found, but a number of picked men were searching for him, and there was little doubt that he would be caught before dawn.

There had been much feasting during the early hours of the evening, and when it was over Don Pedro's guests had come to his house to rejoice with him and to congratulate him. And Don Pedro, standing on the edge of the portico of his house looking at the assembled people, was thrilled as he had never been thrilled before.

The lights, having been out for two nights, were now gleaming brightly again. All over the mesa they were glowing their vari-colours, loops of them swinging down between trees, strings of them hanging over tables and camping places, festoons making spots where impromptu gathering places had been arranged. Single lanterns swung idly in the slight breeze that swept over the mesa. The lights gleamed and glowed through lacelike moss that hung in filmy veils upon some of the trees.

There was no moon, though in the flood of mellow light from the swinging lanterns Don Pedro could see many of the faces that were turned to him. He himself was revealed to the people by several lanterns that were hung above his head at the edge of the portico; and arrayed as he was in his blue uniform with its red facings, its narrow gold lace, the white vest and knee breeches, low shoes with silver buckles, he made an impressive appearance.

It was apparent that he knew that he was appearing to advantage, for he stood, his chest swelling, his eyes glowing with satisfaction.

Behind the house, sitting in the hammock in which she had been wrapped when she had been taken prisoner by Zorilla's men, was Juana. From where she sat she could look through the rear door of the house, through the front door and upon her father, as he stood preparing to speak to his people.

The rear of the house was dark. There was no light inside. There were no festoons of light back there, no light of any kind except the faint glow that shone through the front and rear doors from the portico where Don Pedro stood. That glow did not penetrate to Juana; she was in a darkness so deep that she could not even be seen by Nolan, who stood within two paces of her.

She and Nolan had been talking. She had been questioning him about his experience with Zorilla. She had learned that Zorilla had marked him for death at the foot of the cliff; she had listened while he had told her of his later experiences.

Nolan had been brief. He felt that his part in the incidents of the past few days was insignificant. He was in no mood to talk. Now, glumly, he was listening to Don Pedro.

"My people," said Don Pedro, "it is only because of Divine interposition—and my good sword—that I am able to stand here to-night and talk to you. If God had not been with me—or if I had forgotten my good blade—this great pleasure would have been denied me.

"The fates fight best for those who fight for themselves!" he added, his voice rising. "Fortune ever favours the brave. The coyote runs from the daylight, not knowing that he is a coward.

"You are aware that Don Pedro Bazan is no coward. When Zorilla captured me I was taken by surprise, and before I could object my hands were bound and I was helpless."

He gazed at those near him, scowling.

"The great Don Pedro Bazan helpless!" he repeated. "You can imagine how that thought irked me. I was thrown into a vile ox cart and hauled to Devil's Cache, where I was held in one of the caves, still bound and helpless.

"Knowing that great things were expected of me, I lay there, straining at my bonds in an effort to escape and come to grips with my enemies. I was tortured by the futility of my rage.

"I was in the cave for many hours. I do not know how many. I did not know what had been done with the Señorita Juana. I was maddened by the uncertainty; my hatred of Zorilla grew terrific. And yet I could do nothing. If I had been a lesser man I must have cried tears of shame.

"At last, after I had been in the cave for many hours, I felt there was someone in there with me. There was! It was that Señor Valdez who had tried to steal my horses in the days before the feast. He had escaped from my private cuartel. I had planned to shoot him. My people, if I had shot Señor Valdez I should not be here at this minute talking to you!

"I shall not tell you what Señor Valdez said to me. This only shall I tell you. It was Señor Valdez who cut the throat of the prowler who would have knifed Señor Nolan on the very night we came here. It was Señor Valdez who cut my bonds and made it possible for me to leave the cave.

"*Bastante!* I left the cave. For an instant I paused at the entrance. The light blinded me. I saw no one on the level in front of the cache. It appeared to me that all had deserted me. I would have to fight alone!

"I did not hesitate. Beyond the gulch in the cache I caught a glimpse of the carts. Drawing my sword, I ran over there!

"In front of me I observed at least threescore of Zorilla's men. They were armed with rifles and pistols. I had nothing but my great sword. I stood at the crest of the gulch, looking at them.

"They might have shot me. I do not know why they did not. I shall feel that it was my great bravery in facing them alone that confounded them. They had never seen such bravery. They had never realized that any man could be so reckless. My appearance must have awed them. Their muscles were paralyzed.

"Three of them charged me. So quickly that they did not know what happened, I sent them rolling down the side of the gulch. They were so negligible as fighters that I merely struck them with the flat of my blade. So great was my strength that they fell as if dead!

"My terrible ferocity must have affected the others, because they raised their hands above their heads and begged for mercy. I walked boldly among them, took their weapons from them, and threw them down the face of the cliff. You will find them lying there!

"I do not boast, my people; I relate in as few words as possible what happened there at the cache.

"Still terrified at my rage and bravery, the outlaws were docile. When I ordered them to the carts, they instantly obeyed. You know the rest!"

Don Pedro paused to listen to the cheering and shouts that greeted his recital. Presently, when the plaudits ceased, Don Pedro went on again.

And now Señorita Juana spoke.

"Don Pedro Bazan is a great man," she said in a low voice.

"Yes," answered Nolan, from the shadows.

"His very recklessness keeps him from harm," added Juana.

"Yes," answered Nolan.

"There were threescore of the outlaws," said the girl. "Yet he did not hesitate. The instant he was free of his bonds he attacked them all."

Nolan was aware that Juana was taunting him. Being free for two days at least, Nolan had seemed, in the light of Don Pedro's exploit, to have been almost criminally inactive. He knew Juana had expected him to rescue her; he was now certain that she resented his failure to do so.

All through the days of the feast, through one unfortunate circumstance or another, he had been unable to perform any deed that would make him more attractive in Juana's eyes. Everywhere Don Pedro had been before him. Don Pedro had dominated. There had not been a single opportunity for him to distinguish himself. Not until he and his friends had scaled the mountain wall had he been able to attempt an aggressive movement, and even that feat had been made to appear ridiculous because of Don Pedro's greater feat in single-handedly capturing the outlaws.

There was, then, he felt, a great deal of justification for Juana's taunts. Juana could not see his face, therefore she could not perceive the glumness of his expression.

"Your father is a brave man, Juana," he admitted. "And yet——" He paused.

"Yes?" she said encouragingly.

"He was fortunate in his opportunities," he answered.

"La, la. Señor Nolan, I believe you are envious! Tell me, would you have attacked threescore of Zorilla's men, armed as they were, with nothing but a sword?"

"No," he admitted truthfully.

Juana laughed. "In that Don Pedro was fortunate," she retorted. "He had the courage to attack against terrible odds. His own life he did not value. Tell me, Señor Nolan, do you value your life?"

"Not as much as I did," he answered.

He could not see her face, and yet he felt she was smiling at him—a smile in which there was some disappointment and not a little contempt.

He sighed; kicked savagely into a hummock.

"You sighed, Señor Nolan," she said, mocking him.

"Did I? I wasn't noticing."

"Is it that you were wishing you were as brave as Don Pedro?" she asked, with maddening sweetness.

"I will never be as brave as Don Pedro," he declared.

"And yet you are brave, Señor Nolan. One can see that. And yet, being brave, you permitted me to remain Zorilla's prisoner."

Nolan was silent. He did not intend to make excuses for himself. He had had the will to rescue her, but not the opportunity. And he was aware that he would not have seized the particular opportunity that had presented itself to Don Pedro. The latter's action in facing threescore of the armed outlaws had in his opinion been foolhardy. He mentally admitted that he would not have thought of facing them without a gun in hand. And even then the odds would have been very great.

"Did you not, Señor Nolan?" Juana persisted.

"Yes," he admitted.

She was silent for an instant. Then—

"Why did you come to the feast, Señor Nolan?"

"To be near you."

"Ai!" she breathed. "Then you remembered that first day—the day you came to the Rancho Paloma to talk to my father about cattle—when you stood there in the courtyard with your hat in your hand, looking at me?"

"I shall never forget that day," he declared.

"You will," she said. "You will some day marry a girl of your own race. You will forget poor Juana."

"I reckon not."

"You have loved many girls, señor."

"None—until you."

Silence again. Then—

"Señor Nolan, was your hair always that curly?"

"My hair? Hell! I hadn't noticed."

"Not noticed your hair? Señor Nolan, you are not like a woman!"

"I reckon not. If I had a head under my hair I might have noticed that. I'm pretty nearly convinced that I have none."

"The señor is disconsolate." She paused, laughed lowly. "And he has lost his courage! How—what do you say?—unfortunate! And yet the se-ñor seems to have courage. Looking at him, one would think he would go through fire for anything he wanted. Is there no courage in blue eyes like yours, Señor Nolan?"

"Not much, I reckon," he answered.

"*Peste*, señor!" she said suddenly, impatiently. "Why do you always agree with me?"

"I reckon it's because I ain't got nerve enough to disagree," he returned with some bitterness.

"*Ay de mi!* That is too bad, señor. And yet you had courage enough to scale the mountain wall," she said.

"That?" he said. "It was nothing."

"And you risked your life at the crest, when a red cap shot at you? Only Señor Clelland's quickness saved you! Tell me, does Señor Clelland like you?"

"We've been together a great deal. Yes, I reckon he does."

"You don't know?"

"Well, say yes."

"How can you tell when anybody likes you, Señor Nolan? Does one who saves your life love—like you?"

"Maybe."

"You don't know?"

"I've saved the lives of men I didn't like."

"Tell me, Señor Nolan. Why did you climb the mountain?"

"I reckon maybe I had an idea we could get at Zorilla's men from that direction."

"You only wanted to punish Zorilla's men? You had no thought of me?"

"Well, I reckon we figured to get you at the same time."

There was another silence.

"Señor Nolan," she said, "you do not like to make yourself seem important, do you?"

"I reckon I never thought of that," he said.

"*Ay de mi!* Not you! Never that! You are not brave, nor are you important. And yet I think it required more courage to climb that steep wall while the red caps were firing at you than was required of my father when he faced the threescore red caps on the level."

"Shucks!"

"Because," she went on slowly and distinctly, but with a queer little note of tenderness in her voice, "because, Señor Nolan, you were risking your life. While my father, possessing courage, did not risk his life at all.

"Listen to me, Señor Nolan," she went on when he tried to interrupt. "I think, since you take the matter so hard, that you should know the truth. When my father ran out to the level where the red caps were I ran after him and stood at a little distance, watching. Not one of the red caps was armed, señor. Someone had disarmed them before my father reached them. Ai! he is dear, señor; and it was brave of him to face those men even if they were not armed. But he is a glorious blusterer, Señor Nolan, and he loses no opportunity to make himself a hero before his people. But he really has courage when he faces a woman, señor. You observed how it would have fared with that little Señora Balano who came at his command to be reprimanded."

And now Nolan became conscious that a subtle change had come into Juana's voice. It was mocking, and yet in it there was a note of gentleness which was almost like a caress. Over Nolan swept an astonishing conviction, an enchanting knowledge that all along she had been merely playing with him in an effort to bring to his lips a fervent confession of his love for her. She had been trying to stir his cold Northern self-control to passionate utterance.

He moved toward her.

In the darkness he found the hammock, being guided to it by her low laugh. And then for half an hour they sat there, close together and silent; she lying against him, her head resting upon his shoulder.

CHAPTER XXXII

As they sat there in the darkness, listening to Don Pedro, who was still speaking to his "people," they became aware of a stealthy sound which seemed to come from a point near them, to their left. The sound came during a pause in Don Pedro's discourse. It was a sound such as might be made by the breaking of a twig upon the ground, sharp and quickly smothered.

The sound might have been made by one of the feasters moving toward the front of the house, yet a person abroad upon an honest errand would not be coming toward the house on its darkened side, but would approach it from the front or sides, which were lighted.

Juana and Nolan listened. Nolan had felt the girl start, and he knew that in her mind was the thought that was in his—that the person approaching the house meant ill to someone he expected to find inside.

Sitting in the darkness, however, Nolan smiled. He felt that had it not been that Zorilla was still at large neither himself nor Juana would have paid any attention to the sound. For in the darkness behind them there might be two lovers abroad. There might be the Señora Balano and the husband she had been trying to steal.

The sound occurred again. This time it was closer. A twig breaking with a sharp crack, quickly dulled, as though the twig had been ground into the sand by a heavy weight, a foot.

Then came a slight rustle of the dried grass. A light footstep on the hard sand, a scuffling as of a leather sole rasping on the flintlike grains. Presently a low-drawn breath.

Nolan felt Juana shiver. His left hand was resting upon her shoulder, and he drew her to him reassuringly. He was afraid she would cry out and frighten the intruder away before he disclosed his purpose.

There followed a space when apparently the presence did not move. Juana and Nolan could hear him breathing heavily, as if excited. By keeping his gaze in the direction from which the sounds came, Nolan was at last able to make out the man's shape, dimly outlined against the faint star haze that came through some trees at a little distance.

Presently the man began to move toward the house. He was now within thirty or forty feet of Juana and Nolan. Nolan waited until he had approached to within a dozen feet of the house; then he gently pressed Juana's shoulder, silently got out of the hammock, and moved away from it to a point twenty or thirty feet distant.

He could now observe the man more clearly, for the latter had moved closer to the house and was standing near the open doorway, back from it just a little, where the light from the portico, shining through, did not quite strike him.

It was evident that the man did not know of the presence of Juana and Nolan, for he did not once look back toward the hammock. He was interested in what was before him. For a time he stood motionless, in a listening attitude.

Nolan and Juana could hear Don Pedro, still talking to the feasters. He was amusing them now, for there were shouts and laughter.

Nolan heard a sound from the man. It seemed the latter was cursing. Then, stealthily, he moved closer to the open door and peered through at Don Pedro, who, standing on the portico, was still talking, his back toward the rear doorway, where the man stood.

Juana could plainly see her father. She was also watching the man. Yet she could not recognize him because his back was toward her and the light coming through the doorway shone on his face.

However, Nolan recognized him. The man was Zorilla.

Zorilla stalking his enemy; Zorilla contemplating murder.

For now the outlaw chief had stepped full into the light from the doorway. He leaned forward a little, his face working with passion.

He had found a pistol. He drew it from the holster at his hip, glanced at it, evidently to make sure of its readiness, and then slowly lifted it and aimed it through the doorway, at Don Pedro's broad back.

At that instant there was a slight commotion at the front of the house, near the portico. Shouts of laughter rose.

One of the lanterns adorning the portico had fallen. It struck the ground at the corner of the house, in front, and its vari-coloured paper sides took fire, creating a lively blaze which illumined the spot where Nolan stood, watching Zorilla.

Zorilla heard the commotion. He straightened, turned, saw Nolan standing there bathed in the light from the blazing lantern.

Juana screamed. A lance of fire belched from Zorilla's gun, straight at Nolan. Two flaming streaks from Nolan's gun leaped at Zorilla. Zorilla's gun went off again. He stood revealed in the light from the doorway, slouching a little, seeming deliberately to fire his gun into the sand at his feet.

Nolan did not fire again. The light from the blazing lantern had died down. Darkness rushed upon Nolan and engulfed him. Only Zorilla could now be seen. He was still standing in the light from the doorway. He had sunk a little lower, his knees had sagged, his head was sinking to his chest.

He seemed, in a sort of stupefied bewilderment, to be examining his gun. And finally, as though unable to understand what had happened to him, he permitted the weapon to slip from his fingers. For an instant he stood looking at it, where it lay in the sand at his feet. Then he seemed to reach for it, and pitched forward upon his face.

CHAPTER XXXIII

The feast was on again. There still remained several days of the seven that Don Pedro had specified.

Nolan was sharing honours with the magnificent one, who insisted, in view of the fact that Nolan had saved his life, that Nolan should witness the games with him from the portico of the house. Therefore, with Juana hovering near, and giving Nolan smiles that enthralled him more and more, Nolan watched and feasted.

There were riding contests, roping, dancing. The days were full of action, the nights vibrant with music. At every opportunity Don Pedro discoursed to his people. He told again and again the story of his heroic fight at the cache. With each telling he added something to the recital. Lurid details which he said had escaped him. Some of the outlaws had, it appeared, not been so submissive, after all. He had had several bloody fights with them before he could subdue them. Had any of his people observed that several of the outlaws bore grievous wounds and that he himself bore none?

He had had more trouble with them than he had at first admitted. He had wanted, in the first flush of victory, to be modest. But he had been forced to fight desperately to get their guns away from them.

Manville, the moonshiner, had several times listened to Don Pedro relating the story of his adventure at the cache, and at such times he screwed his brows together as though in an effort to remember something.

To-day, troubled and preoccupied, he left the western end of the mesa and made his way eastward into the broken section that led to Devil's Cache.

When he reached the cache he stood on the level after crossing the bridge and stared about him. His only recollection of the bridge was as he had seen it when leaving the cache with Don Pedro and the others after Don Pedro's capture of the outlaws.

He felt something stirring within him—a vague feeling that something momentous had happened to him while in the cache.

Certainly, he remembered the cave. He remembered releasing Juana from her bonds. He remembered Zorilla running before him out of the mouth of the cave. He remembered seeing Don Pedro driving the red caps before him; his recollection of the massing of the vaqueros around Don Pedro was clear. He could still see Zorilla jumping from rock to rock on the mountain side in an effort to escape. All these things he could remember, but as to what had happened to him and where he had been before these things had occurred his memory was almost blank.

True, he had drunk much wine. That might account for the failure of his mind to register impressions. He shook his head as he wandered around the base of the escarpment, walked through the gulch, and at last mounted to the level near the escarpment.

He stood there long, scratching his head and revolving Don Pedro's story in his mind.

Almost, it seemed, the adventure had been his own. Out of the haze that dimmed his knowledge of yesterday and the day before he seemed to visualize himself doing the things that Don Pedro had done. But he could not be certain. Yet he had an impression that he had been on this particular level before. He had done something here. What?

He walked around the edge of the cliff, peering over. At last, at the base, far down among a rank growth of weeds, he saw a number of rifles and revolvers lying in the sand. He stood looking down at them, scratching his head thoughtfully.

He shook his head again. He could not remember. His memory was likely playing him a trick. He had heard of such things. An incident related by someone which one's brain grasps quickly and makes a double impression. Two photographs for the memory. The first becomes memory. Troublesome. He had heard of such things. A dream, maybe. Well, at any rate, if anything had happened to him here, he couldn't remember it. He had lost it; it had vanished.

He stood still, gazing down at the plains. He heard voices, and he looked around with a foolish grin and saw Don Pedro, Señorita Juana, and Nolan coming toward him out of the gulch.

"Ai!" exclaimed Don Pedro. "It is Señor Manville. Have you come to look at the place of my adventure?"

"It sort of interested me," responded Manville.

"A battlefield!" declared Don Pedro. "Worthy of the genius of a master painter! Never was there a fight against such odds! They assailed me from all sides. Twenty of them felt my steel. Once a dozen of them leaped upon me at one time. I was buried under them. The weight of their bodies stifled me. Yet I gave one great heave and threw them off. Perhaps you observed that some of the outlaws had broken arms. I did that over there near the rock wall when they knocked my sword from my hand.

"Ai! they backed from me. They knew they had cornered a terrible fighter. Not one dared to stoop to reach my sword. I took it up and renewed the slaughter. Several of the outlaws I threw bodily over the cliff!"

"*Ay de mi!*" gasped Juana. She looked down to the base of the precipice, where the rifles and the pistols were lying. She looked back at her father, her gaze innocent and inquiring.

"I see none of their bodies down there, Father," she said.

"No," returned Don Pedro quickly, "you do not. There is a reason for that. As soon as they fell a band of horsemen that was down there picked them up and carried them off."

"A band of horsemen?" gasped Juana.

"A score of riders," returned Don Pedro. "I do not know how they came there or who they were. They appeared to be nomads. I did not recognize any of them. But I distinctly heard their leader shout to his fellows that I appeared to be a demon. Twice the horsemen shot at me. If they had been good marksmen, I should not be telling you this tale."

"Gosh!" exclaimed Manville, "I should say you wouldn't!"

Manville's eyes were bulging with awe and admiration.

Don Pedro's manner was convincing. Banished was Manville's vague and hazy recollection of his own adventure. A dream, most likely. He moved slowly away from the others, found a nook amid the crags of the escarpment, stretched out, and went to sleep.

When he awakened darkness had come. He sat up with a start, for he heard voices near him.

"I loved you from the first, Señor Nolan. It was when you stood in the courtyard with the sun shining down upon you. You looked so—what shall I say?—masterful."

That was Juana.

"And when did you first love me, Señor Nolan?" she continued.

"You came into my thoughts years ago. You were an ideal. When I saw you that day in the courtyard I knew I would never love another woman!"

Nolan, decided Manville. H'm. Nolan. Manville wondered why he had not observed that they had appeared to be attracted to each other.

Manville did not get up. He leaned back against the rock and smiled.

They would be hours sitting where they were. He could not escape without letting them know that he had heard them. He didn't want to let them know. So he drowsed. His thoughts were fragmentary.

Always the way. Love. A man and a woman. Meeting. Growing acquainted. Getting more and more intimate. Loving. Differing. Fighting. Loving again. Talkin' nonsense. Was it nonsense? Maybe not, since so many people talked it. He himself had talked it. Of course, then, it couldn't be foolishness. Anyhow, it was foolishness that men were wise to enjoy. It would go on that way forever, he supposed. Forever and ever—to the end.

THE END